ASHES OF THE AMAZON

MILTON HATOUM was born in Manaus, Amazonas, and studied architecture in São Paulo and comparative literature in Paris. He is Professor of Literature at the Federal University of Amazonas and a visiting Professor of Latin American Literature at the University of California. He lives in São Paulo.

BY THE SAME AUTHOR

The Brothers

Tale of a Certain Orient

ASHES OF
THE AMAZON

Milton Hatoum

Translated by John Gledson

B L O O M S B U R Y

LONDON · BERLIN · NEW YORK

First published in Great Britain 2008
This paperback published 2009

Copyright © by Milton Hatoum 2005
Translation copyright © by John Gledson 2008

First published in the Brazilian Portuguese language
by Editora Companhia das Letras, São Paulo

This work is published with the support of the Ministry of the Culture of Brazil/
National Library Foundation/Coordenadoria-Geral do Livro e da Leitura
*Obra publicada com o apoio do Ministério da Cultura do Brasil / Fundação Biblioteca Nacional /
Coordenadoria-Geral do Livro e da Leitura*

Bloomsbury Publishing Plc
36 Soho Square
London W1D 3QY

www.bloomsbury.com

Bloomsbury Publishing, London, New York and Berlin

A CIP catalogue record for this book is available from the British Library

ISBN 978 0 7475 9672 1

10 9 8 7 6 5 4 3 2 1

Typeset by Hewer Text UK Ltd, Edinburgh
Printed in Great Britain by Clays Ltd, St Ives plc

The paper this book is printed on is certified independently in accordance with the rules of
the FSC. It is ancient-forest friendly. The printer holds chain of custody

FSC

Mixed Sources
Product group from well-managed
forests and other controlled sources

Cert no. SGS-COC-2061
www.fsc.org
© 1996 Forest Stewardship Council

For João, who was born with this book

I'm from where I was born. I'm from elsewhere.

João Guimarães Rosa

I READ MUNDO'S LETTER in a bar in the Beco das Cancelas, an alleyway where I found refuge from the hubbub of the centre of Rio, and endless discussions about the future of the country. The letter had no date, and was written in a clinic in Copacabana, the words jolting up and down in a small, tremulous handwriting that revealed how much pain my friend was in.

'I thought of writing my life over again, back to front, or upside down, but I can't, I can barely scratch the paper, the words are blotches on the surface, and writing is almost a miracle . . . I can feel the sweat of death in my body' – that's what I read, just before the end. In the margin of the last page, these words: 'Just after midnight.'

He may have died at dawn that same day, but I had no desire to know the date or the time: pointless details. Some twenty years later, Mundo's story comes back to my memory with the intensity of burning embers shrouded by my childhood and youth. I still have his notebook with drawings and notes, and the sketches for several unfinished works, noted down in Brazil and Europe, in the course of the wandering life he fearlessly threw himself into, as if he wanted to tear himself open from inside, as if he were repeating, over and over, the phrase he wrote on a postcard sent from London: 'Dumb obedience, or rebellion.'

1

THEY WALKED TOGETHER, in sunshine or rain, Fogo and Jano, his master. The dog went ahead, turned his nose to one side, waited, reared up a little, sniffing the man's scent, listening to the hoarse sound of his voice: 'Come on then, Fogo . . . Come on, let's go.'

They were inseparable: Fogo slept next to the couple's bed, something Alícia couldn't bear. When the dog brought ticks on to the bed, she shooed it: Jano objected, the animal howled, and no one slept. Then Fogo would come back, quietly, silently, and curl up in his own corner, on a *jaguatirica* skin. She went to sleep in the son's room. In the last months of Jano's life that was the way: Fogo and his master in one room, and the woman, alone, where the absent son slept. The dog had some yellowish marks on its coat, which the boy hated because one day his father had said: 'Marks that shine like gold. And after all, Fogo is one of my treasures.'

Before we became schoolfellows in the Pedro II, I saw him once in the centre of St Sebastian Square: scrawny, his head almost completely shaven, sitting on the stones with their black-and-white wavy patterns. Sitting next to a girl, he was staring at a bronze ship representing Europe; he was looking at the ship on the monument, and drawing with a look of astonishment on his face, biting his lip and craning his head from side to side, like a bird. I stopped to look at the drawing: a strange, twisted boat in the midst of a dark sea, which could have been the Rio Negro or the Amazon – beyond the sea, a strip of white. He folded the paper with an insolent gesture, glared at me as if I were an intruder; then suddenly he got up and stretched out his hand, offering me the folded piece of paper.

'Mundo?' I asked, before I thanked him.

He gave a slight smile, his dark eyes still blinking.

'Naiá, is this Ranulfo's nephew?'

The girl grabbed him by the waist, and the two went off, Mundo's face turned first to me, then to the monument.

It was the first drawing I got from him: a ship heeling over in the wind, sailing towards an empty space, and, every time I went near the *Europe*, I remembered Mundo's drawing.

I only met him again in the middle of April 1964, when the classes at the Pedro II were about to start again after the military coup. The monitors seemed fiercer and more arrogant, enforcing discipline to the letter, treating us with mocking disdain. Steelhead, their boss, messed around with the girls, made fun of the shyer boys, and boomed out, before he inspected the uniforms: 'C'mon, you gang of idiots: no noise. Left, right, left, right.'

That morning, the school's main gate was shut during break, and the rain forced the boys and girls to shelter under the marble-lined porticoes. Before the siren blew, a woman appeared holding a small red parasol that only protected the pupil beside her; they were almost the same height. Steelhead rushed to open the gate for the two of them, and they went slowly up the staircase. The schoolchildren moved to one side so they could cross the patio; they looked at nobody, but everyone observed them. The monitor led them to the headmaster's room, and when the siren sounded, the woman reappeared, alone, her hair wavy and damp; her silk blouse, which was wet, attracted whistles from the older boys. Dark-complexioned and about thirty, she hurried down the staircase; when she reached the bottom, she opened her parasol and came close to the iron bars. She saw me leaning against a column and called me over: it was absurd I hadn't been to visit her, but from now on there could be no more excuses; her son was going to study at the Pedro II. I agreed with a timid gesture, and she added: 'I think of your mother as if she were still alive.' It was Alícia, Mundo's mother.

At first, he was just another schoolfellow: shy, the strangest of all, and given certain privileges. On rainy mornings, a black DKW came along Rui Barbosa Street and parked in the side courtyard. Mundo came up the stairs, protected by an umbrella held by the chauffeur, who said to the monitor: 'Here's the boy.' But when Mundo came late, he had to wait for the next gap between classes. We watched him as he wandered round the bandstand in Acacia Square, then sat on a bench and drew a sloth, or an egret, or the face of some passer-by. The school rules were a torment to him; even so, his laxity about his uniform and his general appearance increased, maddening the monitors: his hair unkempt, his face half-asleep, his hands smeared with ink, the gold medallion on his tie askew, the knot loose inside the collar, his epaulettes unbuttoned. His socks were of different colours; he rolled up his sleeves and didn't polish his belt-buckle. Steelhead wouldn't let him into class and threatened him: lazy and offhand, did he think being daddy's boy cut any ice here? Mundo didn't answer: he sat behind the back

4

row, isolated, near the window opening on to the square. When it rained heavily, he spent break-time standing at that window, observing the trees blown down by the storm, the alligators amongst the stones, the birds sheltering at the edge of the little lake, someone sitting on a bench, alone, at the mercy of the gusts of wind, and further off – at the time the horizon was still visible – the little wooden houses flooded or submerged and the boats and canoes capsized or floating aimlessly in the waterways of the centre of Manaus.

During breaks, he showed no fear when he was surrounded by the brash older boys, paying no attention to their threats, even at the risk of being cuffed or slapped. In the nervous silence of a maths exam, we heard the noise of his pencil on paper, sketching people and things; even so, he answered all the questions and was the first to finish the exam. At the end of the year, Mundo gave us all a surprise: he passed in every subject.

When I came up for a chat, he would show me thumbnail-sketch caricatures, and ask me if I liked them. He shut the book if certain of the boys came near, showing a haughty contempt that irritated them.

'We work like slaves, so how come he manages to pass into the next year?' Minotaur complained. And Delmo said: 'His parents must give backhanders to the teachers and monitors. He's even got off the games in the arena.'

These 'games' were a freestyle wrestling match in a circle of dirty sand. On Saturday afternoons, the PE teacher chose the ones to take part from amongst the older pupils and the new boys. The pupils of the Pedro II surrounded the arena, and, on the pavement, boys from other schools and soldiers on their day off watched the spectacle through the bars, cheering the wrestlers on and having a good time, as if they were animals outside our cage. Gradually the competitors lost their fear and became ferocious, like cornered animals.

In one of these tournaments, Chiado died. His opponent, a boy from the final year, was so loudly applauded that he didn't even see the head stuck between the iron bars. He lifted his arms in victory while the other was bleeding; someone let out a cry, he turned around and came face to face with Chiado's closed eyes. With hands like metal hooks, he pulled the bars apart, the crushed head fell, and we saw the bloody mouth, then the body being carried to the teacher.

During a week of mourning, the sand circle stayed empty. We looked at the arena and remembered Chiado, his face pummelled and kicked by his squat, thickset rival. His death was talked about all that year. In November, after a court case that led nowhere, the older boy was expelled from the Pedro II, and the games started again; now they were even more violent. Some of the competitors promised vengeance and pointed to the bent iron bars, alluding to the prowess of their punished friend – cowards beware!

Mundo took no part in these tournaments, or in any of the other sports: he had been let off thanks to a medical certificate Alícia had managed to get; but he had to stay in the playground and be there for roll-call in PE classes. She came two or three times more with her son: they arrived arm-in-arm, and said goodbye at the gate with kisses and caresses; he came up the staircase turning round to look at his mother, and, with every step, his suffering seemed to increase. She left before he went in, walking quickly to the car, while Mundo followed her with his eyes, hoping for

6

a wave. When he was thirteen, he was already taller than Alícia; he had inherited her angular face and big dark eyes, somewhat almond-shaped, 'from some forgotten tribe' as he himself wrote years later. When it rained, the older boys surrounded him on the patio: 'Hasn't your mother come? When she's wet, she's even prettier,' and he, his face set, bit his lip and returned their stupid jokes with a menacing look. We soon saw that his power came not only from his hands, but from the look in his eyes.

The first cartoons caused a sensation in the Pedro II: they appeared on the cover of the four hundred copies of *Element 106*, the grubby little magazine put out by some of the older boys. The drawing of the scowling face of the marshal-president stood out: the heavy, spotty, prehistoric head of a tortoise, his small hunched-up uniformed body covered by a shell. At his feet was a whole brood of little animals in helmets, with grotesque features; the biggest of them, Steel-head, grasped a rod, and sported the Pedro II's badge on his forehead. A month's suspension for the editors, ten days for the artist; the magazine was impounded. Even so, the cover of the *Element 106* was on display everywhere: in the toilets, the refectory, on the blackboards, in the school's head office. It was taken down and torn to shreds, only to reappear the next day, in spite of the monitors' vigilance, threats of punishment and even expulsion.

When Mundo came back, the PE teacher reprimanded him: another escapade like that, and he'd be out! He was branded a subversive by Delmo, insulted by Minotaur: 'Some artist he is, the useless *galego*.' He stayed by himself at the back of the room, watching our gestures, fixing his eyes first on one person, then another; he'd push his chair back, leaning it against the wall, and lower his head, concentrating, with his face close to the paper.

While the players were warming up, he sat in the shade of the awning by the laboratories and discreetly kept his eyes on everyone; the big eyes with their thick lashes following us, more than likely despising our exertions, indifferent to the teacher's shouting: 'C'mon, lad, get stuck in, for Christ's sake!' When the whistle blew, and the teams rushed on to the cement square, Mundo went up to the spectators' seats, opened his pencil box and drew the bodies as they ran, collided, twisted, turned, and fell.

Fallen Bodies was the first series he left on his desk one morning when he went to the refectory. We saw our bodies on the ground, our faces distorted, grimacing: the Minotaur, almost monstrous, the only one without a head, Delmo with a face like a grasshopper, and the teacher, in the middle of the square, a squat harlequin, with his head separated from his body. The drawings twisted and jumbled our bodies; we recognised bits of ourselves and others, so everybody felt insulted. Delmo, in high dudgeon, wanted to tear it all up and get his own back: 'How about a good punch-up?' Minotaur, who was much stronger, pinched Delmo's neck with his great big hand: 'Nah, kid, that's not the way. I've got a better idea.'

It was on a Saturday morning in November, before the second-year final exams. Minotaur came up to Mundo: how about going to the square? The girls were dying to see the drawings. OK, he said. A circle of girls surrounded the bench while Mundo was showing the fallen bodies; with a ball of gum made from a sticky plant, Minotaur stuck a paper tail on to the artist's backside, lit it with alcohol and stepped back; I was going to run and warn him, but Minotaur grabbed me, covered my mouth with his great hand and pushed my head down. Surprised by the girls' laughter, Mundo saw the smoke between his legs, jumped up and flung himself into the lake. Then he sat on the little stone bridge, took his shoes and belt off, and stayed there, soaked to the skin, looking at the animals, listening to the jeers of his fellow students, dozens of them. He didn't budge; he waited for the signal of the end of break, when the square was emptied of uniforms, howls and guffaws. He seemed more sad than angry. 'I'm used to it,' he said, without looking at me. He didn't answer when I asked if he was going to complain to the headmaster.

Later, from the classroom window, I watched him as he walked slowly away, in bare feet, with no shirt on, his belt round his neck, his shoelaces wound round his hands. His figure disappeared into the winding paths of the square, reappearing in the shade of the acacias. He passed near the bronze sentinels of the Military Police barracks, and went round the building, as if on his way to the port.

2

AT THE BACK of the classroom, Mundo's chair was empty. He hadn't done his final exams; he failed the year and went to study in the Colégio Brasileiro, where he could draw as much as he wanted, get up late, arrive in class in the middle of the morning and play truant without being hassled. I kept the notebook with the drawings he'd dropped in fright when he jumped into the lake in the square. Later we met in the doorway of the Casa Africana store. He walked slowly, with a heavy tread, the jacket of his green-and-yellow uniform over his shoulder; he poked at my chest with his index-finger and smiled ironically: 'Your tie's loose – and where's the emblem of the emperor got to?'

I tried to give him back the *Fallen Bodies* sequence. He refused, I could keep the drawings; he got some magazines out of a leather folder and leafed through them; weren't Daumier's cartoons brilliant? 'These are Brazilian, Guignard, Volpi, Portinari. These ones are French . . . and the magazine's about African art.' It was the Masters of Painting series.

He spoke enthusiastically about famous and unheard-of artists, and seemed inebriated by the images. He began to read bits of a book, unaffected by the burning midday sun; he read and showed me the photo of a painting or a sculpture. He got a fright when the DKW sounded its horn.

He put the books and magazines back in the folder and spoke to the chauffeur: 'What is it, Macau?'

'Coming for lunch?' the man said, with his head out of the window.

I tried to see the father's face in the back seat, but it was turned the other way. Mundo said goodbye and went into the Casa Africana. I waited for the car to go, and crossed the square in the direction of the Vila da Ópera. I could see old underpants on criss-crossed clothes-lines at the end of the short street. Uncle Ran! He doesn't even wash *them*! He demands everything of his sister, and won't leave her in peace. I gathered his washing, smelt limes, garlic and pepper, and saw Aunt Ramira in the kitchen, putting slits in the fish to season it. I took my belt off, and was undoing my tie when I heard barking.

'That's Fogo's welcome,' said Jano.

He couldn't persuade Mundo to have his lunch at home and came straight here, I thought, looking at him. It was the second time I'd seen him close to, with his small greyish eyes and his head wrinkled as if with a permanent frown. Illness had aged him in a few years, but he still had the same haughty pose. His linen shirt was starched, blue with mother-of-pearl buttons; his trousers white and loose. Just what I'd remembered from the first encounter: the thick, dark-grey belt, almost the colour of his eyes. His voice, a bit hoarse, sounded deeper: 'Where's your aunt?'

She appeared, and her expression revealed surprise and shame. She smelt of raw fish, and before she greeted the visitor, she cleaned her hands on her apron. 'Mr Mattoso . . . You here?'

'Fogo smelt new people in the area a while back.'

They looked at each other for a while, until she raised her arms and lifted her head: she apologised for the mess the room was in, the mould on the partitions, the warped ceiling-battens.

'All the same, you know, it's a big advantage living in the centre. You were miles away from everything, out in that jungle.'

Fogo seized a red dress she'd sewn, and dragged it round the room, circling his master. Ramira didn't react to the animal's insolence – she tried to stroke it; it dropped the dress, growled and went to sniff the old scents coming from the Morro da Catita.

'My brother's going to paint the walls and do the house up. Well, he's been saying that since we moved in here. When it's ready, you must come and have a coffee,' she said, servile and flustered.

'Is he living here, or still wandering round like a gypsy?' Jano asked, annoyed.

'A gypsy,' Ramira echoed him. 'He appears from time to time, then vanishes.'

Jano clapped me on the left shoulder, and put his fingers on the three green stripes on my shirtsleeve: 'Your nephew's got promise . . . much more than his uncle and my son; up to now he's shown no promise at all. You were together at the Pedro II, weren't you? Mundo didn't do his final exams in the second year. By the looks of things, he'll flunk again at the Colégio Brasileiro. I knew he wasn't going to his PE classes. His mother's proud of the fact; she thinks Mundo's too delicate to be playing sports. My chauffeur saw the two of you near the Brasileiro. What were you talking about?'

'Art,' I said. 'That's all he talks about. Paintings . . .'

'That's why he's shown no promise,' Jano interrupted. 'Art . . . who does he think he is?'

He said goodbye to Ramira, looked at me out of the corner of his eye and whistled the dog; the two went to the door side by side; Fogo gave a jump and went trotting out of the street, his yellow marks shining in the sun, with the echo of Jano's hoarse shout: 'Come on, get going, we're off.' My aunt was left complaining – it was a disgrace, receiving such a refined gentleman in the midst of this clutter; Ranulfo's promises were worthless.

Our house in the Vila da Ópera was never tidied: her sewing work brought piles of cloth, remnants and patterns, and once in a while Uncle Ran took Corel and Chiquilito there, two friends who began smoking and drinking before Saturday's fish stew; they ended up sleeping on the floor near the door on to the street, for Ramira forbade them to step into the room where the sewing was done; on Sunday mornings we awoke to their speeches, each of them defending crazy ideas about a revolution in Brazil. They had all kinds of topics: agrarian reform, fishing for *tambaqui*, a party on board a ship, the newest brothel in Manaus, called Eve's Verandas. They drank a toast to the Verandas, and Corel, with a cigarette butt in his mouth, shouted enthusiastically: 'The Rose of May is still the best!' They'd forgotten the revolution and agrarian reform, and remembered nights spent in their youth at the Rose of May, Here and Now, or Shangri-la. They left when they could hardly recognise one another, leaving a pile of cigarette ends and dead matches, glasses with dregs in, and a sourness that impregnated the room until it was next cleaned. The rest of Sunday dragged; it was so tedious at home that my aunt and I went to the Fifteenth of November bathing club. She put up with these drunken sprees because her brother, since my father's death, had become the 'man of the house'.

At the beginning of 1961, when we moved to the centre, the Morro da Catita still consisted of little houses, some with gardens, scattered through a stretch of forest that began in São Jorge and went as far as the edge of a vast military area. A narrow path linked Castanhal do Morro to the Ponta Negra road, opposite the barracks of the Jungle Infantry Battalion. When Aunt Ramira needed to buy cloth or take some sewing work to a client in the centre, she went along the path to the entrance to the barracks and waited for a lift in a jeep or a military truck. The journey took hours, but she refused to go by canoe: she couldn't swim, and she was afraid of drowning in the Cornos creek. She complained about the isolation too, the lack of electricity, the animals prowling outside the house, the tree-porcupines falling off the Brazil nut trees, shattering the baked clay tiles with a frightening crash. My aunt wanted to fell the trees, but her brother wouldn't let her: they gave shade, and fruits that attracted the animals he hunted. Ranulfo stretched a hammock between the trunks, hung a night-lamp on a branch and sat reading all night; when it didn't rain, that was where he awoke, in the damp morning air, his book open on his bare chest, with dry leaves covering part of his body. Uncle Ran's books! They came from a long way off, from the South, and lay piled up in the little room at the bottom of the garden where we lived. He would read a paragraph or a long sentence to me, and become excited, forgetting I was still a child and couldn't understand complicated stories, written with difficult words;

even so, he went on reading out loud, only stopping to slap his arms and legs, and then I saw the mosquitoes' blood on his bronzed skin. I remember once, in the middle of a weekday afternoon, Ramira found him reading and making pencil notes on a strip of white tissue paper. She asked him why he was reading and writing instead of looking for work.

'I am working, dear sister,' said Uncle Ran. 'I'm working with other people's imaginations, and my own.'

She thought it was a strange expression – later, I would understand it as one of the definitions of literature. When he gave me some little books with drawings in, Aunt Ramira pointedly asked him: 'Were they stolen from a bookshop or bought with that woman's money?'

I grew up listening to my aunt and uncle quarrelling because of Alícia, who had lived in a nearby neighbourhood, the Jardim dos Barés. It was a story dating back to before I was born, but which was still raked over on the Morro da Catita, and seemed to have no end. One time, my aunt and I saw Alícia and Jano on the Rua da Instalação, coming out of the Vinte-e-Dois Paulista store. They were coming, arm-in-arm and smiling, in our direction; Aunt Ramira slowed down, nervous, and pulled my arm, as if to turn round. We stopped in a ridiculous position, and the two came towards us, but only Jano greeted Ramira with a smile, raising his hand. I saw Alícia's face with its make-up, felt her hand brushing through my hair, her perfumed fingers touching my lips, and heard her voice say: 'How he's grown, he's the image of his mother.' She leant over, gave me a kiss on the edge of my mouth, repeating: 'The image of Raimunda.'

They went, and my aunt murmured: 'What an unbearable woman. And how she manages to pretend she loves him.'

When Ramira unexpectedly announced she was buying a small house in the Vila da Ópera, her brother reacted like a peevish child: 'You want to live near Jano, don't you?'

'My nephew and I are going to get out of here,' she said calmly. 'My clients can't even get into the Morro. I'm bound to get more clients in the centre.'

He did nothing, thinking it was just a threat. But, on the day Ramira shut her sewing machine and put away the patterns, magazines, reels, needles and pieces of cloth, Ranulfo watched the process with an air of defeat. Then she said to me, out loud: 'Your uncle threw up a great job in Vila Amazônia . . . he chucked his fate into the dustbin. Last year he was still playing at being a radio announcer. Two flops. If he wants to stay here, he can get a steady job and pay the rent on this hovel.'

He himself took charge of the move to the Vila da Ópera. He boxed up the sewing machine, wrapped the furniture, the kerosene fridge and the stove in worn-out rags, and transported the whole caboodle in Corel's old wagon. In the back, I saw my aunt gripping the machine, her panic-struck face next to her brother's mocking features. Corel and Ranulfo carried everything into the new house, put everything in place, and we all went quiet.

The five little wooden houses of the Vila da Ópera, in line abreast, intruded like a scar into a block of large, austere houses; access was by a short street about three yards wide, and on the right, an iron gateway barred the entrance to a modern mansion, whose garden surrounded the small patio of our house. The Vila had been built by workmen who, in 1929, had worked on the construction of a pair of large houses, and they ended up taking possession of what had been part of a building-site.

Uncle Ran looked at the whitewashed partitions, with patches of mould, walked theatrically round the tiny room and muttered: 'I'm not going to live here. Where are the nut trees to set a hammock up? It's very cramped, Ramira. Far too gloomy.'

'Where will you sleep?'

He nudged his friend and said: 'Where, Corel? In the back of your wagon? And where am I going to keep my books?'

The two of them started laughing, and then Aunt Ramira cottoned on. 'You can sleep in Lavo's room, in the kitchen or the patio. Only you're not allowed in my room and the sewing room.'

He understood too.

Ranulfo did the heavy work and solved problems his sister hated dealing with. In exchange, he was allowed to sleep on the living-room floor after his all-night extravaganzas; days went by without him appearing, and then suddenly he'd come depressed, with not a cent to his name, and cadged the food he often brought with him still alive and kicking: peccaries, agoutis and wild ducks, tied on to the back of Corel's wagon. Uncle Ran killed the creatures with a machete, and handed pieces round the neighbours. There was food for two weeks. He got drink at the Bar do Sujo, where the bill hung for a month, and then sent for it to be paid at home. We got a strip of greasy wrapping paper with his signature under the total amount of the debt.

Many people in Manaus still remembered the stories and conversations from his radio programmes; when I was a child, I stayed up till midnight to listen to them; Aunt Ramira pretended to hide the little battery-radio, fearing her brother's fiendish voice, but she listened to it all: the people in a nearby house raised the volume of their powerful set. I got the impression that all the people living in the Morro da Catita, the Jardim dos Barés, Santo Antônio, São Jorge and Glória laughed and cried along with the presenter and his non-stop chat. I remember the sad Christmas of 1960, when he arrived in silence and instead of coming into the house, climbed up a Brazil nut tree and perched there high-up, smoking rope-tobacco and staring at the riverbank and the Cornos creek. He'd been sacked from Radio Rio-Mar: the priests who ran the station thought his weekly programme *Midnight and Just the Two of Us* had got too nonsensical and obscene. But Uncle Ran was proud of the only work that had given him pleasure and made him a name in the capital and in the interior of Amazonas.

'Anyway,' he said years later, 'after the coup they'd have sacked me in the end; the censors after that wondrous event weren't going to put up with my political comments, let alone the love stories I related at the dead of night.'

3

O NE SUNDAY MORNING, Ranulfo was sleeping on a straw mat when a boy whistled at the door of the house and handed my aunt an envelope and a turtle. She opened the envelope and read the note out loud: 'A gift from Vila Amazônia.'

Uncle Ran stretched his arms and yawned: 'Gifts don't just come from heaven, sister. With a neighbour like that, you won't have to buy anything, just do the cooking.'

'Jano's already been here. He came in without the least fuss, and brought the dog in too. He's a simple man.'

'He'll come back, with or without the dog. And if he doesn't, he could send more animals with shells on.'

'We're not starving.'

'I am. Just this minute I was thinking about what I was going to have for lunch – that animal, for instance. And by the looks of it it's a female.'

Ranulfo filled half the tank with boiling water and let the turtle slip to the bottom. He bit his lip, giving little stifled laughs, and looked at the waving legs of the capsized shell with a strange pleasure. He only stopped pouring hot water in when the animal quietened down.

'It's better than drilling a hole in its neck or clubbing it to death,' he said, seeing how shocked I was. 'That's barbarous – the suffering must be greater.'

He put the turtle on the kitchen floor, picked up a hammer and a machete and told me to keep my distance: he was going to take it out of its shell. He chopped the head and legs off, cut the body out, took out the innards and sliced the breast to make a mince. In the front room, with his bloodstained hands holding a half-gourd full of eggs, he said: 'If the cook will allow me, I'm going to take the eggs and eat them with sugar.'

Aunt Ramira turned her face away in disgust, and I went to clean the kitchen, which looked like a slaughterhouse. Then she fried the *farofa* in turtle-fat and made the mince with parsley, coriander and onion. She put a portion on one side in a gourd and put it in the fridge. Uncle Ran didn't use a plate: he stuck his spoon into the shell, mixed the mince and *farofa*, bit into a pepper and ate with relish. His mouth full, he laughed: 'A gift from Vila Amazônia, that's a good one. Jano knows how to negotiate. What does he want out of you?'

His sister reprimanded him with a hostile expression; he shook his head suspiciously, the question still in his eyes. He put the spoon down and ate with his hands, bent over the shell. He went back to the mat, snored till the end of the afternoon and went away taking the half-gourd, now empty of eggs, with him.

Next day, at lunchtime, I got the large gourd out of the fridge and went to take it to Jano. Naiá asked me to wait a bit, and came back flustered: the master and mistress wanted to see me. Alícia noted it was my first visit to their house. 'Lavo's very shy,' she went on, talking to her husband, 'he was an orphan before he could say "mummy". And what a mother he'd have had.'

The mansion's main room was sober, without much furniture or many *objets d'art*. I noticed the glass cabinet, panelled with glass on the sides too, containing miniature soldiers and weaponry; next to the gramophone, a shelf with books and records. On the opposite wall, there was a photograph of a big house facing the River Amazon. The greatest show of luxury was above: old stuccoing with lyres, harps, easels and paintbrushes. I stood staring at the ceiling till I heard Jano say: 'It's painted by Domenico de Angelis: *The Glorification of the Arts in Amazonia*. It's an imitation of the one he did for the auditorium of our opera house.'

Mundo wasn't at the table; Fogo was sleeping off his meal on the sofa. Jano put his knife and fork down: 'I adore turtle stew, but my illness prevents me eating fatty meat. Did your aunt do the cooking?'

Alícia spoke before I could: 'Ramira's always been a dab hand at cooking and sewing. Good at everything she does, in fact. Quite different from your mother, incidentally.' She got up with her glass in her hand and went on: 'Your mother and I got pregnant at the same time. She was the opposite of her sister. Ramira was always strange, terribly jealous of your mother, of everyone . . .'

'Alícia knows a lot of the families in the city,' Jano interrupted. 'If she had her way, there'd be no one left standing, not even the dead.'

'Quite a lot of the dead were admirable people.' She laughed and looked me in the eye. 'Don't you want to try Naiá's dessert? Naiá does everything – and she still has time to spoil my son.'

'Everyone's got time for him.' Jano got up from the table. 'That's why he hasn't got time to study, or any desire to go to parties or play football.'

'Aren't you going to finish lunch?' asked Alícia.

'I'm going to show you the house,' he said to me.

Fogo jumped off the sofa and accompanied his master along a corridor leading to a spacious pantry; further on was the kitchen and a veranda opening on to a cement square, and two adjoining rooms, with doors and windows painted green. At the bottom there was a garden full of palms and other trees, which ended in forest. We went down to the garden, and Jano pointed out the little white building housing the generator, in a corner, protected by iron railings. At the side was a zinc roof sheltering a black DKW, a jeep and an Aero Willys.

'You've got time for lunch, Macau. We're only going out in a short while,' he said, looking at the chauffeur's sleepy face in the window of the DKW. He whistled for Fogo, who ran towards him, making a noise in the foliage.

'It's strange . . . He has no friends.'

The dog came out of the vegetation with a lizard in its mouth, dropped it on the hot cement and scratched at the reptile with his foot till he'd torn it to shreds; the tail, separate from the body, was still twitching; Fogo snatched the quivering thing in his teeth and devoured it. Then he growled at the animal's mutilated body and looked at us, posing and showing off.

'He's got no friends in the neighbourhood, or at school. I know why he wanted to leave the Pedro II. He got good marks, but the discipline got in the way of his mania. He wanted to spend his time drawing. It's a vice, an illness . . . That big guy played that trick on my son, didn't he? Instead of reacting, fighting back, he took a ducking in the lake and sat there like an idiot. The headmaster told me the other boys laughed at him. They must still be laughing . . . they always will be.'

He put his hands behind his back and stood on tiptoe as if he wanted to see something, but it was just a gesture of irritation. 'I want Mundo to get out a bit and drop this mania of drawing, drawing all the time . . . He gets away some-times – I've found out where he goes. His mother says she doesn't know anything. Come on, I'm going to show you something.'

We went back to the living room; Naiá was cleaning the glass cabinet and saw the look in her employer's eye.

'Dona Alícia's gone out,' she said. 'She's gone to visit a friend.'

'Why didn't she go with Macau?'

Naiá didn't answer him and went on with her cleaning. Jano stood looking at her, with a serious face, without blinking. Suddenly, he said under his breath: 'She's gone to visit a friend . . .' The maid didn't turn round, or register that she'd heard. Then he spoke to me: he wanted to take me to his son's room, the last room on the upper storey. The solid-wood flooring along the corridor shone. Jano took a key out of his pocket, unlocked the door, and began to cough. Sheets of paper, paintbrushes, pencils, tubes of paint, birds' feathers, dried plants and seeds scattered over the floor; in a glass cube were creepers rolled up in a cone and, on the walls, drawings with indigenous symbols.

'No maths books on the shelves. Just art, poetry . . . Worse still: no photos of women, except his mother. My son can't go on like this.'

He locked the room again, went downstairs and from the kitchen veranda ordered the chauffeur to open the car doors. Fogo jumped into the front seat, and Jano invited me to go out with him. Where were we going? The DKW went up

23

the narrow Dona Libânia Street. Near the Law Courts girls in T-shirts and shorts came out from the shade of the *oitizeiros*. Red lips glistened, then disappeared. They saw the black car and came, together, down to the paved street. Jano looked at me and gave a dry laugh: 'Macau, we're going to go by the General Osório barracks.'

The DKW turned into Epaminondas Avenue and stopped a few yards from the sentinels; on the sunlit General Osório Square soldiers were jumping over barriers, running in zigzags holding bayonets; they had a flask and a knife at their belts, and knapsacks on their backs.

'Military training,' said Jano, greeting an officer. 'That's what my son needs . . . a bit of fearless running and jumping, just like these lads with their weapons.'

His voice was more sure of itself than it was hopeful. He stood admiring the olive-green figures with their weapons; now they were crawling through the thin, dry grass. I felt a little fear and asked again where we were going, what did he want to talk about? He clapped me on the shoulder and smiled. Self-confidence. He wasn't concerned that I was there, against my will, watching military exercises, or observing his triumphant expression, as if he was in change of these exercises. He walked on to the square and exchanged words with an officer.

'Now we can go,' he said to Macau.

It looked as if everything had been planned. The car passed along Sky Street, through Pedro II Square, and went along Seventh of September Street. Marshal Deodoro Street was chaotic: pavements jammed with peddlers and people selling fruit who clapped, shouted and rushed towards the DKW. Macau hooted the horn and gesticulated, trying to drive them away. At the end of the street, Fogo recognised his master's office, jumped out of the window and stood on his hind legs against the tall door. The chauffeur waited in the car, and the three of us went up. A smell of old paper exhaled from the shelves stuffed with papers and boxes of documents.

'I don't throw anything away,' said Jano. 'My father's life is stored there. He came from Portugal without a penny in his pocket. All he had was courage and the will to be someone. He was a religious man who believed in civilisation and progress.'

On the desk stood the replica of the firm's first steamship, the boat that had begun the regular line between Manaus and Vila Amazônia.

I asked for the windows to be open; he paid no attention: the mould and dust on the papers didn't bother him. He lit the lamps and sat on the high chair in front of the desk. His figure looked down at me from above, with Fogo at his feet. The dull light only lit part of his face. Jano began to speak, fingering a piece of blotting paper.

'You're a young man already, Lavo. I'm talking man to man. I'm a sick man, but I don't give up.'

Then he made me swear not to tell my uncle and aunt anything. He pressed the point: I was to forget everything he was going to say to me that afternoon. Wasn't I Mundo's friend? Maybe the only one. His other friend was just a cheap artist.

Who was this other friend?

He punched his thigh and sighed. 'Don't you know him yet? A bum. He paints junk, things with neither head nor tail. He makes sculptures too . . . twisted stuff, rubbish, all of

25

it! Mundo spends all his time in this leech's house, even sleeps there sometimes. My wife thinks our son's going to be a genius.'

He spoke with his finger pointing at my head, as if his son was there instead of me. His white shirt was darkening with all the sweat, and his face was red; he rested his hands on a pile of paper, absorbed, staring at the dusty windows blocking off the afternoon sunlight. Muffled peddlers' shouts could be heard; I was listening to the hubbub, when a noise brought me back to the room. Jano had opened a drawer and had an envelope in his hand. His look moved to the dog on the floor; he waved the envelope, playing with Fogo, and calmed down somewhat.

'I know you're an orphan, Lavo. I know your uncle and aunt . . . All that ex-radio announcer thinks about is having a good time, but your aunt's an honest woman. I know you have a hard life,' he said, with the remains of a smile. Then he went on, in a harsh tone: 'But that's not the reason for what I'm going to propose to you. I've got my difficulties too – just they're different. My health . . . my son . . . this moral inferno. I want him to meet a woman and get away from that artist's house. A woman . . . old or young, a widow, a whore, any woman'll do! And keep out of that bastard's house. I'll pay you a lot of money for that. I want to save my son, before it's too late. Think about it, Lavo. It's a job like any other.'

He waited for a word or a gesture of assent, without a thought for my humiliation and shame. The dull light protected me. The man was offering me, with his right hand, an envelope full of money, as if he wanted to share the flames of this moral inferno with me, when it was his, and his

26

alone. Even Fogo's yellow eyes were trying to corner me. I felt small, stunned, faced with this father who wasn't mine.

I still remember the punch Jano landed on the table, his reaction to my silence or perplexity. The dog jumped up on to a pile of old papers, stared at me, and let out a threatening snarl. The two of them faced me, demanding a reply.

I remember the oppressive silence, stifling the noise in the street, my anxious walk back to the little house in the Vila da Ópera, and the powerful voice of a sick man, tormented by his son's artistic vocation, or, perhaps, by something else.

I never told Mundo about this generous, infamous offer.

When Jano visited us for the second time, he pulled over near the door and whispered, with a smile that seemed to recall his offer: 'You're all really in a hole, my lad.' He kissed my aunt with calculated effusiveness.

He'd seen that no object or piece of furniture had come into our house; the only novelties were the French and Italian magazines the customers brought for the seamstress to copy the patterns.

'I wish I could earn a bit more money! Or a friend would lend us some. Your uncle spends it all on women!'

Had Jano hinted at something? Aunt Ramira said this as soon as he'd gone, leaving us expensive presents: a cut of pure silk for her, of cotton for me; he also left a stronger sense of our penury behind him. He was the must illustrious visitor to come to the Vila da Ópera; even the neighbours came out into the road to see him go. One neighbour came over to get the gossip, and said my aunt was too full of her own importance, and stingy with it: she didn't ask for coffee, sugar or flour. Nothing, no favours at all. Before, we got leftovers from local birthday parties: slices of coconut and manioc pudding, or trays full of stuffed prunes and dates, and Brazil-nut biscuits; Ramira never returned these favours, maybe out of pride, or, in the case of this particular neighbour, for fear that if she got too close, she would come into our house and get into Jano's good books.

Macau, who sometimes appeared in a white jacket, was also given respect. Not many of the seamstress's clients had chauffeurs, and only one, Dona Santita Biró, was always in a hurry because a black Aero Willys, with a black number-plate with gold numbers, was waiting for her. She was the wife or the mistress of an important magistrate, which provoked whisperings. However, Jano impressed everyone much more: he had a neoclassical mansion, which attracted the attention of tourists, and a property, far from Manaus, much talked about, Vila Amazônia. For Aunt Ramira, what mattered above all was his great reputation, which had grown after the Second World War and still shone with the force of authority. This combination of material wealth and moral correctness made Jano a perfect being. 'That's a real rarity,' she'd say. 'The poor man's only fault was to fall under that woman's spell.'

Mundo's refuge was his mother, but there was another one too, whom I discovered by accident one Saturday afternoon, when I was doing some research for a history project. I was looking at the low-fronted, colourful houses of the old Tocos area, in Aparecida. Mundo was near the church, in front of a rusty fence blocking the entrance to an abandoned house. His green-and-yellow uniform gave a garish air to his thin body; he was holding a black leather briefcase, the same he'd used when we were at the Pedro II. He bent down, put his hand through the iron bars and stayed like that for a few seconds; when he came away, I saw a family of Indians picking up the coins he'd thrown; that was where they lived, between the fence and the façade of the ruined house. Then Mundo went along a ravine and came out at the Beco da Indústria; I only caught up with him on a piece of wasteland, between a boatyard and a sawmill, near St Vincent's creek. He looked all around him, as if someone was spying on him. There was a smell of burnt oil and freshly cut wood. The canoes beached on the sand rocked back and forth as the boatmen waved at him; one of them shouted at the visitor, but Mundo paid no attention. He went into the boatyard, its ramp covered in mud, and reappeared rowing a red canoe.

Did anyone know that lad?

'Luti, the captain, has been around with him a bit,' said one of the boatmen, pointing at a pontoon.

'Where does he go?'

'He comes without warning and goes rowing out towards São Raimundo. He only comes back when it's dark.'

I went by canoe to the pontoon, where four men were playing dominoes round a beer crate; the boatman whistled to a little fat man, dressed only in a pair of shorts, and tapped me on the shoulder: 'Luti, this lad wants to follow that strange-looking guy.'

'Raimundo?' asked the other one.

Mundo's canoe had already disappeared. Luti rowed quickly up the Rio Negro, went towards the right bank and waited for the ripples from the wake of a pleasure boat to pass. Since when had he known my friend?

'Two or three years ago . . . He carried a satchel full of

paper. He said he was going to see an artist, his teacher. I took him lots of times; then he got hold of a canoe in the boatyard and went on his own. The so-and-so did a drawing of my head . . . my wife threw it out, said it looked like the face on the Devil.'

In Franco's creek, we passed amongst the boats of a floating market. After the bridge, to the left, the channel widened, and the hills of São Jorge appeared, covered with houses built of rough stones and wood. On a small island in the middle of the channel, a silk-cotton tree shaded a white house. Luti lifted up his oar and jumped on to the bank. Mundo's canoe was on land, upside down. There were bits of wood piled up in the garden, and strange objects stuck into the sand.

Mundo, in uniform, appeared on the veranda and walked slowly in our direction. He recognised Luti and straight away asked me: 'Does my father know?'

A faint whistle came from somewhere in the garden.

Mundo's gaze swept the banks of the river looking for someone. 'Did Jano tell you about the studio?'

'No one said anything. I saw you in Aparecida, and Luti brought me here.'

His face relaxed: 'We'll go back in my canoe.'

Luti was given some loose change and left.

There was a more distinct whistle, and a tall, dishevelled man appeared, with rounded features and small eyes. He was barefoot, dressed only in Bermudas, his hands yellow with sawdust. He opened his arms in an expansive gesture, embraced me and said in a deep voice: 'You must be Mundo's friend, right? Come on in. Another young man in Arana's studio.'

He stopped in the garden and pointed at a sculpture stuck in the ground: it was made of wood, slender and convex, full of circular holes and red gourds. Arana put his head into one of the holes and made a face: the local children did it too, for a game.

'A holed canoe,' I said, almost in spite of myself.

'Much more than that,' he observed. 'It's a false canoe. I made that sculpture with the children that live on the riverbank.'

Until then, I'd only seen the pictures in the State Art Gallery and Government House (the former Schulz mansion), and the Italian paintings in the Opera House. Now I found myself in a studio with tables, carpenter's tools, lathes and a circular saw. Chunks of wood had the form of a cat, a bird or a reptile; on the walls were sheets of paper with Arana's drawings on them. What attracted me most was a series of objects painted in strong colours: little clay women, sitting or lying down, giving birth to fish and serpents. They had a strange expression, all with their mouths open and thick red lips; they were looking upwards; on their heads was a veil of tulle, frayed and stained.

'The guy who made those was crazy,' said Arana.

'A madman?' I said, addressing Mundo.

'They're crude objects,' said the artist, with disdain.

Mundo touched the face of a sculpture and crouched down to look at it closely.

'I bought these things just to help the poor fellow, but that's not art,' said Arana, on his way up to the mezzanine. 'The neighbours think my house is a joiner's workshop. They don't know that a sculptor gives a new form to nature.'

In the passage round the mezzanine, he showed me books and reviews with reproductions of the works of his favourite artists. A narrow gap led into a large room, with only a bed and a console in it, in contrast with the downstairs room piled up with objects and machinery. From the window I could see the building of the Military Club, and, closer, the two channels of the divided creek. I had the impression of being in a house that was cut off, on an island. I remembered the canoe trips with Uncle Ran in the Cornos creek; from there, we went out to the centre and other neighbourhoods.

'When I was a boy, I came past here, but you couldn't see the house,' I said.

'The jungle hid it all,' said Arana. 'I knocked down some trees and used the trunks for sculpture. I left the silk-cotton tree, which gives shade and good luck.'

He became thoughtful and looked at me with curiosity: 'Where do you live?'

'In the centre, but I was born in Castanhal, on the Morro da Catita. I was brought up by an aunt . . . Ramira.'

'The seamstress? That's a long time ago . . . What I mean is, my profession has isolated me in this studio.'

Something had left a bad taste in his mouth; he looked at me and twisted his lips in what looked to me like a comic grimace. Suddenly, he clapped his hands: the noise of running and shouting filled the house.

'Neighbourhood kids', he said. 'They're going to get a snack.'

They devoured the manioc cake, and then went to look for mangoes that had fallen from the trees; they tidied the garden, swept up the shavings scattered round the studio and put it into bags. Arana watched the work out of the corner of his eye. In the end, he told the children they could go.

It was already getting dark, and Mundo had to go. The artist gave me a tree-porcupine shell with a hole in it, full of

Brazil nuts, tied to a red cane. I shook the shell, making a sound like falling rain.

'It's a real rattle,' he said, with a serious face.

I saw he hadn't liked my gesture. He'd embraced me, given me a present, and had made an effort to please, but in that first meeting I felt a hint of hostility, or mutual antipathy. Maybe it was a false impression left over from Jano's words, I thought.

Mundo took a torch out of his briefcase, and while he was rowing, I kept it focused on the stretch of water in front of the prow. Remains of the floating market bobbed on the water by the bank, where shanties built out over the water loomed in the darkness. Near Aparecida quay, I asked him how he'd met the artist.

'It was on the day of Chiado's death. I got home in a state of terror, and my mother got a shock when I said he'd died in a fight with one of the older boys.'

He told me that Alícia, that afternoon, to distract her son, had taken him to a matinée in the Polytheama cinema, and then to the 'Castelinho', the shop owned by the Booth Line; on the way back, when they went by Customs House, they'd been drawn to a group of foreigners taking photos of objects piled up on a mat, and picking them up to look at them. Mundo was curious, and wanted to get closer; his mother pulled him by the arm – it was just peddlers' trinkets. He insisted, and Alícia went off in a hurry – Jano would be home soon.

'She didn't look as if she was in a hurry – she looked as if she was afraid,' said my friend. 'She of all people, who was never afraid. She seemed nervous, frightened. I pulled myself away and went alone, into the circle of people, and saw the artist for the first time. He looked like a clown, or a mimic.

He was making mad gestures, stammering out words in English . . . I think he was trying to translate the name of the animals he'd sculpted; he pretended to understand the questions, answered "yes" or "no" in English, and sold the objects. He accepted any foreign currency, threw the money into a straw basket and wrapped each piece in tree bark. He did everything at the same time. When the tourists left, I stayed on my own, looking at the animals. Then he put his hands on my shoulders and asked as naturally as could be: "Would you like to visit my studio?"'

'Does Alícia know you go to Arana's house?' I asked, remembering my encounter with Jano.

'My mother's not bothered about it. Jano's different; he's suspicious of everything. He spies on me all the time, pursues me . . . at heart, he despises me.'

We left the canoe in the boatyard. There was no one on the beach. The dogs were barking, and the sound of a radio came from a wooden house on a vacant lot. We passed in front of the church, and further on saw some figures behind the fence of the abandoned house. They were eating, sitting on the ground. There was the sound of children crying, and incomprehensible voices. Mundo touched my arm; if Jano were to see those Indians, he'd say they were lazy vagabonds.

He pointed at a noisy corner, with lights on; he wanted to go to the bar and have a beer. He buttoned up his collar, knotted his tie, and combed his hair. He said to me in a low voice: 'Van Gogh and Matisse, my lad. Brancusi . . . Arana has reproductions of all of them. When I next go to Rio, I'm going to buy those books.'

In the bar, he wanted to know if I'd liked the artist.

'He doesn't seem very friendly.'

'Unfriendly and a know-all, isn't he? No one likes him on first acquaintance. Later he puts people at their ease, you'll see.'

'He made a strange face when I said where I came from.'

'Arana was very poor,' said Mundo. 'Before, I never talked to anyone about art. Well, only with your uncle, but Ranulfo isn't an artist.'

'Have you known my uncle for a long time?'

Mundo looked at me sideways, drumming his fingers on the table. I was going to repeat the question; he picked up his glass and said mockingly: 'I'm going to drink to my father's birthday. He's forty today, but he must only be celebrating the years he's lived without his son.'

He paid the bill, and we walked through the streets of Aparecida; on the pavement in front of the hospital of the Santa Casa he stopped and asked: 'Your uncle?' and started walking again, without me answering. Near the Music Conservatory he slowed down and insisted I came in: 'Just stay for a short time. You'll see Jano's best pals. It's worth seeing some people close to.'

Cars were parked in both streets, and the mansion was illuminated. We went round the front, and Mundo preferred to go in by the back entrance; he banged on the iron gate until Macau appeared.

'Your mother wants to know where you are,' said the chauffeur.

'Doesn't she know where her son hides himself?'

Mundo pulled me into a corner in the kitchen, pointed to the guests and whispered: 'The big one over there is Albino Palha . . . a friend and adviser to my father. He exports jute, Brazil nuts and rubber. If it was down to him, he'd export the Vila Amazônia employees too. He's an old bachelor, and melts when he's with the military. Look how he fawns on those guys. All he needs to do is comb Colonel Zanda's moustache; he's the tallest, and Jano keeps saying he's the darling of the Amazonia Military Command. The other one's Lieutenant Galvo, Zanda's aide-de-camp. That hunchbacked skeleton is the president of the Chamber of Commerce. He's got various nicknames: the whiskered skull, Herodotus . . . He knows all the big dates in history by heart. When he speaks, you'd think he was in parliament. The halfwit thinks he's a historian, and his wife, that twisted broomstick, makes fun of her beloved Herodotus all the time. The others are arse-lickers or gatecrashers. My mother hates these people. She's drinking already . . .'

At the centre of the table was an iced cake, a miniature of the Mattoso family mansion, surrounded by a circle of red and green candles. Mundo went in front of me, greeted his father, then straight away went to kiss Alícia; several faces stared at us, and some of them focused on Mundo's dishevelled state.

'Lavo, your uncle would have had a fine time here,' said Alícia under her breath. 'If he was still on the radio, the whole city would be laughing in the middle of the night . . . *Midnight and Just the Two of Us*. He was funny.'

She waved to Naiá, made a gesture with her thumb near her mouth and said: 'Whisky'. She went to whisper, but said it louder than intended.

Jano left Albino Palha and touched his wife's arm: 'Would it be better if you stopped drinking? Not even on my birthday . . .' He looked hungrily at his wife's plunging neckline and turned to his son: 'You and your mother can't even behave on my birthday. Are you going to stay here with that dirty uniform and those filthy hands?'

'Leave the boy in peace,' said Alícia. 'Your guests want to talk to you. They admire you, and you need them.'

'Why don't you talk to the women?' asked Jano. 'They'll say you don't like them.'

'Those women . . . all they do with their mouths is gorge themselves and spout nonsense. I'm fine with my son.'

Jano went back to the men, and I heard a voice praising the new general-president; the same voice recited a poem in homage to his predecessor, the late Marshal Castelo Branco, 'A knight of Amazonas'.

Mundo let out a savage laugh: 'That's Herodotus. When he gets going, that's the end of the party.'

The orator, in suit and tie, looked as if he was suffocating: he stuck out his neck and breathed out heavily, his fingers stuck in his shirt collar, as tight as a dog's; then he looked around to get attention. He was praising the dead marshal to the skies, and his voice was getting louder. The man wouldn't stop. He was possessed by these eulogies, by his own voice, indifferent to his wife's pinches and nudges, which were now undisguised. A twisted broomstick! She was tall and skinny, her crazy neckline revealing her wrinkled skin.

'Didn't I tell you?' Mundo made a face. 'A first-class idiot. Our very own Herodotus.'

Colonel Zanda emerged from a circle of officers, crossed the room and firmly interrupted Herodotus's speech. 'You're right, the late marshal's decree will bring lots of industries to Amazonas.' He put his hand on the orator's shoulder and went on: 'But the president's death isn't the end of the world, much less of our government. We've still got great generals, don't you agree?'

Herodotus lowered his head: he obeyed, shut up, taking

37

his arm away from his wife's bony hand. He looked at her angrily, felt he was being looked at, and withdrew into his shell.

Alícia took a sip of whisky and looked with disgust at the table: 'They can't half eat . . . it looks like a hungry ant-hill.'

The guests were tucking in to the platters of fish and meat. Lieutenant Galvo tried to balance a plate of a huge pile of fish, but the mashed manioc slid over the side and fell to the floor. Naiá, attentive as always, cleaned it up with a cloth.

'A real lackey and pushy with it,' Mundo murmured.

Jano and Albino Palha didn't eat. With his back to the wall, Palha was smoking and looking at his friend. He had a cold face, and his gestures were rehearsed: he shut his eyelids when he drank, and then stroked his ring. He spoke and moved to one side, observing everyone around him; his enormous head and shoulders made his friend's body look smaller. I caught something of what they were saying: the price of jute . . . a buyer from São Paulo . . . a firm in Taubaté . . . the Military School. Alícia was looking at them sideways, her empty glass in her right hand. The conversation was taking a while, and the noise of cutlery and chewing drowned their whispers. She went over to the men, said a few words and left them. Naiá lit the candles on the cake and called her employer. Alícia turned round, and was already on her way out of the room, when her son stopped her – he didn't want to be left on his own.

'You've got your friend and Naiá . . . and your father, it's his birthday.'

She invited her son to go upstairs too. Still with her glass in her hand, she opened her mouth, showed her full wet lips, and blinked. The two of them stayed still, looking at one

38

another; then she said she was feeling a bit dizzy and was going to her room.

Jano saw his wife moving towards the stairs; he looked disorientated, put his hands together, embarrassed. Suddenly he asked where Fogo was, and lost any composure he had possessed. The dog appeared behind Naiá, someone put out the lights, and the maid began singing happy birthday. When Jano blew the candles out, I looked for Mundo and couldn't see him. I left the room straight away, guiding myself by the kitchen light until I got down to the patio. Macau was sitting, his legs stuck out in front of him, beside the building with the generator; he was propped up against the wheel of the jeep, holding a plate. He picked up the food with his hands and devoured it, alone in the garden.

What a telling-off my friend got from his father the next morning! While Naiá was doing the cleaning, he listened to the threats: no holiday in Rio; if he was going to travel, it would be to Vila Amazônia; he'd see lads of his age were working themselves to death.

Alícia had asked Mundo not to answer back: Jano had got up in a bad mood, accusing his wife and son of ingratitude, and swore there'd be no more celebrations; he didn't want to celebrate his own survival.

After the fortieth birthday party, I saw him only from a distance and hesitated to greet him. He was waving out of the window of the DKW without looking at me. It was towards the end of November when the car stopped at the top of the alleyway and Macau called me over with a whistle. I stuck my head inside the window, and Jano was stroking Fogo's ears.

'In January we're going to Vila Amazônia. You're coming with us,' he said, as if it was an order or a summons.

Someone lit a kerosene lamp, and the shadow of a woman stained the screen over the window. It might have been your mother or Algisa: the same angular profile, long neck, and wavy hair down her back. That September night, I remember, the sky was completely dark, the day's heavy downpour had left the jungle and the earth wet, and I hid to see who was coming out of the house, if it was a man . . . This was after midnight. Your mother and I'd had a nasty quarrel at the wedding party of a man she thought was a distant relative: the last Dalemer in the city, a boor who'd never paid the least attention to the two sisters. Even so, Alícia wanted to go to the do and insisted on wearing new clothes. I hadn't got any money to be buying expensive clothes, and I had to steal a linen dress that Ramira had just sewn for a customer. It was too big for your mother, but even so she wore it with petticoats belonging to my elder sister, Raimunda, who also lent her a pair of pointed high-heeled shoes. Algisa refused to go to the party: the Dalemer was no relative, near or distant, he was nothing. I waited for the rain to pass, put a plank between the entrance to the house and the dirt road so your mother wouldn't step in the puddles, and we went slowly along the dark path to the Ponta Negra road. We were lucky to get a lift on an Army lorry that was going to Chapada and would pass by the Bosque Club. About nine, Ramira surprised us in the middle of the room and said in front of the guests that Alícia had stolen the dress. Your mother had no time to reply: she was humiliated by Dalemer, who said: 'How did you get into the club? Were you invited?' She didn't answer: she pulled me by the hand and demanded I go with her. I heard some sniggering around me and reacted with false, aggressive courage, saying without thinking that she could go, I was going to enjoy myself. She shouted: 'Stay here then with these filthy-rich whores and never darken my door again.' And before she left the club alone, she raised her finger right in Ramira's face and said: 'One day you'll do sewing *for me, and I'll give you a few remnants out of the goodness of my heart.' Her angry voice lit up her gypsy eyes, and she looked even prettier in her stolen linen dress, its neckline showing half her young breasts. I tried to stop her, but she pulled herself away with brazen gestures, threw her shoes down and ran out amongst the women and the girls, who looked at her with fear and envy. I thought it was just one more of the several quarrels we'd had in the last few months; I also thought she'd come back to the club, but the night went by and she didn't return. Ramira went before ten, and seemed happy to have charmed a woman who'd liked Alícia's dress. Another customer for my sister, who'd just humiliated your mother. I decided to stay a little longer and danced with a socialite who didn't know how to dance. She was drenched in such a strong perfume I couldn't smell her body, and I left her at the end of the third* samba–canção; *I started thinking about Alícia again and began drinking. I danced with another beanpole and smelt the same nauseous perfume, enough to make a horse throw up. Dalemer was in a state of euphoria; he was drinking and dancing to music played by some sad, sleepy men, playing out of tune. A distant cousin of the two sisters . . . Your mother wanted to believe that. I left these funereal proceedings and walked as far as the creek, where I found someone to row me to the Morro. I stayed hidden in the jungle, eaten up with jealousy, thinking there might be someone, a man in the house: I was keeping watch, given over to a tame, melancholy madness, chewing over the quarrels and whisperings of the past, chasing any will-o'-the-wisp I could. In the open doorway there appeared a girl holding a lamp. By her height and her walk I recognised Algisa. She was wearing a T-shirt that went halfway down her thighs. She hung the lamp from a branch of the* pitombeira, *and with a jump she sat on a low wall, slowly swinging her legs, smoothing out her braided hair and then rubbing her bare arms. Some boys going by made themselves a nuisance, whistling and smacking their lips. She picked up the lamp, stood in front of the door as if afraid. I came out of the jungle and shouted: 'Get out of here,' and the kids ran off. I went over to speak to her: she lifted the lantern as high as her shoulders, a part of her face shone in the light, and her big anxious eyes looked at me as if seeking help in the humid, sleepless, almost starless, night. 'What are you doing out here?' I asked. Then I demanded to know where Alícia was. Algisa, with a voice like your mother's, asked: 'Didn't she go to the party with you?' 'She left the Bosque on her own,' I said. After that I suspected: 'Your sister's in there with someone.' Algisa stuck out her lips: 'Go and have a look.' I went in, searched all round the house, and then I realised something had happened in your mother's life. I looked at the kitchen, went out the back and saw a new fridge, came back to the little room where the two of them slept and opened the wardrobe I myself had ordered from a joiner on the Morro, and my blood began to boil. 'Who is it?' I shouted. Algisa got a fright. 'What d'you mean, who is it?' 'The man, Alícia's lover.' She stammered: 'There's no one, no one at all.' 'Oh no? What about the fridge, the new clothes? Why's she been lying to me? You haven't got money to be buying that kind of stuff. Who gave it you?' Algisa stopped and looked at me; then she went to the kitchen, came back with a bottle of beer, offered me a glass and said: 'Is my sister the only woman in the world?' That was what your aunt was like, the other aspiring Dalemer. We only stopped drinking in the hammock, and she was fiery, just like your mother, only she pretended to be afraid, and was madly jealous of Alícia's beauty. At some moment in the early morning, I looked at Algísa and saw your mother, and murmured her name. Algisa reacted with jealousy, and there we were, the two of us, locked in an embrace and prey to jealousy. Both of us were jealous of Alícia. Then she told me her sister wouldn't be sleeping at home, and spoilt the rest of that night, a night which would go on for more than thirty years. Who was Alícia seeing? Algisa didn't answer the question, but said something worse: 'My sister's . . . found a rich young man, and she's going to marry him.' That was when, drowning in the body of the aunt you barely knew, I began to hate your father. I felt hatred and jealousy for Jano, and I'm sorry I never told you everything . . .*

4

V ILA AMAZÔNIA – the name and the place had always
attracted me. At the back of the little house on the
Morro da Catita, those two words had never been forgotten.
Uncle Ran said it was an imposing property, near Parintins,
on the bank of the Amazon: a big house with a swimming
pool at the top of a steep bank, from where you could see
immense islands that looked like the mainland, like the
Tupinambarana.

When I mentioned Jano's invitation, Ramira stopped sewing and fixed her eyes on me with enthusiasm; then they lost
their shine and wandered into some kind of daydream. 'I very
nearly got to visit Vila Amazônia. Your uncle disappointed me.
What I mean is, he pulled the wool over everyone's eyes. The
truth is he couldn't keep far away from that woman . . .'

'Alícia?'

'That's the one . . .' she confirmed, chewing the edge of
her mouth.

I suspected that there had always been something hidden
behind the arguments between my uncle and aunt. Now I
was going to visit the place, I wanted to know what had
happened there. Why had Uncle Ran disappointed Aunt
Ramira? Why had he fooled everyone?

My aunt stuck her needle into a piece of red cloth and
told me: 'Ranulfo was married to Algisa, Alícia's sister.

44

The one's as clever as the other's idiotic. A stupid, loveless marriage.'

'So our family's related to the Mattosos?'

'Indirectly . . . and not for long. Well, as you're going to Vila Amazônia, I think there are a few other things you should know.'

She leant her elbows on the machine and told me about the farcical, ephemeral marriage. The couple had spent some time in Vila Amazônia, and after they separated, Ranulfo never set foot in the property. When he was married to Algisa, Alícia avoided any intimacy with Ramira, and never invited her to her house in Manaus or the Vila. Jano didn't want to accept their engagement, and said Ranulfo was debauched, a man of the worst kind: he never settled down, lived on the hoof, with nothing but a hammock and a bundle of clothes, sleeping anywhere and with any woman. But, when he married Algisa, he turned inside out: he was like a saint, did everything for his wife – they slept together in a little house rented for next to nothing, in a group of shacks in Nossa Senhora das Graças, near the Amazonense Park. It was when the idyll was at its height that Jano suggested Uncle Ran work in the Vila Amazônia.

'At the start I didn't even suspect,' my aunt went on. 'I didn't think it was a trap . . . I thought it might be an opportunity for my brother, and for me too. Your friend's mother smooth-talked Jano into it, saying Ranulfo was willing to work. Your uncle puffed his chest out and said: "Look, sister, from now on I'm going to be a responsible man. An administrator!"'

Persuaded by Alícia, Jano wagered on Uncle Ran: he offered him a reasonable salary and two per cent of the profits from the jute exports. He gave the couple a big room in the basement of the house. Every six months, the two of them would spend a fortnight in Manaus. Ranulfo agreed and left with his wife for the middle reaches of the Amazon.

Five months later, Ranulfo disappeared; Algisa came back to Manaus in a pleasure boat and went to live with her sister. Aunt Ramira tried to get in touch with her sister-in-law, but in vain: Algisa refused to see any of her husband's relatives; she wandered round the house barefoot, dressed only in a nightgown, mouthing absurdities, incoherent, cursing Ranulfo and all the workers at Vila Amazônia; when Alícia asked her questions out of interest, her sister would start to tell a story and burst into tears. After some time, Algisa got hitched to a river trader, one Feliciano, and they moved to Rio Branco. Jano helped them make a new start in life: he bought rubber and Brazil nuts from Feliciano sight unseen – Feliciano made good, got some money together, and the two of them went to live in Minas Gerais. Algisa and her husband sent a letter to Jano, thanking him for his help, without even mentioning Alícia's name. They stayed in Minas, and she never reappeared.

My aunt's dream of a jump up the social scale never came off. Two months after her brother's disappearance, she got a message from a boatman: Ranulfo was travelling around the area of Santarém, Oriximiná, Óbidos and Monte Alegre; he was going to go as far as Belém, and then come back to Manaus.

'He appeared on the Morro da Catita in November 1955. I looked at him, thin, tired, and his clothes dirty with oil and grease. I started crying, and he hugged me and carried me down to the riverbank. He sat on the ground with a pose like a nabob and said, in that voice you know so well: "Sister, I wasn't going to exchange my freedom for two per cent of the jute sales. I wouldn't do it for a hundred per cent of all the production of Vila Amazônia." Then I said: "But for God's sake, Ranulfo. You put up with it for five months. Why didn't you stay longer? Was there something wrong with the place? Or the work? Or was it some woman?" Then your uncle gave a laugh and repeated, shouting: "A woman?" I know my brother . . . it wasn't a roguish laugh, he really was nervous. He knew that sooner or later I'd find out. He said the house was great, the place was pleasant enough, but when the jute was being cut, there were accidents every day. Workers . . . He was told they cut the jute standing in water, and they were bitten by all kinds of creatures. They came back to the house with wounds to their feet, hands and legs, and he still had to put up with Algisa's shouting. He called his wife a weakling, said she couldn't stand the sight of a drop of blood. She got nervous for no reason, wouldn't let him go on his own to Parintins, much less to Santarém, and one day he abandoned her in the basement of the house and left. He crossed the river, went to visit places like Nhamundá, Faro . . . wandering round . . .'

'What did he do in Vila Amazônia?' I asked.

'Nothing. It was show. He didn't administer a thing. He put all the blame on Algisa and the overseer, an ex-corporal in the Military Police that he railed on about. He said he forced the *caboclos* and the Japanese to work day and night and only talked about increasing jute production.'

I reminded my aunt that in my childhood I listened to Ranulfo telling stories of his trips round Amazonia, going as far as Belém; on the journey from Belém to Manaus he was

47

cook and ship's engineer, and nearly stayed behind in Parintins; sometimes, right at the beginning of *Midnight and Just the Two of Us*, Uncle Ran would sigh: 'Ah, Parintins, that enchanted isle.'

'Yeah, that enchanted isle,' Ramira echoed angrily. 'Now you're going to see what he lost.'

She didn't let me go with my pockets empty; she gave me a little bit of money, and on the day we left gave me motherly advice: chew your food without making a noise and don't whistle before the dessert, a childhood habit that had survived her irritated complaining. And if father and son quarrelled in my presence, I should tactfully get out of the way and go to my room. She walked nervously round the room and came up to me: 'What hurts me more than anything is that he left a child there somewhere. He must be a grown lad by now.'

'A son?'

'Yes, your cousin. I don't know him; don't even know his name. Ranulfo never talks about his son, but everyone knows about it. See if you can't find a way of seeing that lad.'

Out of pride, she didn't go with me to the Mattosos' front door. In the living room, I heard steps on the staircase. Fogo circled round me, and lifted his paws up in front of me. He's in a good mood, I thought, looking into his yellow eyes; his ears stood up, and in a trice, he had turned his nose towards the door: it was Jano. The others followed him. Mundo, between Naiá and his mother, came forwards to speak to me: 'Good thing you're coming,' he murmured. 'I couldn't have put up with this trip with my father.'

'Isn't Alícia coming with us?'

Mundo looked at me as if returning the question, and I realised he didn't want to talk about the subject just then.

Naiá called a taxi and opened the front door for the dog to get in.

'Macau's down at the harbour already,' said Jano, taking Alícia's hands. They hugged one another, caressing and whispering in each other's ears, with an intimacy that even surprised my friend. I got out of the way, thinking there was love between the two of them. Suddenly he lifted his head: 'But I've left it . . . in the same place.'

'You've left small change. There are things to be paid for in the house,' said his wife.

'How much?' Impatiently, Jano took some notes out of his wallet, folded them, and she took the money with a quick, insolent gesture; then she kissed her son, hugged him close, and went to the car with him. Her husband still tried to persuade her to come with us: a week was nothing; she could stay on the veranda, the swimming pool or the yacht. He looked at her in fear, his body rigid, defeated by his submission to her. Alícia, wearing a transparent blue night-dress, backed into the doorway and covered her breasts with her bare arms. She was dishevelled, her face still sleepy from her siesta, but her beauty won out over the neglect.

As the car moved away, I saw her once more next to Naiá, the two of them waving and laughing all the time. By my side, Mundo, with a serious face, didn't look back.

The *Saracura* was one of the most luxurious yachts in Manaus: it had an aluminium hull, six cabins with bathrooms and a sitting room with air-conditioning; an internal staircase led to the bridge. Macau, in a white uniform and a kepi,

49

went to the taxi and carried the food Naiá had prepared; then he cast off, and the yacht began to go down the Rio Negro, sailing close to the Educandos, with its shacks built out over the river. In the cabin, Jano sounded the horn: a deep, long-drawn-out sound attracted the people living in the Baixa da Égua, who appeared in the windows and doorways and waved.

'He wants to show off,' said Mundo.

'Or to irritate you,' I said.

'No, he did that before we set off.'

He lowered his head and covered his ears, until the bellowing horn stopped.

'Does your mother never go with Jano?'

'Last night he asked time and again why she wasn't coming, and what she was going to do alone in Manaus. Then he asked me, and I didn't answer. The day before every trip to Vila Amazônia, he presses her so much she begins to drink and ends up sleeping in my bed. Sometimes I get mixed up in the argument, but yesterday I kept quiet, trying to understand . . . When I was a child, we went together. Then she stopped wanting to go. She can't even bear hearing about the place, and gets annoyed when I ask why. I think she likes to be alone. I don't know what happened . . . nor what she feels . . . She stays beside me, defends me from Jano's rudeness, and then suddenly gets out of the way, as if she was angry about something . . .'

He said nothing more; he picked up a notepad and a pencil and observed Fogo sitting at my feet. In the entrance to the Eva branch of the river, the sun had already half disappeared in the vast surroundings. Mundo began drawing; glancing to one side, I saw what was going to be Fogo's muzzle, but the image looked monstrous. A little later, we were sailing in the dark. He shut his pad, and was going to go down to his cabin, when Jano appeared in the sitting-room doorway and ordered: 'Have your shower and come and have dinner with us.'

'I'm not going to eat.'

'What?'

'I'm not going to eat here,' Mundo repeated, and went down.

'You should have stayed in Manaus. You and that notepad with its obscene scribblings.'

Nervous, Jano stood on Fogo's foot; the dog went to hide under the table. He sat down, called Fogo over, and sat looking at the river between the dark strips of the forest. He asked me to take the captain his dinner; I filled my plate and went to eat on the bridge too.

'Tomorrow very early, we'll stop in Uricurituba,' said Macau.

'Will we be there for long?'

'Half an hour. Depends on what the boss says.'

Jano was eating alone; he threw Fogo bits of meat, and spoke from time to time. Mundo must have been thinking things over, fed up, or maybe drawing. A large boat, to our left, was going upriver. Still hammocks came close by, and only the kitchen, in the poop, was lit. The yacht shuddered in its wake, and a breath of damp air cooled the cabin. In the morning I saw my friend sleeping on the floor, with the lamp lit, and crayons and drawing-pad on the bunk.

We woke up with a commotion on board. Uricurituba. A priest came out of the small crowd to receive Jano. Fogo went after the two of them, towards the little church in the village's only square. Mundo disappeared into the unpaved streets that ended in jungle. I helped Macau carry the boxes to the moorings. Then he whistled, and, in single file, men and women presented themselves; he himself took charge of the bartering. Coffee, soap, salt, sugar, tins of powdered milk and pieces of cloth were exchanged for fruits, fish and turtles. Macau gave the rotten fruit back, threw the smaller fish into the river, and bargained with the *caboclos*: 'Do you know how much a packet of coffee is? A bar of soap? You don't know a thing, you've never seen money.'

In Manaus he was more submissive, and hardly spoke; now his white uniform and his kepi made it look as if he'd been promoted in some way. He gave the *caboclos* orders, selected the products, made fun of them all; he bought a hammock made of *tucum*-palm fibre and put the fish in a box full of ice. Mundo came back before his father; he brought some seeds he picked in the forest. He'd chatted with the locals – in the last flood the water had even got into the church, and they were still living in the dark. When Jano came back, he immediately said to his son: 'See? Macau's filled the yacht with food and got some bales of *malva* fibre for free. All that for a few boxes of trinkets. He's learning . . .'

'Learning to trick people?' asked Mundo.

'Learning to work,' Jano corrected him. 'That was what Macau was doing.'

Mundo murmured to me: 'He thinks I'm an idiot. He's the one that's mad, sick twice over he is.'

He collected the seeds and dried berries and put them all into a straw basket.

'Are you going to take them to Arana?' I asked.

'At his house I'd be learning the techniques of painting, watercolours, drawing . . . learning important things about artists, or leafing through an art book. Jano's not interested in all of that. He doesn't think his son can be different from him.'

'But he likes music, he's got a collection of records, he goes to concerts in the Opera House . . .'

'He listens to classical music only to say he knows such and such a symphony or sonata. He's always citing a famous pianist or conductor, an orchestra . . . It's not hard to impress Colonel Zanda.'

I tried to convince him that Jano wasn't just a collector of books and records, but Mundo moved away to the prow and stood watching the fishermen rowing fast towards the Serpa branch of the river. The warm wind shook the canoes, the fishermen jumped on shore, and a flash ripped across the sky. There was a crash of thunder as the morning ended. From the bridge, Macau told me it would only rain in the afternoon. His voice sounded serious, and bothered me. We ate lunch in silence; the wind was blowing stronger, the yacht shook, and Jano and Fogo sat in a corner of the sitting room. Mundo opened a beer and stood alone on the poop. I took the captain a plate of food: he thanked me, but he wasn't going to eat yet. His big hands gripped the helm, a cigarette butt in his mouth, his eyes on the alert. I looked at the nautical map and asked if we were going along the Rebojal. He said yes, and added, with a chagrined look: 'There's rough water there.' Further on, in the widest part of the river, dense clouds appeared, and a viscous mist covered the banks and the forest, blotting out the horizon. As we went blindly down the Rebojal, we heard laughter, low voices and music. We sailed slowly in the direction of the sounds; at the heart of the mist, a huge dark shape was swaying. The searchlight revealed a greenish boat, with its prow run ashore on the right bank. Macau deciphered the other captain's signals: 'It's a motorboat that's broken down, Dr Jano. We'll give them assistance.' His boss didn't want to, but Macau insisted: it was compulsory to help them or they'd tell the Port Authority, and the yacht would be fined – and heavily.

'I'll pay the fine. Let's get going,' ordered Jano.

'They're important people. The boat's owner is the head of the business association, your friend. There's no one understands about motors in the boat.'

Jano still resisted, and made a face: 'OK, let's get on with it. We'll have to.'

It was a boat full of girls with three or four men on board. Jano wanted to hide in his cabin, but someone shouted his name. Mundo recognised the voice: it was Colonel Aquiles Zanda. He was full of good cheer, glass in hand, his body swaying to and fro in the swell. Behind him was the round face of Lieutenant Galvo. The aide-de-camp wasn't armed: he wore a green T-shirt with the Army's insignia in the middle of his chest. Between two hammocks, half hidden, was a moustache on a haggard face – Herodotus.

'Our motor failed,' said Zanda. 'Jump over, Jano. Bring your son. Let's have a bit of fun.'

Carrying a box of tools, Macau disappeared into the hold of the stricken ship. His boss looked over the rail: he saw his son jump on to the deck, join the men, and mess with the girls. The one close to Mundo was wearing shorts and a T-shirt; dark and small, she laughed for no reason, like a child; she looked less young than the others. Her breasts were growing, and she seemed the most aroused: she was drinking, and started moving her hips in front of him. She gave her glass to a friend, and then Jano witnessed the scene he'd been dreaming of: his son glued to a girl's body, Mundo's hands stroking her neck and arms. Colonel Zanda lifted his glass, calling his friend over – Jano refused with a gesture. He happily put up with the loud music and the smell of burnt oil. He smirked foolishly at me, as if I was an accomplice, unable to see that this drunken spree was just a crazed provocation.

Macau reappeared, his hands dirty with grease; he swigged a drink and waited for the order to leave. My friend was laughing to himself, and already staggering when he let the girl go and grabbed another, then two more, one on either side, pointing at the colonel's belly and guffawing. Lieutenant Galvo pinned Mundo's arms: 'That's not the way we play, my lad.'

'The tarts like it,' Mundo shouted, belching in his face.

Macau and I dragged him to the yacht, as he shouted out: 'The tarts, you lot and the tarts . . .'

'It's OK,' said the colonel to Jano. 'They start like that when they're young. Later they learn to drink.'

Mundo leant over the deck railings and vomited between the two boats. Still dribbling, he stretched out his arms and stuck a finger up, pointing towards Zanda's head. The colonel restrained his aide-de-camp and fixed Jano with a serious look. The yacht went on its way, the music died away, and the girl's face was still hungrily looking out for Mundo's figure.

As we emerged from the Rio Urucará, the sultry air surrounded us with a kind of torpor, and the undulations of the water rapidly grew; the thick rain hid the forest and the horizon. Macau lit the searchlight and sailed near the left bank. From time to time Jano got up to look at his son, who was stretched out on the deck under the downpour. He paced round the sitting room, bit his lips, and said: 'Where does this rebelliousness come from?' He wasn't addressing himself to me: it was as if he was trying to reply to his own hoarse, useless voice, suffocated by the noise of the rain.

At the end of the afternoon, a weak sun lit up the low-level housing of Parintins, which stretched out as far as the end of the island of Tupinambarana; we passed near the ramp leading to the market, the harbour and Cathedral Square. The yacht went round the mouth of the Macurany and the Parananema, rivers shallow at that time of the year, when the cattle were transported to the straight stretches of the rivers and the islands that appeared when the water was low. High up on the bank, a big grey house, built on solid arches, looked out over the Amazon and the island of Espírito Santo; Jano, arms stretched out on the prow, answered the waves of the female employees. He had the status of a little god, and the confidence of an idol.

Mundo was still lying at the stern. He wouldn't go with me: I was to go alone, he wouldn't go up, and he wasn't going to have dinner with his father.

Grass covered the slope down to the moorings. Jano was waiting for me between the garden and the veranda. He said he'd not reproved his son for his drunkenness: he'd always wanted to see him dancing and drinking with women. The problem was his rebelliousness . . . He shouldn't have insulted the military men.

'Thank goodness my father never knew the insolent so-

and-so,' he went on, walking to the edge of the swimming pool.

'Did he never see his grandson?' I asked.

'He saw him as a baby and was happy that I had an heir, but he didn't see him as a boy or a young lad.'

There was a map of Portugal in green and red tiles on the bottom of the swimming pool, and on the walls were carved the names of the same country's cities, kings and queens.

'My father said that decoration was there so that he could dive into his country,' said Jano. 'He never did take the plunge. He had no time for nostalgia.'

On the wall of the principal room was a blue-and-white-tile mosaic portraying the Last Supper. The tiles and several porcelain and silver objects were Portuguese. Then Jano took me to the kitchen and to the six bedrooms ranged along the side of the big house. I asked why there were so many paintings of St Francis Xavier, done by the same Portuguese artist. He explained that, at the end of the Second World War, his father had these images brought to decorate the small houses for the Japanese employees. He wanted them all to worship the saint, but they didn't like the idea, and returned them. In Mundo's room, where I slept too, two of these pictures were on facing walls.

The bedroom was larger than the sitting room at the Vila da Ópera. A tulle mosquito net surrounded the beds, and the wind from the river brought some air to an atmosphere that still smelt mouldy. From the window I could see the islands between the banks of the Amazon, and, to the left, the mouth of the Ramos branch, which goes up as far as the Rio Andirá.

The night we got there, Mundo woke me to say he'd come across an old sick Indian. An artist. He put the light on and showed me a painting on thin fibrous wood bark: strong colours and the half dissolved outline of a dying bird. He took the pictures off the walls, pushed them under the bed, and on one of the hooks he hung the Indian's handiwork. He said those images with their black background had given him nightmares when he was a child. In fact, everything in the house was detestable: the atmosphere, the pretentious decoration, the high-backed chairs, the red towels from Alcobaça, and the fawning maids. 'I'm not even going into the main room, Lavo. You can stick around with him . . . he won't bite you.'

'I'm to spend a week hanging round your father?' I asked.

'Tomorrow I'll have lunch with you,' he reluctantly agreed.

The following day, at eleven o'clock, Jano was already sitting at the head of the table. Two maids were polishing the Last Supper while the cook brought silver platters to the table. We waited a few more minutes for Mundo, who didn't appear. Jano noticed my anxiety, but pretended to ignore his son's absence. He said it was a struggle to implant civilisation in Vila Amazônia. In the old days, everyone ate with their hands and relieved themselves anywhere. 'I had to rebuild almost everything, Lavo. We've got to build all the time. Amazonia gives no respite. Working . . . that's what my son doesn't understand.'

The cook picked the bones out of the fish and served Jano with two slices; from time to time she came in to see if he needed anything. At the end of lunch, she asked after the mistress: it was a long time since Dona Alícia had been to the Vila.

'I don't think she'll come back . . . ever again,' Jano said with regret, looking at his son's empty chair. 'Now let's go and have a look at the property.'

In the warehouse, the jute passed through a mechanical press to be baled and carried to the barge *Santa Maria*, moored in the Ramos branch. In 1945 old Mattoso had bought the property from a Japanese firm. Oyama, the pioneer, whom everyone remembered, had brought jute seeds from India. He'd come with his family in 1934; later dozens of young agronomists from Tokyo arrived, spent a few days in Vila Amazônia and journeyed on to the Rio Andirá, where they founded a colony. They had built a small hospital, an agricultural school and Okayama Ken: a town where the oldest workers still lived. During the Second World War they were persecuted and imprisoned; some managed to escape and later returned. They had children with the local women: young mestizos, half Indian, half oriental, hard working and tough. There were still remains of that time: the ruins of a hospital, of tile-covered houses, and of the *kaikan*, an enormous pavilion, entirely of wood, put up by a master builder, also Japanese. It was used for parties, and to celebrate the Emperor's birthday. The descendants of the Japanese really worked hard, and in a few years they had done a huge amount, a hundred years' worth of work. On their own land, they had everything: maize, manioc, beans, *guaraná*, cocoa . . . They went into the water and cut the jute; they were courageous and well disciplined.

I saw several of them, thin and sad, on Gypsy Island, in Saracura, Arari, Itaboraí, and even on the Limão branch of the river. They cut jute with a machete, dried the fibres on lines, then carried them to the house, where they were compressed and baled; when the river level was high, the leftovers from the jute fed the pigs and cattle. The majority of the employees lived in shacks spread around Okayama Ken; when they fell ill, they were treated by one of the few doctors in Parintins, Dr Kazuma. The only Japanese not to be persecuted during the war, his name was uttered in veneration: Kazuma San. Once a week he visited the workers on the property, and one day he ate lunch with us. He was a man of about seventy-five, tall and very thin, his face turned copper-coloured from so much sun, and alert eyes behind his thick glasses. In a voice almost without accent, he thanked Jano for the medicines he'd brought.

'We couldn't do very much without them,' he said. 'Do you take your insulin every day?'

'When I forget, Naiá remembers. She looks after me well; she's learnt how to apply the injection and finds the right muscle with her eyes shut. The problem, Dr Kazuma . . . I don't know how to say it . . . but, with every day that passes, I feel more nervous and edgy. My life . . .'

The doctor made no comment. He turned his face towards the river and ate little, and silently.

After lunch, the two of them went on to the veranda. Only later, when the sun was less hot, did Dr Kazuma go out to visit the families, going from house to house. Mundo and I went with him. He looked at children and old people, chatted with them and gave them medicines. The local people followed, in line; they asked for advice, showed infusions made with tree bark, and asked if they were good for rheumatism, skin diseases or haemorrhaging. Did dolphins' teeth tied round children's necks cure diarrhoea? Or they said: 'I've got a pain in my backbone'; 'My brother can't walk'; 'My daughter's in the family way'; 'My granddad can't see the light any more.' The doctor calmly replied: 'We'll have a look, we'll take care of everyone.' We went into several shacks covered with straw and earth, their mud walls bound with creepers. In one of them, the most distant from Jano's house, an old man was groaning, lying in a hammock.

'He can't get up,' said his wife.

It was an Indian couple, whose children had gone to live in Manaus. Dr Kazuma knew what the man's illness was, listened to his heart, and looked serious. His wife understood. Mundo was looking at the sick man with fascination; he nudged me and pointed to the objects hanging on the wall. The doctor murmured: 'It's Seu Nilo, the oldest man in Vila Amazônia.'

Mundo talked of buying the objects, but the woman didn't want to take money: the boss was good, he gave food, clothes, medicines. My friend insisted and paid what she didn't know how to, or didn't want to, charge. He stayed there, near the hammock, looking at the sick man and conversing with his wife. He didn't go back to the big house; in the early morning, he woke me with these words: 'The old man's just died.' He sat on the ground, thoughtful, and began to draw.

Years later, I got from Germany a little painting on an aluminium sheet, with a copy by its side, on paper. In the copy, the face had another expression: one side of it had blurred, and cavities had formed in it. The title of the work was: *The Artist Lying in a Hammock*.

In the middle of the morning, some workers came out of the warehouse to keep vigil over the dead man's body; soon there appeared boats and canoes from Parintins and other places. Jano saw everything from far off; he allowed the employees to go to the funeral, and he knew his son was out there, and that he preferred to be with those people. From the veranda, he watched the ritual of the dead, half indigenous and half Christian; in the early afternoon, Mundo got into a launch and accompanied the water procession to Parintins.

'Why wasn't he buried here?' Jano asked me. 'He and his wife always lived here because I let them. Before, these Indians were treated by medicine men, charlatans through and through. We pay Dr Kazuma, and still they're rude and ungrateful. They forget the efforts we make, our dedication to them. They're like children . . . One day they pray to Our Lady of Mount Carmel, the next they forget both the saint and the Church. Their faith's all over the place.'

Mundo only went into the house to sleep. One night, he told me he'd lunched on cooked *bodó* with two Indians from the Rio Andirá who taught him to pronounce words like 'bird', 'sky', 'horizon', 'earth' and 'death' in their language. 'They're all drinking,' he murmured. 'Drinking and dying.' He spent the rest of the night drawing; he didn't ask me any questions or look at me: he just repeated the words he'd learnt, and talked about his conversation with the Indians as if they were there in the room with us, together, frightened in the dark.

The only day he had lunch with us was a disaster. He sat at the other end of the table, facing his father, and began eating greedily. The noise of his chewing was sickening. I wanted to say something, but didn't manage. In the kitchen doorway, Macau, to suck up to his boss, told a joke. No one laughed. Jano broke the silence: he asked the cook where *that woman* was.

'Down by the river, washing clothes.'

'And the boy . . . her son?'

'He's there, helping his mother.'

'Bring them both here.'

Mundo stopped chewing.

A dark-skinned woman appeared in the doorway, holding the hand of a boy, almost a teenager. Her cotton dress was wet: it had little red flowers on a white background. Her smooth black hair ran down over her bare shoulders, her hands and arms had dry sand all over them. Her face had a delicate, tired look. Mother and son, as they stood there on the threshold, were a picture of dignity and beauty. Those eyes, all four of them, which they wouldn't lower, reminded me of Naiá's eyes.

'Take a good look at that child,' Jano said to me.

I saw dark eyes, full of life, in a harmonious face, a high forehead, thick hair and a snub nose. The boy smiled.

'Your uncle came to work here, and just look at what he left behind here on the property. He must have others spread around the place, in Parintins, Santarém, all over the Amazon. Not much doubt that one's his, is there? Your uncle . . . He was even sniffing round our maid, in Manaus.'

Jano gestured, and the boy and his mother left.

Mundo chucked his knife and fork on to his plate and got up abruptly, shouting at his father: why had he done that? So as to humiliate the boy and his mother, or to show off?

He ran out on to the veranda and disappeared into the garden. It was a little time before Jano said: 'What's up with him? What the hell happened?'

He didn't seem either perplexed or indignant. His voice had a forced serenity. Jano wanted to show me his self-control and superiority, even a kind of benevolence, in the way he treated Mundo. Maybe the presence of Ranulfo's child had irritated my friend. It had certainly bothered his father, because of the jealousy he still felt for Uncle Ran.

The day before we were going back, Mundo invited me to lunch in Parintins. Macau gave us a message: we were to be back before seven. He added: 'The boss wants you both at table. It's the last supper.'

'Tell your boss to go to hell,' said Mundo.

Macau smiled mischievously and saluted.

We lunched in the Full Stomach, by the ramp up to the market: beans, pumpkin and *maxixe*; fried fish, rice and manioc flour. Then we played snooker with some of the pilots of the small boats plying the river, and the harbour porters. In the middle of the afternoon, Mundo decided to go to the town centre to pay a debt; he took almost an hour, and came back with a smile on his face, which had something secretive about it. A customer in the restaurant told us the participants in the celebration of the festival of the Red Ox were already working for the June event.

We walked towards the Ribanceira and went inside a noisy, crowded hangar. They were all working. Skeletons of boats and animals stood by a joinery workshop, and from the roof beams there hung mythological beings from the jungle. The little objects sculpted by the old Indian were now enormously large. Mundo already knew some of the people, and joined one group to give his opinion about colours, the final touches, and the surrounds for the objects. He did this with real energy, as if he was in Arana's studio. I observed the enthusiastic crowd, with their allegorical costumes and their fancy dress, and remembered the St John's Night festivals on the Morro da Catita, the clothes sewn by Aunt Ramira, and one of the 'oxen', the Field-Runner, whirling round and dancing in the middle of a gang of kids. Suddenly, a cry went up, and several voices started to sing, accompanied by a rhythm beaten out on zinc sheets, hollow wood and tin cans. Now a lot of people were dancing and singing in homage to the dead artist, one of the founders of the Red Ox. The voices and the drumming got louder and louder, the ground shook, and it seemed as if half the population of Parintins was there. I got up on a bench to watch the dancing, with its rehearsed steps, round the slowly moving wooden animals. I was taken up by the spectacle when I felt a sharp nudge in my side and saw a red mask with one yellow eye poked out. Mundo burst out laughing and stretched his arms out, showing claws made of bones. 'The Song of the Whistling Wind,' he yelled. Without my asking him, he told me he was going to stay there till the end of the rehearsal.

The sun was setting in the forest, behind Gypsy Island. Parintins was quiet: only the noise of the boat going down the river. I went back to Vila Amazônia by canoe. Macau was getting the yacht ready for departure; on the veranda, Jano was talking to the foreman.

At seven he called me to dinner. I sat with my back to the Last Supper and facing the Amazon, where Espírito Santo Island was going dark, in a profusion of shadows. Jano cut a slice of fish, and didn't eat it. The noise of the generator drowned the croaking of the toads. The man's silence was frightening. I asked how the property was coming along.

'Reasonably,' he replied, crumbling a piece of fish. The baling of the jute was almost finished, and he'd bought two tons of rubber from a plantation owner in Santarém. 'An old family . . . Americans who fled from the Civil War and settled in Pará. The heirs sold the rubber plantation to an

English family, and now they're all Brazilians . . . *caboclos* with English surnames.'

From the kitchen door, Macau informed him the yacht was ready.

'If it doesn't rain, we'll leave early,' said Jano.

He'd said he wanted his son at the table for the last night: where'd he got to?

'Parintins,' I said. 'We visited the rehearsals for the Red Ox. He stayed over there, working.'

'Bumming around, you mean.' He pushed his plate away, turned round and saw Macau's shadow. 'Boi-Bumbá . . . a lot of nonsense. They begin to slack this time of year. Already in March they're asking for money for the festival, and by June nobody's working any more.'

He was silent for the rest of the dinner, looking sideways at the clock. He took some pills, and went out of the room. I saw him later, walking with Fogo round the swimming pool; later on their shadows were together on the veranda. There was no moon, and a wavy line lit up the river. The boats coming from Parintins were coming into the moorings. Macau lit the boat's searchlight, so that the boss could come down to the shore. The employees said goodnight to each other and went on their way to Okayama Ken. The light shone on the water, ruffled by the boats' wakes. Macau was waiting for orders, which came in a shout: 'Go to the town now and bring my son back here.'

Fogo barked and his eyes glinted.

Macau jumped out of the yacht, went to Okayama Ken and came back with three employees; they got into a small boat, and the throbbing of the motor disturbed the silence. Mundo's going to spend the night in the hangar, I thought.

He's going to be late for the journey back – he might just come back with the red mask . . .

Before dawn, I awoke to the sound of the maids' steps, as they came out of the basement; the generator was turned off; on the veranda, Jano was waiting for his son.

Macau, sweating and defeated, had to put up with his master's silence. 'We went round the whole town, Dr Trajano. The employees know every corner of it, and there was neither sight nor sound of Mundo.' He cracked his fingers, put his hands together, not knowing what to do. He backed off slowly and leant against the low wall.

The nervousness, worry and hatred I saw on Jano's face when he went into his son's room! He stepped on the dirty clothing rolled up on the floor, opened the windows, picked up the sheets of paper spread out on the bed, and inspected the drawings with a frown: 'Look at your friend's art.'

They were pencil drawings of the little houses of Okaya-ma Ken, of the warehouse and the big house: façades and perspectives. At the foot of each sheet was written: 'The property of the Emperor Trajan.' I gave the sheets back, and he ripped them up one by one; he went over to the wall, pulled Nilo's painting off and stabbed it with a ballpoint pen. He left the room and went to the overseer's house. I only saw him after midday, his face lined with exhaustion and lack of sleep. He was talking to the overseer, and I was surprised that he barely spoke to me. Macau came to me to say we were leaving and that we'd have lunch on board.

'Has Mundo appeared?'

He hid his face in his hands and let out a laugh: 'Don't tell anyone, lad. Mundo's already in Manaus.'

More than a month without kissing her, without even touching her body. I couldn't see her in the places we usually met, she didn't answer my messages, avoided me. One Saturday after lunch, I talked to my sister and brother-in-law, and told them I didn't believe in this marriage story; this is what Jonas said: 'You're the only one that doesn't. You should ask Alícia.' My sister Raimunda agreed with him, and that afternoon she took me to your mother's house. There was no one on the bare earth street; the neighbourhood seemed deserted. Raimunda went in, and I waited until the end of the afternoon, when they came out together, hand in hand. 'Here's the bride,' said my sister. I grabbed Alícia by the arms, and we went to Castanhal. 'You're lying,' I began to say. 'The ring, the wedding day, it's all a lie.' She threw her head back with a laugh, sat on the ground covered with dry leaves, and lay down, saying: 'It's going to be in the cathedral, at the end of October.' Even then I didn't believe it: it's a trick, she wants to provoke me, I thought. She said it again: 'In the cathedral. Go over to the Saúva bar and ask your friends . . . ask the Archbishop of Manaus.' 'Why? His father's that Portuguese moneybags, that's why, isn't it? A millionaire and a widower with only one son, and that fellow's fallen for you, and you think that's going to be your salvation . . . Go on, that's why, isn't it?' To this day I can't make out the expression on her face because she wasn't laughing any more, and it was difficult to see any feelings in her impassive look: no tenderness, no regrets, maybe a bit of pain and despair, I don't know. She was still lying down, watching a canoe slide along the Cornos creek, and the shadow of the evening grew around us, and beyond the river the houses and the church of the Colina were visible. Then, without looking at me, she unbuttoned her blouse and showed her dark breasts. Night was falling in the jungle around Castanhal. Her eyes: her look was inviting me, and her skirt slid down to her ankles, and our bodies entwined, and I breathed in her warm smell and heard a sob, a spasm and then weeping, her arms limp, her legs inert, her whole body given over to convulsive weeping. I kissed her mouth, her wet, salty lips, and went on kissing and stroking her shaking body, which showed no reaction. She didn't want it. She said: 'Not today, Ranulfo . . . Afterwards . . . after the marriage.' Then it's true, I said to myself, and asked: 'You mean you're really going to marry that idiot?' She said yes with her eyes, a real yes with a look I knew. She waited for the sun to disappear and for the darkness to rise up on this side of the world: there was only blurred outline and the huge shadow of the trees and the sound of the insects, and, far from the Morro, the lights on the Colina. Then your mother's voice cut into me. The voice, the words I didn't expect to hear, or ever thought I would, more absurd than the news of the wedding. That was what she resented: I seemed to be deaf, or something in me refused to hear the two words spoken right close to my ear: 'I'm pregnant.' And straight away, louder, fearless: 'Pregnant, expecting.' There was no light to see her face, her eyes, the nakedness of a quiet, still body, refusing to give itself. I felt my jealousy grow like a destructive, explosive madness, while my imagination repeated the two words, 'Pregnant, expecting', until I furiously asked if she'd spent last Saturday night with that idiot. She pulled her skirt back up to her waist, buttoned her blouse and sat down. 'You mean you were already going out with the millionaire's son before the Dalemer party. When was it? Where?' 'It was an accident . . . we met in the Casa Colombo, I was looking in the shop windows, and Trajano was buying something.' 'And after?' She moved her hands, began to plait her hair, and I could feel her big eyes looking at me in the dark, her hands moving through her hair, and I smelt the perfume she was now wearing, and the voice asked: 'Let's go and have a beer at home? There's whisky too. Everything I ask for he gives me double. My fiancé, Ranulfo . . . He works with *his father, he doesn't have to steal . . .' 'Beer? Whisky? Does he give you everything?' I shouted, and pushed her body away. Your mother was still lying down, and I opened her blouse, ripping off the buttons, and she let me, she wanted it, and said once more: 'After the marriage,' and she took her own skirt off, stood up and laid me down, saying: 'I'll get on top of you . . . there are a lot of fire-ants in this forest.'*

5

MACAU'S KNOWING MOCKERY made him less servile – it was as if he was saying: Mundo's a sly bugger, he's pulled a fast one on us all.

On the return journey, Jano brooded over his son's audacity. Faced with his outrage, I didn't know what to say. Early in the morning, I found him in the sitting room, repeating: 'Property of the Emperor . . .' He went up to the bridge, asked Macau how Mundo had escaped, if there was a speed launch in the port. Macau shook his head – it's a mystery, boss – but he'd find out.

Jano prowled round the yacht, dressed all the time in long trousers, a belt, a linen shirt, socks and black shoes, as if he was in town. In Vila Amazônia, too, he'd worn his working clothes. I remembered the trip to Vale Island, beyond the Parintins hills. Macau had woken me early: we were going to go down the Amazon, as far as the frontier with Pará. Four mongrels on leashes barked on the prow. First, we sailed along the Parananema: Jano wanted to see the fibres, more than three yards long, peeled and softened, drying on lines. The dogs jumped off and ran to the grassy area by the edge of the water, sniffing for prey. 'Chameleons, a real plague. They'll destroy the plantation,' Jano had said, holding on to Fogo's collar – he was unsettled by the other dogs running loose. Later, on Vale Island, an extensive and uniform plantation looked like a range of hills covered in yellow flowers. While the yacht was going round the island, Jano explained details of the planting, cutting and drying of jute and *malva*. I listened with interest; it was enough to encourage his enthusiasm, which was something he couldn't share with his wife or his son. On the way back, when we could already see Vila Amazônia high up at the top of the bank, he'd suddenly asked me: what was the future of the property going to be? What if it was abandoned, pillaged, destroyed? His voice was sincere, waxing lyrical about the beauty of the landscape and revealing that, if it was down to him, he'd spend the rest of his life there, he'd die on the veranda, embracing the vision of the river and the forest. That was what he wanted most, so long as Alícia was by his side.

Now, looking at him in this state, nervous and sweating, moving around the whole time and muttering words that escaped me, I feared he would tackle me on the subject of his son. After lunch, he got some release from his agitation, and nodded off for a while. He didn't look as if he was on the yacht at all, but at home in Manaus: sitting down, legs and feet together, his torso upright, his head moving from side to side, as if saying no in slow motion. He woke up as if he'd had a shock, went to wash his face, and started on his rounds again – he made me feel dizzy. I anxiously awaited the end of the afternoon; as soon as it got dark, I went to my cabin to read, but I kept on thinking about the two of them: Mundo and his father. When I couldn't manage to sleep, I went up on deck and saw the figure of Jano sitting at the stern, with Fogo's nose in his lap; he didn't turn around.

Near Marapatá Island, half an hour from Manaus, he seemed less agitated, and came to offer me a glass of port. He thanked me for my company on the yacht and said he'd fallen into a trap, for Mundo had made up his mind to come when he found out I was going too.

'I thought your presence might stimulate my son, but it was no good. He was moved by the death of that Indian. He doesn't know Vila Amazônia, he's grown up with rejecting the place . . . If only I had other sons! That's why I envy the luck of some of the landowners of the region, men and women who've brought up sons and have heirs. I'm going to die without an heir. God hasn't given me one.'

He sniffed the top of the bottle and put a little more port in my glass.

'I can't even have that pleasure,' he said, stroking the bottle. 'But Mundo can. That and other ones . . .'

'His greatest desire is to be an artist.'

'It's a mistake,' said Jano, firmly. 'And I want to be alive to watch the results of that mistake.'

'But it's Mundo's vocation. The only thing he wants to do.'

He gave an ironic laugh and admonished the dog, who was growling. 'A great artistic vocation doesn't just depend on a choice. And anyway, Mundo thinks revolt is an achievement in itself.'

He sighed, lifted his head to see the edge of the Edu-candos. He turned and asked if I'd chosen a profession, a career.

'Law, maybe,' I said, timidly.

'So in a few years' time you'll be working with a law firm.'

'I'll see if I can get an internship.'

'I know judges in all the courts,' he said, in a voice that reminded me of the meeting in his office on Marshal Deodoro Street. 'Without someone to pull strings, it's very hard to get on in this country. That's the hard truth, Lavo.'

At Manaus Harbour, he called a taxi, and ordered Macau to leave me at home.

'Aren't you coming with us?' I asked.

'I'm going to work,' he answered dryly, shaking my hand.

That night, when I went by Mundo's house to talk to him, there was no one in the room. From upstairs came the sound of voices, and in the kitchen I found Naiá washing the supper dishes.

'Your friend's in his room,' she said. 'His parents are arguing. Go up and make the most of it, you can hear quite a bit.'

I stopped near the couple's bedroom door, and heard Jano's voice first: 'He's not inherited a drop of my blood. He lied to the aeroplane pilot, and took advantage of my illness. He's a coward.'

'My son travelled alone, sitting in the middle of boxes and letters. He got off at the Panair aerodrome and walked home,' said Alícia. 'That's courage, not cowardice.'

Jano changed his tone: 'It's a long time since you've been to Vila Amazônia. You haven't seen the fish and turtle hatcheries, the orchidarium, the cocoa plantation; you've not seen the improvements to Vila Okayama . . .'

'I'm not interested in any of that: the hatcheries, the plantations, Okayama. I'll never set foot in that place again. And, if you showed me a map of the area, I couldn't tell you where it is. But I know the name of every street and

restaurant in Copacabana by heart. I can almost see them . . .
God knows.'

'Yes . . . and God knows that, without the jute and the
Brazil nuts, your apartment in Copacabana wouldn't exist.
You don't deserve to have your holidays in Rio. Much less
our son . . .'

'Jano, darling.'

'You don't deserve it . . .'

'Jano, Jano . . .'

Her voice went quieter and disappeared. I turned the
handle on Mundo's door, and asked if he wanted to go to the
Cine Guarany.

'Not today, Lavo. Come on in. Pity you arrived at the end
of the performance. It began before supper. I've been
following it for an hour . . . listening, I mean, but I can
imagine the gestures of the actors on the bed, the expressions
on their faces . . .'

'How did you come back by plane? You could have told
me.'

'I didn't ask you along because Jano would have been
furious with you. There was only room for one person in my
plan: me.'

Then he told me how he'd got into a seaplane, the
National Airmail Service Catalina, which was stopping off
in Parintins. He'd persuaded the captain to take him as far as
Manaus. Crying, he'd said that Jano was a good friend of
Colonel Zanda, and that he, Mundo, needed to go urgently:
his father was very ill. He'd got into the seaplane with the
clothes he had on him, carrying the objects and drawings
made by the old Indian and the seeds and plants he'd picked
up on the journey.

'I cried so much it looked as if my father was actually dying. I wanted the lie to be true,' he said, in a calm voice, with no sign of remorse. 'I couldn't have come back with him, the return would have been a nightmare. Now he wants to stop me going for my holidays in Rio, and so punishes my mother too. But Jano won't manage it, she's much the stronger. Up till now the actress has been sober. Once she begins to drink . . .'

At the beginning of February, mother and son, accompanied by Naiá, went to Rio de Janeiro. I still remember Aunt Ramira's mutterings: it was cruel . . . leaving a sick man on his own . . .

'But Jano has Macau's company,' argued Uncle Ran. 'Not counting the wondrous Fogo.'

That holiday in Rio was a melancholy time for Ranulfo, who waited for Alícia's return like a hungry wolf, anxiously walking round the square, his eyes looking for light in Mundo's room. When Corel and Chiquilito went to cadge lunch in the Vila da Ópera, my uncle talked about Alícia's absence with an exasperated look, as if fighting off a cloud of mosquitoes. His friends changed the subject and talked politics, but their notions had no substance, just the dust of dead ideas. Uncle Ran was riled, wished them in hell, demanded that the woman's name be present at table, or that'd be an end to the festivities.

Alícia's house was sad too without her, the bedroom windows shut, and only one lamp lit on the sitting-room veranda. There was no dinner with gambling afterwards, and Naiá didn't prepare a grilled *tambaqui* on Sundays. At night, as I passed by the mansion, I heard the chords of a Mozart sonata, and imagined Jano and Fogo quiet in the solitude, under the ceiling painted by Domenico de Angelis.

One Saturday morning, I saw Macau and his boss at the harbour by Remédios Square, where the *Santa Maria* was moored. The heat was crushing, and amongst the shouts of fishermen, hawkers and porters, Macau was counting the boxes and bundles to be taken to the firm's warehouse. The smell of jute and Brazil nuts took me back to Vila Amazônia, and the memory mingled with that of my friend and his mother in Copacabana. Jano is the link between those two worlds, I thought, as I came nearer. Sweat was running down his wrinkled forehead, dripping on to his wet shirt. He said he was taking advantage of his wife's absence to keep an eye on the transport of his products. That way, he didn't stay at home on his own, and also avoided theft – the place was riddled with it. The chauffeur agreed with a nod of the head, without interrupting his inspection.

'The jute will be exported to São Paulo, Argentina, South Africa and Germany,' said Jano, mopping his forehead. 'I read your name on the list of the freshmen in the law faculty. Alícia will be proud of her son's friend.'

'When will they be back?'

'Tomorrow . . . tomorrow without fail,' he exclaimed, lifting his head and smiling, his mouth open to the sky. It was a broad smile.

Naiá and Alícia came back purple from the sun: Alícia, her skin peeling, was full of the delights of Rio. 'Oh, our apartment in the Labourdett building! In the heart of Copacabana, Lavo. You're not just on the Avenida Atlântica, you're floating in the ocean, and your eyes swim in the sea. D'you see what I mean?'

The Labourdett building was one of the holiday's refrains. Just like the Yacht Club, the Country Club, the chic restaurants and the shopping. Lots of shopping: boxes of shoes, dresses and decorative objects. The sitting room was crammed with packages, and visitors envied this prodigality. One of them, Dona Santita, a partner at cards and a client of Ramira's, asked: 'Did the money from the jute pay for all this?'

'Lots of people spend and don't know where the money comes from. Where does yours come from?' said Alícia.

She opened the packages, drinking whisky all the time; she said with a look of surprise or disappointment that she didn't know why she'd bought that awful lampshade, or that necklace only fit for an old woman, or a red velvet jacket – who could wear that in such a hot climate? Naiá was piling the objects up, keeping those her mistress liked, separating out the ugliest for the Home for Poor Children. Alícia seemed a different person. She spoke with an affected Rio accent; it didn't just echo the pleasures of the city, but the more intimate pleasure of contrasting the splendour of the metropolis with the stagnation of the provinces. Her accent wore off as Manaus life became harsh and even hostile. The embarrassments she had to endure when she was playing cards, when she lost and her husband refused to pay up, his fights with his son, the stories invented or hinted at about her, the envy she saw in everyone's eyes: all this separated her from the Labourdett, with its balcony overlooking the ocean. A few weeks after Carnival, she went back to being the Alícia we all knew. But she didn't hide from anyone that one day she'd go away for ever.

'I'll go and never come back. Dead or alive,' she said one night when her luck was out. Jano was already asleep, her card partners had just left, Naiá was picking up the tokens, cards, glasses and bottles. Alícia, tense and hoarse, was sweating so much her blouse clung to the contours of her breasts. When she saw me come down the stairs with Mundo, she leant on the banister and repeated: 'Dead or alive. I'm just saying it as a plain fact, no promising or swearing. I'm going away with my son and the books . . . your art books, my love.'

When he saw his mother drunk, Mundo went back upstairs and said: 'Don't come into my room. Go and sleep with my father.'

She threw a beseeching glance in the direction of her son, and sat on the bottom step. 'Naiá, make some coffee . . . I'm feeling dizzy . . . What a ghastly night . . . My gold choker's disappeared . . .'

That night, while Alícia was throwing her jewellery away, Mundo was telling me about Alexander Fleming, an artist he'd met in the Museum of Modern Art. Then he showed the drawing and painting materials and the art books he'd bought in the Leonardo da Vinci bookshop. Who, in the Pedro II or later in the Colégio Brasileiro, didn't envy him, when the papers published the photograph of him behind Alícia on the staircase of the *Constellation*, she with her dark glasses and a huge smile spread over her face? Mundo was one of the few who could study German with Gustav Dorner or Frau Lindemberg, and French with the French consul's wife. And only he could pay for private English classes with Mrs Holly Hern, in one of the houses in the Vila Municipal.

The Minotaur and Delmo were eaten up with jealousy about these privileges, but each for their own reasons. Still in their last year at school they were commenting on the time my friend had been humiliated.

'Wonder if he still remembers when we set his arse alight?' Delmo asked, nudging the other, who said: 'Mundo's a fool. He should get his teeth into his father's fortune.'

Delmo, the only son of an important businessman dealing in metal goods, wanted to move into his father's position: why study, if he could begin work as a boss? Minotaur, with his bulky body and tiny head, was going to get a place in the State Department of Public Security by hook or by crook. In December 1969, at the farewell for the final-year students, he showed off in the school arena, violent and arrogant, punching up the first-year pupils, forcing them to eat soil and clumps of grass crawling with ants.

In March, when I was already studying in the law faculty, Uncle Ran criticised my choice; he expected something else of me. 'You should spend your life reading and living, wandering around, with no profession. You'll end up just like your aunt, locked up in a little room and praying for clients . . . Or running from one law court to another.'

'I don't know if I've got a vocation for it, but I can write, put cases together, defend and prosecute . . .'

'D'you believe in vocations? I've got no vocation for anything; I spend all my time inventing one . . . Invent, lad. Or go looking for something. Mundo's looking, why don't you do the same?'

'One way or another, Mundo's still studying at the Brasileiro.'

'He'll get out of there. He's just putting things off to fool his father.' He hooked his fingers on to my throat and whispered, as if he was telling me a secret: 'You'll go mad putting cases together. The big fish'll swallow you up, Lavo. Every law case is a fraud, nothing more than a lie. It's better to write, paint, be an artist.'

The afternoon the Minotaur and Delmo came by the Vila da Ópera, as if to seal the outcome of the friendship at the Pedro II, Aunt Ramira examined them with her seamstress's eyes, and, leafing through a fashion magazine, asked innocent questions: 'Where do you live? Have you chosen a profession yet? Where do your fathers work?' Then she served *cupuaçu* tart, bourbon biscuits and Brazil nuts, and left the table to look at them out of the corner of her eye. When they left, she said Delmo thought he was God's gift. 'That Delmo's really ignorant, Lavo. See how he laughed at your books? I killed myself working to buy dictionaries, law books and that Roman law thing, and the idiot makes fun of them. Isn't his father the one that sells barbed wire and hammers?'

When she could, Ramira made cutting remarks. She said the other one would lose all his teeth, but it would make no difference: he didn't chew, he devoured everything, with the greed of an animal. The Minotaur's patched clothes, his big rotten and blackened teeth and the place he lived – a shack without a number at the bottom of the Buraco do Pinto – made an impression on her. 'When it rains, what happens to his family?' she wondered, perhaps thinking of the risks our own family ran, always living from hand to mouth.

November and December were better months: Ranulfo got commission on his sales in the Booth Line shop, and Ramira did sewing for the end-of-year parties and the fancy dress for the carnival balls; that was the time when she saved for the next few months, and a relative calm lasted until April or May; from then on, we collapsed like a house of cards. July was the beginning of penury, which Uncle Ran, with a mixture of superstition and sarcasm, associated with the 'flames of summer'. 'The river's low, our pockets are empty. We'll have to grate manioc, eh, sister? Aren't your girls making their debut in August?'

Even so, he brought his friends for lunch; his sister indignantly dragged him into the kitchen: 'There's not even food for the cats, and you dare bring those wastrels round?'

'Those wastrels aren't hungry, dear sister – just thirsty. A bit of *cachaça* and fried *jaraqui* and we're in seventh heaven.'

Days later, Ramira would get a basket full of goodies imported by the Booth Line. She knew Ranulfo pilfered things from the English shop, but she sent nothing back: she hid the packets of biscuits and the tins of toffee, and offered them to her clients. As time went on, she got more tight-fisted, and her brother more spendthrift, attitudes that reflected what each of them expected out of life. My aunt was terrified of the future, while her brother squandered everything, asked for loans from women, and kept saying they owed him God knows how many nights of love. The delicacies he filched kept his lovers sweet, calmed his sister down, and there was something left over for me. 'Never save, Lavo. Sufficient unto the day . . .'

In the second week of the month Ranulfo was already plagued with debts; in the third, when he came to eat at home, Ramira locked the sideboard, fearing he'd pillage it. When things were at their worst, my uncle surprised us by flourishing crispy new notes, which he counted in our presence, whistling and smiling; then he threw two or three of the highest notes on the work-table, hypnotising Aunt Ramira, who didn't even ask how he'd got the money. Hardly had her brother gone, she picked up the notes and hid them in her room. As Ranulfo's ties with Alícia were not completely clandestine, news from Jano's mansion came on his tongue. And what a tongue it was! But one subject Uncle Ran always avoided was his son at Vila Amazônia. He got irritated when his sister asked him if he wasn't going to visit the island. For her, the island meant 'the son you've abandoned'.

One time, when I told Ranulfo I'd seen the child and his mother, he hid his feelings and controlled his anger. Later, with malice and hatred in his voice, he said Jano always found a way of humiliating people.

'He showed the two of them to everyone, eh? And what did he say? I can just see the great coward accusing me. He's not just jealous of me . . . he's jealous of his son too, of his son's relationship with me. D'you know what Jano's cooking up? Mundo's going to suffer like hell . . . And the thing is, he's got the strength to counter his father's tricks. The two of us are going to confront Jano.'

It was Alícia who revealed the trick, which was to have disastrous consequences for Ranulfo. One afternoon, about three o'clock, she unexpectedly appeared: with a red silk blouse, a plunging neckline, tight white shorts, her buttocks in high relief. She came in without announcing herself, and spoke to me: 'I heard you had a good time on the trip to Vila Amazônia. Jano talked to you, didn't he? He's got pull, he can get you a job, an internship in one of those courts.'

She went into the front room, and opened a package: 'Ramira, I bought this Swiss brocade. Isn't it lovely?'

My aunt looked at the cloth in amazement and smoothed the silk embroidery with the tips of her fingers.

'I want a dress to go to a recital in the Opera House a month from now.'

'Fine.'

'Jano's made me a member of the League of Volunteers for Progress. He believes in philanthropy – another of my husband's fine qualities. And more work for you, Ramira. I'm going to need a suit to go to a charity lunch; it's for lepers. Naiá'll bring the money for the work. Any cloth left over's for you.'

The two women faced each other, not saying a word. Alícia's tone of voice, her words, her daring, her neckline and her shorts all irritated Aunt Ramira, who lowered her eyes and went on sewing.

'Well, are you going to take the job?' Alícia asked me.

'I don't want to work in the courts,' I said.

'It must be your uncle's influence. Good thing he's coming now, I don't like waiting.'

My aunt looked at me; she realised they'd fixed a rendezvous. Ranulfo was given an embrace by our visitor – a long squeeze, in fact.

'Do you want lunch?' Ramira asked her brother.

He didn't even reply; he put a cigarette in his mouth and went over towards the door with Alícia. They sat on a little bench, and talked in low voices. They could have recited whole poems without being heard, but Mundo's name burst out of the whispering, like an explosion. The neighbours were passing in the street, staring at the couple and laughing. Aunt Ramira muttered her fears: some neighbour might tell Macau! The chauffeur might open his mouth . . . If Jano appeared, there'd be a scene, and she'd lose customers. The city's full of bits of jungle, why did the two of them have to snog just there?

My ears were on stalks, as I looked at the woman's red lips. When Alícia crossed her legs, pushing her fingers right into her flesh to loosen her shorts, Ranulfo gave her a look that made her smile. She licked away the sweat on her upper lip with her tongue, and he was smoking greedily. Their ease and their appetite kept growing, and I watched my uncle letting himself be enveloped, servile, head over heels.

Mundo was the subject of the conversation, without a doubt. I heard some of Alícia's words: 'Jano wants him to live and study in the Military School . . .' 'Discipline . . .' 'One of my husband's idiotic dreams . . .'

Then my uncle spoke louder: 'Boarding? The Military School? Is he mad?'

'Jano thinks it's the best solution for our son.'

'Solution?' Ranulfo protested. 'That's your husband's idiotic dream?'

He put his cigarette out with his foot and got up, punching the doorpost: a boarder at the Military School! She and her husband were going to destroy Mundo's dream. Where and when did they think they were living? Mundo would run away: didn't she know her own son?

Alícia got up, and her lingering look disarmed him even before she said: 'Every mother knows at least one person in her life – her son. I haven't spoken to Mundo yet about the boarding. That's not what worries me; he'll make up his own mind. There's something else bothering my husband: for a long time he's been warning me about an artist . . . Jano won't put up with that guy.'

85

'I've already told Mundo who Arana is, but I couldn't persuade him . . .' Ranulfo whispered. He looked at the workroom with a severe expression, as if disapproving of his sister's presence.

My aunt went into her room, but left the door open. Alícia turned her head, saw I was listening to the conversation and laughed: 'Your nephew's got sharp ears, he's catching every word.'

'And the worst thing is, he believes in the word of the law,' he said. 'Tomorrow I want to talk to you, Lavo. Come by the Bar do Cabaré at lunchtime.'

The two of them stood for some minutes at the entry to the Vila da Ópera; then went in opposite directions. I heard Aunt Ramira's voice: 'What does he want to talk to you about?'

'It must be about Mundo.'

'That shameless hussy didn't come to order a dress . . . She came to lure my brother into some kind of trap.'

She wasn't addressing me: she was talking to herself, or the sewing machine.

6

I N THE Bar do Cabaré, on Frei José dos Inocentes, Uncle
Ran ate the eyes of a fried fish, sucked the head and
chewed it hungrily. He wiped his greasy hands on a towel,
and lit a cigarette.

'What is it you want to talk about?' I asked.

'Alduíno Arana,' he said, blowing smoke into his plate to
chase the flies.

'The artist?'

'That's the one. Well, all three: the boy Alduíno, the artist
and Arana. Three in one. He's the greatest artist in this
wondrous hemisphere, but he's the only one who thinks so.
Get some of that money your stingy aunt hides and even I'll
make a work of art and sell it you at bargain price. Then you
go and sell the masterpiece at Manaus Harbour.'

'I don't much like Arana, but he has good ideas . . .'

'Fabulous ideas,' he interrupted, pointing to the whore-
house on the other side of the street, where two women
were haggling over some fish.

'See that fishmonger? Arana takes his tray, hangs it up on
the wall, fish and all; then chops off some of the heads, makes
a pyramid and smears them with red paint. He calls that art
. . . but that's *passé* now. Now he's exchanging these daring
experiments for paintings of sunsets. He must have been
overwhelmed by the grandeur of our natural surroundings.'

'Mundo thinks his art is revolutionary.'

'I know all about his revolution.' Uncle Ran laughed till he started coughing, and tears came into his eyes. He asked for another beer, sat watching the fishmonger going knocking from door to door: the eyes and scales shone on his tray, along with his wilting bunches of parsley and yellowed tomatoes. The fishmonger turned his face to our table, and my uncle greeted him.

'He'll die in the doorway of a house on Frei José dos Inocentes before he sells his last string of sardines. He'll drop dead, with his feet swollen, scorched by the heat. But an artist like Arana is more interested in the beauty of the dead fish, the visual effect of his tray and the price it'll fetch. Arana and I played all kinds of tricks in the Castanhal and in those muddy streets in the Jardim dos Barés. We left our bills unpaid in the same bars and drinking dens . . . but he went much further. I'm just a petty thief compared to my ex-neighbour.'

'Neighbour? Did he live on the Morro da Catita?'

'That's right. Later, we became sworn enemies.'

He threw the remains of the fish to a stray dog prowling round the table. The dog came closer, famished, and was pushed out into the street, with the remains and the manioc flour. Ranulfo laughed at his own mean trick, and drew the lesson: 'He's hungry, he doesn't react or take revenge. He goes for the safest thing, and that's fish remains. Are you sorry for a cowardly stray dog?'

He bent forwards and shooed the animal away with his knife. 'Your aunt was sorry for Arana. She feels really sorry for scum, except for me, of course. We used to go fishing in the Cornos creek, then he went to look for star apples, Brazil nuts in their shells, and sweet olives in the Castanhal; he sold all that rubbish on the pavements in front of the shops in the centre. "Poor lad, the only reason he's not poorer still is that he's on his own," Ramira said. The same poor lad gave her a fish from time to time and turned into a saint. Then he got in with Pai Jobel, the madman on the Morro da Catita. Pai Jobel lived in the forest round the Castanhal; he went around naked, went up on the hills with his arms open, went into São Francisco church and preached from the pulpit. Alduíno Arana would bring the madman out of the church, the two saints coming out in each other's arms. Only one of the two, Jobel, was a sculptor. No one was interested in the clay figures of *caboclas* he made, squat women giving birth to animals. Jobel painted the statues with twisted geometrical patterns . . . red, yellow, blue patterns. Father Tadeu liked him, and gave him paint and brushes for him to work. They were beautiful objects, just like *marajoara* ceramics. Arana bought everything for a pittance and sold it on to the tourists. He must have a collection of those statuettes in his house. The scoundrel began copying those women, only they began to grow, and the animals they gave birth to turned into monsters . . . and Arana became an artist. Then he got interested in other women.'

He lifted the empty bottle and whistled to the bar owner. He banged the bottle on the table: 'Real women! Widows, all of them! The one who really got taken in was Luciete Velina, who was loaded with properties. And no children! Rich as they come . . . she owned land and houses in São Jorge. When your parents died, Arana had already got himself in with the woman, went out in public with her; they went to Mass, to the best restaurants, even to the Bosque and the Guanabara Country Club. He met politicians and painted the portrait of a minor bigwig . . . a populist banned from political activity by the military in 1964. Not because he was a communist or subversive, it was for robbery on a grand scale. On the Day of the Dead, Alduíno used to go with the widow to the Colina cemetery, and the two of them prayed for the soul of the dead husband. If he'd only known . . . They didn't marry, she refused; her brothers and nephews would have waged war. But they went to Rio and São Paulo . . . and round the North-East. She even bought some pictures by Brazilian artists for Arana. Then they travelled by ship to Europe and, when they came back to Manaus, they went to live in the house on the island, one of the woman's best properties. Arana knew how to reciprocate, and painted several portraits of Luciete, at every age: girl, young woman, wife and widow. He painted the late husband's portrait, the lot! There was even a face he'd painted in her bathroom. The widow swore it was a proof of love. Time's ingenious: it plays all kinds of tricks. Luciete Velina died and left the house on the island to Alduíno Arana. That was at the beginning of 1955, before I went to Vila Amazônia. He must have some talent, but the charlatan's more genuine than the artist. The real, true artist is the mad Jobel. He was put away after the mischief he got into in the church. He insisted he was in love with Our Lady of the Conception, and kissed and hugged the saint's statue. Then the faithful got angry with him, and even your aunt was hopping mad. Jobel spent more than ten years shut up in the asylum. He died there. He had no family, no one . . . He was a madman alone in the world. I went to the asylum several times, I took soft clay, paint and pictures of women saints. He adored the saints, he was a truly passionate man . . .'

'Mundo doesn't know about that,' I said.

'He's blind, that's why, but one day he'll find out who Arana really is. Now what I really want is to get Mundo away from Jano.'

He called the waiter, told him he'd owe the money and got up: he had an appointment in the middle of the afternoon.

A job?

'What bleeding job?! I've not got a job, my lad,' he said scornfully.

In Pedro II Square, in front of an old ruined nightclub, he picked a mango off the ground, bit into it and sucked it down to the stone, smearing his hands and mouth with the juice. Near the bandstand, he shouted: 'Tell Arana I know his story from top to bottom.'

He picked a flower from the border and offered it to a prostitute sitting on a bench. The two of them went to the bandstand and began to dance in a tight clinch in the middle of the square.

In the studio we saw a cage made out of wooden battens. Kneeling down, Arana was scorching wooden animals with a torch; his face red and sticky with sweat, his hands blackened, the artist seemed truly inspired that afternoon. He got up, put the torch out, took his apron off and opened his arms in the middle of the smoke. 'I thought you were going to stay in Rio,' he said. 'And when you're in Manaus, your friend disappears.'

'I've brought some drawings I made in the holidays,' said Mundo. 'But first I want to show you the objects Seu Nilo made . . . an Indian from Parintins.'

Arana came out of the cage and picked the objects up. He said the Ticuna made sculptures like that. They were light, like birds, and looked as if they were flying free. In a professorial tone, he added that many European artists had imitated indigenous and African art. But Nilo's real work was different.

Out of a box he took some small wooden objects the Indian had sculpted twenty years before: a face that was disfigured, or had a tortured look; men and women together, with terrified expressions.

Mundo asked him for one of the older pieces.

'One day, when you start really working properly.'

'I've already begun . . . and an artist in Rio liked my work.'

He told us that in Rio he'd gone to a course on engraving, and to museums and galleries, and he'd met Alexander Fleming, an artist who lived in Berlin and was taking part in an exhibition in the city. With Alex, he'd learnt new techniques, and had been impressed by the materials he used in his three-dimensional works. It had been Alex who had taken him to see a strange work of art: people went into a tent, put on a plastic cape full of folds and began gyrating and shouting, trying to free themselves of a lot of things.

'The body participates in the work; it's part of the art,' Mundo said excitedly.

Arana listened, but his attention was forced. He made no comment. And when Mundo showed the drawings of faces of people living in a Rio favela, Arana looked at the sheets of paper and, after a quick glance, folded his arms and went quiet. His silence irritated me. Then I said I didn't understand art, but it had all impressed me: the colours, the human figures, the perspective, the light.

'It gives you a feel of the people and the place,' I finished with enthusiasm.

'Is it your uncle teaches you to look at a work of art?' Arana asked. 'He's good at drinking and partying, but art . . . I somehow doubt it.'

'True, but Ranulfo knows about lots of people's past lives. He doesn't just like parties, he likes talking. He says it himself.'

Mundo saw the furious look in my eye and tried to change the subject, but couldn't find a way to do it.

'Let's forget the big talker and look at something serious,' said Arana, lighting all the lamps.

On the floor of the cage was a miniature forest with bits of animal bones and pieces of metal ore. In one corner, I saw a skull, curved ribs and rosaries of vertebrae. A pile of bones. Mundo saw it as well: was it a monkey's skeleton?

'A monkey? Of course not,' Arana objected. 'These are the remains of our people . . . Indians and *caboclos*. I got them in an abandoned cemetery by the Castanho waterfall. When the river rises, the tombs collapse, and when the waters recede, the bones appear on the beach. When I saw that, the idea of the work took shape in my head. Nature on its own isn't good for much. The bones of anonymous people are more than just a symbol.'

He spread the bones round the miniature forest and stopped, thoughtful, as if he was waiting for something.

'But they're not anonymous,' Mundo observed. 'Was there no inscription on the stone? The dead person's name?'

'Nothing. Time had wiped it all away,' Arana replied.

Mundo walked round the cage, then stopped and held on to the battens, with a vague, melancholy look in his eyes; he opened his hands and rubbed his blackened fingers over the charred wood.

'That's it,' Arana said with excitement, his voice somewhat affected and with a semi-idiotic look on his face. 'You want to know what the secret themes of this work are? Devastation and death. The burnt forest is dead humanity.'

He'd spent the last month working day and night: the work was going to be exhibited in the Art Biennale, and then in galleries in Rio and São Paulo. He was proud of this, thinking about these events all the time. Mundo asked him what the title was.

'*The Suffering of the Tribes . . . The Suffering of All the Tribes*. That's suggestive, don't you think?'

Arana lit the torch and went on scorching the wooden animals, moving around in the cage, opening his arms and twisting his mouth. I wanted to laugh; Mundo still had a serious face. Suddenly Arana stood still and excused himself: now he wanted to be alone. 'Today the saint has come down,' he went on, his face lit by the torch. 'It's a day of powerful inspiration.'

When we came out of the studio, Mundo said he'd been disappointed by Arana's silence about his drawings. 'He was rude about Ranulfo,' he murmured. 'I think Arana's mad . . .'

I thought of the bones, of him looting the mortal remains of those anonymous human beings. I tried to tell my friend what I thought and revealed what Ranulfo had said about

Arana. Mundo became despondent – he didn't want to talk any more.

Days later, I came across him on the pavement in front of the Colégio Brasileiro, squatting with his head between his knees; he was gripping his hands, which looked like a red ball. When I touched him on the shoulder, he lifted his head, hitting the palm of his hand with the fist of the other.

'I've been thrown out of the school,' he said. 'My father caught me unawares. There was nothing my mother could do.'

The news of your mother's wedding attracted journalists and photographers to a forgotten place: the Jardim dos Barés. They came by canoe, and climbed up the ravine on a little wooden ladder; others came by the São Jorge road as far as the barracks of the Jungle Infantry Battalion, entered the Castanhal forest and visited the houses, principally the oldest one, known as 'the Stone family's American country house' — its wooden architecture was impressive. The reporters wandered around between the mango trees and the jambeiros *growing in the unpaved streets, and stopped to chat and have a drink in the bars and drink shops, observing the place and the people with curiosity. They found out I'd been Alícia's first boyfriend, asked if it was true and I said yes: the first and only one. Then they wanted to know what I did, I said: 'Nothing', and if I studied. I said: 'I gave up school and I read books lent me by Father Tadeu and the owner of the Académica bookshop.' Then I said I helped my sister Raimunda and my brother-in-law Jonas to sell all kinds of items in the interior, and that Alícia sometimes went with us. I showed one of them a photograph: your mother and I embracing on the prow of the* Fé em Deus. *He asked me to lend him the photo, which was published with the interview. Even though the image was small and grainy, your mother and I were there, embracing. Next to it, the news item with details of the wedding: the French cloth bought in the famous Paris in America store, in Belém; the dress made up by a Rio couturier; the reception in the Ideal Club for eighty illustrious guests, and the bridegroom's father's present for the bride: four kilos of Portuguese jewellery. My brother-in-law Jonas brought the papers to the back of the little house where we lived, and while Raimunda read and laughed, Ramira was trying to provoke me with a look that spoke of revenge and anger at the same time. Your mother flew off the handle: I shouldn't have lent the photo, or told the reporters what I had. Pregnant, expecting . . . she*

96

accused me, over and over. I prowled round the two sisters' house, and Algisa told me Alícia wasn't there, or couldn't see me. It was strange: after years of intimacy your mother hid herself from me in her last week as an unmarried woman. Only once, at night, when I stood like a statue near the pitombeira, she appeared in the window with the lamp lit: she was naked, and looked at me with a touch of pain or despair, which the smile attempted to hide. I went to go in, she withdrew and, before she shut the window, I saw her naked body for the last time before her marriage. She was already dreaming about her move to a big house two hundred yards from the Opera House. The neighbours came to talk to the bride, asked if they could get a job in her house and buttered her up. Or they went just to see her. She appeared in the window wearing a pearl necklace over a white silk blouse with black buttons. On the day before the ceremony in the cathedral, a launch moored by the creek bank, and a man of about forty – tall, strong, with a white suit, his collar tight as a dog's, and dark glasses that looked like a bandage or a bat – came up the ladder carrying a cardboard box as big as an adult's coffin. He was immediately surrounded by a gang of kids, impressed either by the suit and the stature of the stranger or by the box he was carrying; the man bent over to ask one of the children something, he was pointed to the end of the sloping street, and down he went, with the kids behind him, laughing and pulling at his jacket sleeve. He stopped in front of the sisters' house; Algisa came out first, followed by Alícia. The man handed over the box, and they went back into the house; he went up the street, stopped to whisper to one of the children and started walking towards Castanhal. I had already jumped down from the branch of a Brazil-nut tree and was smoking, leaning on the trunk. Two yards away from me, he took his glasses off, fixed his black eyes on my face, and with a voice so formal it sounded put on, asked if I was Senhorita Ramira's brother. I laughed: Senhorita Ramira? He wiped his puffed-up neck with a handkerchief. 'I'm an employee of the Mattoso family, and I've come to pick up an order. Seu Jano's father is a customer of hers. The Portuguese man, the father of the bride.' I couldn't disguise my feelings, and the man came to my assistance, pretending he'd not noticed I'd changed colour. I tried to get out of the situation and cool my anger by looking at his shirt wet with sweat, his tight jacket with dark patches, and his shoes so tight they seemed lined with stone. I asked what was in the box he'd delivered to the sisters. 'Dona Alícia's wedding dress,' he said. Very chic, really expensive. He held his hand out and bowed his head: 'Macau, chauffeur in my spare time and professional mechanic.' We went into a short cut in the forest and came out at the back of the house. I clapped my hands, and just to irritate my sister, I shouted: 'Senhorita Ramira, there's a gentleman here to speak to you.' Ramira, a bit embarrassed, appeared with a white tissue paper parcel. She said to the man: 'Why have you come here? It was me who was supposed to go to the firm and deliver it . . .' 'I've come to bring the wedding dress, and thought I might as well pick up the trousers,' he said. He took the package, pulled an envelope out of his pocket, gave it to Ramira and said no more to me; he took the short cut, went down the ravine, followed by a line of children. On the afternoon of the wedding, I was drinking with Corel and Chiquilito in the Saúva bar, when he came back: dressed the same, with enormous glasses, the same slow, easy-going walk, and this time he was accompanied by a slim dark-skinned girl dressed in white. The two of them stopped in the doorway of the little house belonging to the two sisters, and waited. Now it wasn't just a group of children that surrounded them: many people from the Morro, from Jardim dos Barés and even from São Jorge were hanging around, as if they were watching the guests arriving at a carnival ball in one of the city's posh clubs. It must have *been about four when I saw Alícia dressed as a bride. My sister Raimunda ran over to talk to her, and the two embraced, then stood holding hands, whispering before they said goodbye. Chiquilito tapped my arm and asked how I could be such a fool as to let Alícia marry that idiot. He said: 'I'll throw mud over the dress and put paid to the fucking ceremony.' No, it would have been an evil trick, and useless, Alícia would have hated me for ever. Corel, who was already in cahoots with some smugglers, agreed. Then someone came out of the crowd and tried to give a clay statue of a saint to the bride; I saw it was Pai Jobel, his naked body covered with sand. He must just have escaped from the asylum, for there were strap marks on his arms, and he had a frightening, staring look on his face. Your mother picked up the clay statue and threw it on one side, for fear of dirtying her dress. The man, Macau, pushed Jobel, who fell over and was dragged away by some of the bystanders. Algisa and the girl in white held the dress's train while the bride went down the steps, looking at the ground, leaning on the man's arm. No one else went down, not even the children. The man got into the launch, helped Alícia to step in at the prow, and the girl, behind, rolled up the train and held it as if it were a cotton cloud. Algisa stayed on the riverbank. From down there, your mother saw me and waved goodbye once more. She wasn't saying goodbye to me, but to the whitewashed house on the unpaved street, to the India road, that years later would become an avenue through the centre of the Cidade das Palhas, to the settlement around São Francisco's church, to the Jardim dos Barés, where she would never return, not even to visit her sister. She said goodbye to a whole period of her life, and the launch left a frothy wake in the brown river, the girl holding the dress train, until the white stain grew smaller and disappeared round the curve. The locals dispersed. Algisa was left by herself, looking at the river, then climbed up the bank and went home. I came out of the Saúva bar, followed her close behind, touched her shoulder and saw her reddened eyes. She was crying with anger and envy. I only had shorts on, and she had shorts and a printed blouse; she had leather sandals, made in the neighbourhood by a cobbler from Ceará. I went into the house, opened the wardrobe and saw the old clothes that Alícia had left for her sister. I smelt the rotten wood, the toilet with no septic tank, the cockroaches and bedbugs, the stagnant rainwater. Heat, stink and sweat. Alícia hated those smells. I asked Algisa if she still had beer and whisky. She sat on the hammock and said in a weepy voice: 'That cow of a sister must be nearly at the cathedral now.' 'Are you going to work today?' She nodded her head: there were ships in port, she'd go by later. 'How much do those gringos pay you for a night?' I asked. She looked at me and said: 'What about you, you old cuckold? You stole from the gringos and gave everything to Alícia . . . and just look what she's done to you.' Algisa went to slap me, I pushed her and she fell into the hammock, I fell on top of her, grabbing her by the hands and feeling her calloused fingers and skin hardened by rubbing clothes and scouring pans with sand when she was a child and a slave, maybe unaware that she was both things at the same time.*

7

'EXPELLED OR SUSPENDED?' asked Albino Palha.

'Expelled. He argued with a history teacher who praised the military government. They say he drew a frightful caricature of the teacher, then tore up his uniform and nailed . . .'

'There's no need to tell the whole story,' Alícia begged him. 'Dr Palha's come here . . .'

'He tore up his uniform, nailed the pieces to the windows and appeared almost naked in front of everyone,' Jano went on. 'My son has made a ridiculous spectacle of himself, made fun of the headmaster and even made another caricature of the poor man. That's why he's going to study at the Military School. More for the moral discipline, the character formation, than the quality of the teaching.'

Alícia saw I was peering in by the pantry, and beckoned to me to come in. I said I'd come back later to talk to Mundo.

'Are you frightened of anyone in this house?' she asked.

Albino Palha got up and stretched his hand out to me. Jano offered me a seat; I wanted to leave, and stood where I was.

It was the first time I'd seen Albino in daylight: tall and fat, with watery green eyes in his unsmiling face. His loose white jacket made him look more robust; an orange-coloured satin handkerchief flopped out of his pocket, giving a strange lustre to his clothes. He still had the habit of wearing a hat; the one he had on, of grey felt, left a line of sweat on his forehead. For Jano, Albino Palha was much more than a man – he was a career model. One time, Alícia had said: 'He's gloomy and formal, but he's like a joker in a pack of cards – he can fit in anywhere; he even gets on with my husband. Jano adores Palha, from his shoes to his hat.'

Palha changed his posture and moved around almost without anyone noticing. His bulky form shifted to a corner of the room, and suddenly I saw his lustreless but watchful eyes and heard the voice of the mediator, slow and mono-tonous: 'He needs to be understood, Trajano. Your son's a dreamer.'

'He's a destroyer of dreams, you mean,' Jano answered. 'Where is he? Alícia asked our son to come to this meeting, but at times like this he disappears. He must be hidden somewhere, doodling great works of art. He thinks he can build the future with daydreams. A dreamer can't ignore the work of half a century! Vila Amazônia . . .'

He stopped talking and followed Fogo's steps to the door. Mundo, on the threshold, had his eyes on his mother. He took off his sandals and came in slowly, carrying a bag full of paper. There were paint marks on his Bermudas and T-shirt. He avoided the dog, dropped the bag and opened his dirty hands, so as not to have to greet anyone.

'Let's talk, Raimundo,' said Albino Palha.

When Mundo looked at me, I don't know if he saw complicity or betrayal in my face. I didn't want to be there, taking part in an intimate family conversation. As for Palha, my friend was not in the least intimidated by his presence. In fact, he hardly seemed to hear him say that our region was marvellous, nature was prodigal and monumental, and that it was only now, with the military, that Brazil was discovering and protecting these infinite riches. Didn't we agree?

Alícia moved her head in a gesture of hopelessness; the father turned to the son, who returned his look. Albino Palha ran his index finger round the brim of his hat and touched on the subject: 'It's very difficult to be an artist here, Raimundo. Nature inhibits every artistic vocation. Your father's right: a painter or a sculptor has to be a great man. It's as an entrepreneur or a politician, not as an artist, that you'll rise from obscurity. That's why you have to study.'

'Who wants to be great? And what's nature got to do with my work?' Mundo rebutted. 'I don't think about such things. And I don't need to study in a college. I learn through books, and the works of artists.'

'Why don't you go and live in Rio? You could study in a boarding school,' Palha suggested.

'Far from me – never,' Alícia intervened.

'Rio, or any other city, will be a disaster for him,' said Jano. 'Mundo's wasted three years, been humiliated at the Pedro II and expelled from the Brasileiro. Now he's going to face boarding school here, near his father. Now he's going to live with people from the lower ranks, get orders from officers and show proper respect for good values.'

'Get orders?' repeated Mundo, furious. He pointed his finger at his father. 'You can give orders to your dog and your employees. I don't take orders.'

'No shouting,' begged Alícia.

'We're just talking, Raimundo,' Palha declared. 'Your father knows I don't like extreme positions, he knows I admire the military . . . I myself brought Zanda to dine here.

I know some people in Brasília. I defended the creation of our Military School here, but I do recognise it's not for everyone.'

He sat between father and son, his arms and hands open, trying to bring them together, but both avoided his clutches. Mundo, alarmed, rubbed his paint-stained hands together; Jano shoved his into his trouser pockets. Albino Palha made a compromise suggestion: Mundo should study in the Miltary School, but not as a boarder – life as a boarder was tough.

'Boarder or not, I'm not going,' my friend said.

'Your opinion counts for nothing,' Jano said. 'I'm not going to allow it . . . You've been influenced by that idler Arana. You and your artists . . . a load of useless layabouts.'

Mundo's face contracted, and his breathing seemed to make his body grow.

'Mundo, go up to your room and stay there,' Alícia begged.

Jano came over to his son and roared: 'Never in the world will I let you alone!'

Mundo laughed in his face: it was a harsh, edgy laugh.

'No one's put you in your place. No one can be totally free, no one. Colonel Zanda'll find the way.'

I tried to guide Mundo to the stairs. He resisted and faced his father: 'Zanda? What a charlatan. Those friends of yours . . .'

'How can you say that? I'm one of your father's friends . . .'

Albino Palha's voice fell silent with the crack of a blow: the father's belt had hit Mundo's neck; next he whipped his shoulders, and I ran to grab Jano's hand. Alícia shouted for Naiá and Macau; I was brought up short by a ferocious snarl, followed by a whine; I saw my friend kicking the dog and then being immobilised and dragged out of the room by the chauffeur. Alícia and the maid surrounded Jano. His eyes were fixed on the wall, and only his lower jaw was moving – his body seemed anaesthetised.

'He's pale,' said Palha. 'Let's call the doctor.'

'There's no need,' said Alícia.

The friends eyed one another.

'My son's going to learn . . .' murmured Jano, dropping the belt.

Albino Palha said goodbye coldly, without addressing me.

'Let's go up,' said Alícia.

Jano walked slowly to the stairs between the two women. While he was going up, I heard him say: 'Take care of Fogo, Naiá. He's been kicked by a savage.'

Mundo wasn't on the patio; Macau said he'd already gone out: he had a gash in his neck and was bleeding. This time the boss had really hit the mark, he wanted to cut the kid's veins open . . .

'This time?' I said.

'The boss has lashed out like this since way back, Lavo. When the two of them are together, they can't bear the other's shadow.'

In the middle of the next week, the classes at the law faculty were cancelled in protest at the murder of a student at the Polytechnic School of the University of São Paulo. The press had said little, and obliquely, but the reports sent by the Law Association pointed the finger at the military. As well as rebelliousness, there was fear. They said that one of the teachers was an agent of the federal government. Students met on the steps, and the president of the union was beginning to make a speech, when I saw Mundo in the garden of Remédios Square. Sitting on the grass, he was drawing a child's face. When he'd finished, he gave the drawing to the boy, who looked at the paper, burst out laughing and ran across the square to the Escadaria harbour. My friend got up and came across to me on the pavement.

'Zanda's pals have hit the bull's-eye again,' he said, touching the wound on his neck with his fingertips.

'How did he have the gall?' I asked. 'How did he have the strength to hit you like that?'

'When I'm around, Jano's illness vanishes. He lost his cool because I criticised his friends. Palha thought he was being got at. I should have attacked them both, but instead I caught poor Fogo. A father shouldn't love a dog more than a son.'

He said he was off, and I asked him where to.

'I talked to Arana, and I'm going to sleep in his studio for a few nights. My mother wants me to stay away from Arana . . . she's afraid of Jano.'

'One day you're going to have to go back home. Ranulfo mistrusts Arana too – he told me . . .'

'Your uncle's fallen for my mother's story,' Mundo interrupted me angrily.

'Ranulfo's known Arana for a long time, and he wouldn't lie to me.'

'Arana . . . I still don't really know who he is or what he wants . . . But I'm never going back home. I'm going to take up my father's challenge, Lavo. First, I'm going to fulfil one of his greatest dreams,' he said, with a malicious laugh.

'What challenge is that you're going to take up?'

'I'm going to study and live in the Military School. I told Arana that, and he made the same face you're making. Arana's sure I won't be able to stand it. He even suggested I go to Rio. He said he can help me, he's got some friends . . .'

'Wouldn't it be better than staying here? Your father's not going to let up.'

'I don't want to run away. Now I want to go right to the end.'

'What d'you mean, to the end?'

'The end of life . . . mine or his. Isn't that his challenge?'

'That's an absurdity, Mundo.'

'Absurd? It wasn't the first time my father's landed one on me. In Vila Amazônia, he came up from behind, shook me about and called me queer in front of the employees' children. Only because he saw me laughing and playing with the boys at Okayama Ken. My mother argued with him a bit, but Jano didn't give way: he forbade me to go out and stopped my games. I was alone for all the holidays. Then my mother threatened to go back to Manaus. It was just a threat – I don't know why, but she backed down and didn't go. I think she was frightened of something . . . I still don't know what. She listened to my father's insults and went out of the room when he said I had a laugh like a little tart . . . that the boys from Okayama Ken were always up to tricks in the forest, and it was her fault . . . He always blamed Alícia. That's what he kept saying: "Look at the dreadful education you're giving our son. You've never taken that child to church. He's growing up like an animal, and that's why he likes to play with the workers' children. None of them go to church, but our son's worse than they are." My mother put up with all this. I remember she'd drink and look at him as if she were saying: things aren't going to go on like this . . . it's only a matter of time. Then she would go to Naiá, and they would talk in whispers. One day he got it into his head that they were laughing in her room, and wanted to know what they were laughing about, but they weren't even laughing, and he spent the rest of the holidays forbidding them to laugh. My father hates laughter. Now he's going to see his son, the little tart, parading in uniform.'

From the steps up to the university came the noise of howling and booing. Mundo noticed my books and looked at the façade of the old, imposing building. I was going to join the group of students, but instead I decided to accompany my friend, who silently moved away from the square. On Joaquim Nabuco Avenue, you couldn't hear the protests any more. Mundo went into a grocery store to buy beer; I helped him carry the bottles to the end of the street – from there he was going to get the boat to Arana's studio. Before I went, I asked about boarding at the college: he was joking, wasn't he? No, he wasn't. His game with Jano was no game. He told me his father used me as a stick to beat him with, saying I was a university student and was doing well. I came from nowhere, but I was going to be a lawyer, and he, Mundo, was nobody, nothing . . .

8

'DID YOU SEE my son in the Mascots Parade? He looked like a real cadet.'

Naiá had her attention fixed on the needle on her boss's thigh, Alícia was looking at her nail-clippers and biting her lip, both of them far removed from Jano's enthusiasm.

The procession commemorated one more anniversary of the military government, and it had caused a sensation in the city. The new recruits, with red berets and green canvas jackets, marched with rhythm and panache, and seemed to be marching in the direction of a promising future. Mundo was the oldest, the tallest and the most ungainly. That Saturday, he had promised to go by the house after the parade. Alícia blew on her red-painted nails, called me over to the glass cabinet and told me her son wasn't coming: he was going to take part in an excursion in the jungle, near a river; it must be a college encampment. She was worried; he could get ill, catch malaria . . .

Mundo hadn't spoken of any 'excursion'. We met once or twice a month, during the boarding-school breaks, almost always in Arana's studio. He didn't talk about daily life in the college, or the rigours of the discipline and the training, but, when he was bathing in the creek, we could see the scratches and wounds on his arms, legs and shoulders; however, the scar left by his father's belt was more visible and more shocking.

Mundo would feel his neck with his hand, to make sure it was still there. When the break was ending, we left together, rowing down the river. My friend, already with his uniform on, said a sad farewell to Arana, as if he was off to war.

I told Uncle Ran that Mundo was a bit low, with scratches and bruises on his body; it didn't surprise him. He said that the cadets had taken part in their annual training with the legionnaires from French Guiana. Mercenaries . . . They were instructing Brazilian soldiers. They were fierce and cunning, with years of experience in the desert and the jungle, but the French always learnt something with their Brazilian colleagues. The commander led a group from the Centre for Jungle Warfare to the training sessions, and the students from the Military School learnt exercises and techniques of survival and combat. Many of them had no experience of the jungle, and were shit-scared of the military.

Ranulfo let on he knew all about day-to-day life in the Military School and everything Mundo did on his time off. There was no doubt in my mind: the ex-radio compère knew a lot of people, and could charm the devil himself. He gripped my arm, looked around him and dissembled: 'I'll let you into a secret. Some three years after the military coup, a band of young Amazonians organised a guerrilla group around here. The Military Commander of Amazonia called an officer from Rio to harass the guerrillas and capture them . . . an officer from a parachute regiment . . .'

He lowered his voice to say: 'Captain Aquiles Zanda . . . was promoted and decorated when the job was finished. He captured and tortured everyone in the group. The leader was jailed in Belém and then executed. A Venezuelan . . .'

'Captain Aquiles Zanda,' I murmured. At the university

we talked about the government's atrocities in other places, but no one had talked about that guerrilla group in Manaus.

'Not many people know about that, Lavo. The information was censored.'

'And Mundo? Does he know about it?'

'No, but one day I'll tell him how Jano's friend made a name for himself. Zanda's one of the hardline military. He has directed all the military institutions in Manaus and today he's still in control of everything. He wants to be prefect, governor, the lot. He thinks he's a god in uniform. He likes to chuck the students into the jungle, just to test their resistance. When someone falls ill, he strokes his medals. I don't even want to talk about it, it's disgusting . . . Mundo must have come back from a training session.'

'Tomorrow he's going to Arana's house. He spends the last Sunday of the month at his studio.'

'Is he still going to see that scoundrel? I've warned him . . . Does Mundo want to defy me? Is that it?'

I told my uncle that during the latest visits the artist had scarcely looked at my friend's drawings; even so, Mundo had been interested when he'd shown his most recent work.

'The big cage, eh? The charred cage. Mundo told me. Devastation and death. Another lie. Arana exhumed some poor devil's body. Even that . . . Now you've got something to do with your laws.'

After my conversation with Uncle Ran, Mundo fell ill. I still remember the hallucinated look in his eye that Sunday in the studio. He'd not even been to see Alícia. As soon as he came in, he talked to Arana a little, then said to me: 'Lavo, I've not been feeling well since yesterday. I'm going to draw over in that corner.' He stayed drawing on a little table at the bottom of the stairs, in front of a photograph of his parents' wedding. Arana asked what was going on.

'I'm tired,' said Mundo. 'I sleep very little . . .'

'What does your father want to do with you? Why don't you run away?'

'I don't see him for weeks on end. That's the best way.'

'No, that's not the best way,' said Arana. 'Let's talk about you going to Rio, we've got to think . . .'

'I want to rest . . . my head . . . Or I'll be on my way,' said Mundo angrily, struggling to speak in an assertive tone.

Arana looked resentfully at me, and went to get a painkiller; my friend took two pills, bent his head forwards, pressing his temples and looking at the photograph. Arana wanted to show me one of his recent paintings: a landscape, of a river fringed by dense jungle and birds in a luminous sky.

I looked at the picture and watched Mundo out of the corner of my eye.

'What do you think?' asked Arana.

'It looks like something painted by a naturalist or a traveller,' I said. 'Isn't it the opposite of what you taught Mundo?'

'It's commissioned,' he said, justifying himself. 'It's not just got to be to my taste, it depends on the onlooker.'

Always when the artist spoke about his own work, Mundo listened attentively, but this time he seemed in-different. I saw he was moving his right hand with a struggle, his hand only drawing his mother, leaving an empty space, a blank, in his father's place. I looked again at the commis-sioned painting and heard Arana asking again what was happening. Mundo's stiff arm was leaning on the table, with his pencil hooked in his hand. When we came close, we saw the dark blotch spreading on his green shirt, sweat running down his face and dripping on to the drawing. He had a high fever.

'Let's go to the Military Hospital.'

Mundo stuck the point of the pencil into the drawing as if he was stabbing it, and his body slumped on to the table, knocking everything over. He fell to his knees, but soon lost his balance and was flat on the floor. He muttered: he wasn't going to any Military Hospital, not likely . . . he tried to undo the knot of his tie and take his shirt off, but couldn't manage it. Arana and I tried to help, and he got irritated – he could do it himself, and he began to say strange things: he was going to cross the river with his knapsack on his back, he knew what the enemy's position was . . . He murmured Brazilian and French names, and stammered: 'The ambush . . . enemies in the trees, up there . . . the noises . . .' His hands opened and closed, trying to lay hold of something, and cracked to the ground. He asked for his knapsack, his flask, he was thirsty . . . His shirt was already soaked, and not just with sweat: blisters and cuts on his shoulders, chest and back exuded pus. Arana decided to take him forcibly to the Hospital for Tropical Diseases or his parents' house.

'If anything happens, his parents will demand satisfaction from me,' I said nervously. 'I don't want trouble with Jano.'

Naiá stopped sweeping the veranda and went to call Alícia. Before she embraced her son, she said to the maid: 'I knew it, he got ill in that hellish college.'

I told her what had happened in the studio, and Alícia straight away asked me not to tell her husband, and to invent some story. Mundo kept saying he wanted to sleep; then he asked about a friend from the college, Cará. In bed, he was still talking about him. He would knife a peccary, biting a piece of raw liver and holding his hands out to the officers. Cará covered his face with the peccary's skin and laughed at his fellows, a load of gutless cowards. Mundo started laughing and coughing, and his mother's eyes widened, asking me: what kind of madness was this? What had they done to her son? I knew nothing – they should go and ask the college director. When the doctor arrived, my friend was no longer delirious. Jano stood with his back to the door, holding his index finger to his mouth; from time to time he stretched forwards and looked sideways at the bed.

'Where did you meet?' he whispered.

'In the college,' I lied. 'I went round there, it was his monthly break. I went into the bedroom; he had a fever already, he couldn't even get his uniform off.'

'He'll have to have a blood test,' said the doctor. Then he opined: 'His glands and spleen are swollen . . . and he's got a fever. It might be the kissing disease.'

'What the devil's that?' asked Alícia.

'A virus . . . Infectious mononucleosis,' the doctor explained. 'Two weeks' rest and no alcohol. One injection a day.'

Outside the room, Jano asked some more questions about the infection and asked the doctor to sign a certificate: his son was going to miss a lot of classes, and that might go against him.

In the middle of the week Mundo was still pale and a little feverish. Alícia, sitting beside him, didn't react to his caustic comments on Jano; he wanted to go back to the college as soon as possible, he couldn't bear listening to Fogo's barking, announcing his owner's arrival, or the sight of a grey eye spying on him through a crack in the door. The eye observed him from the corridor, as if he was a caged animal. Was that all a father could do for a sick son?

'Jano still feels awkward,' Alícia said, trying to justify his behaviour. 'Since that day . . .'

'Since the day I was born, he's never been sorry about anything he did.'

She sighed; she didn't want to argue.

'I sent a note to Arana,' I said.

'You had an argument in the studio, didn't you?' asked Mundo. 'My head was burning, but I heard your comments on that picture. I no longer know if Ranulfo's right about Arana. Does your uncle know I've got that kissing disease?'

'I told him. He wanted to come here . . .'

'And why doesn't he come?' Mundo turned his face to his mother.

'Your father's jealous,' she said firmly. 'I've always played poker and rummy with several partners, and Jano's only jealous of people that have never been in the house. What can I do?'

'No one can do anything,' Mundo said angrily, sitting up on the bed to take his T-shirt off.

Alícia frowned when she saw her son's shoulders and back covered with wounds; she wanted to put *copaíba* oil on to help them heal; he wouldn't let her; the scratches and blisters were healing, the trouble was he felt tired all the time . . .

'Are you still going to take part in the jungle training?' I asked.

'That wasn't why I got ill,' he said, with a look that accused me of stupidity.

'I thought they were excursions? The director never said anything to me about training,' Alícia protested. 'You should just study, and let the others bury themselves in the jungle. What do you do there?'

'No student is obliged to participate in the training exercises,' Mundo lied. He went on in the same vein: he didn't eat too badly in the Military School, and had a good relationship with the teachers and officers. It was only the patriotism that was over the top, truly awful. No one was allowed to complain about anything, and punishments were severe. Others suffered more than he did . . . One friend, Cará . . .'

'It doesn't matter what happened to Cará, or anyone else,' said Alícia. 'I just hope you can bear it until you graduate. Then . . .' She paused, and asked if he didn't want to study in Europe; Jano would agree, and if he didn't, she'd get hold of some money, sell jewellery. 'Not here or in Rio. In Europe, Mundo.'

His pale face looked straight at his mother, with a mysterious expression; then looked away towards the drawings on the wall, and he lay down with his back to the wall. I saw he wanted to be alone. I said I'd come back one day that week and went downstairs. I stopped in the sitting room, when I heard the notes of a piano concerto. A voice cut through my daydreaming: 'He's better, isn't he?'

Jano was buried in the sofa, half hidden.

'Thank goodness,' I murmured.

'Lavo . . .'

I looked at the head in the semi-darkness, and the man was smiling. 'This infection is just a weakness; it'll soon be over. From now on, my son will be known for his acts of bravery.'

A madman, I thought, as I hurried out.

9

EVEN THOUGH HE was ill, Mundo went back to the college alone on the Friday afternoon. Naiá couldn't stop him: her mistress had waited for the boy to nod off to go out for a while; he feigned sleep, took his medicines with him and escaped.

I waited a little while for Alícia and, before Jano came in, I left. Without my friend's consent, his mother began to keep watch on him and invent stories about him. Macau got a tip for doing this work. In fact, the chauffeur had been in her pay for a while. Since the Mascots Parade, Macau had been lying to Jano: he said that Mundo was having a great time with the girls from the Teacher Training College, the Rui Barbosa School and the nuns' schools; he told his boss about his son's erotic prowess, pursuing the girls when he left for his break on Saturday mornings.

'You're a phenomenon,' Jano said every time he heard news about Mundo. Alícia, more subtly, also praised the chauffeur: her husband's life would be a lot harder to bear without him and the dog.

Uncle Ran assured me that Jano was so enthusiastic about his son's performance in the Military School that he hadn't seen Alícia's trickery.

'I've known Macau for a long time,' he said. 'He's an honourable man, but he's hungry, like the rest of us.'

Macau put on a show for his master and mistress with malice and a touch of cruelty. He gesticulated, attempting to imitate Mundo's grimaces when he let his hair down on his afternoons and nights out of college. Alícia watched the farce, laughing out loud. The actor even dragged a sincere smile out of Jano, which gave some life back to his face.

'I think the future cadet is going a bit far, sir. I saw him last Saturday, in the Castanhola, drinking and dancing on the pavement. He really let go. He was hitched up with this woman dressed only in an off-the-shoulder number . . .'

The Castanhola was a narrow stretch of pavement, crammed with bars and little restaurants that had taken over part of the Rua dos Barés. Mundo took me there a couple of times; he adored the atmosphere, which began in daylight, enlivened by out-of-tune female singers – their almost naked bodies adorned with cheap jewellery – who also danced for the taxi-drivers, dock-workers, sailors and the people who worked in the Port Authority. My friend left his uniform in the Recanto bar, bought beer, fish kebabs and boiled manioc, and had a good time with the women, completely anonymous, until the strains of the guitar went quiet, in the early morning.

The second time I went to the Castanhola, I caught a glimpse of Macau's head behind the counter of a tobacconist's, enjoying Mundo's performance. He stayed there, watching, until it went dark. He went away when, drunk, Mundo began to urinate over the chairs of the Recanto, and huskily to call out for his favourite women: Libelina, Daiana Cleide, Aminadab. Then he angrily uttered the names of the commanders of the training exercises, shit-houses, bastards, the same French and Brazilian names he'd pronounced in

Arana's studio. His eyes red, his body shaking, he began to kick everything; the shop owners of the port area tried to hold him down – what a madman! They should call the police and have him arrested as a vandal. But the owner of the Recanto liked him, and the women spoilt him; they sang: 'Goodbye, love's over,' stroking him, making seductive gestures, with his head on their breasts or in their lap. Then Mundo began to say: 'This night is just for me, Lavo,' pushing me away and saying in a loud voice: 'Your uncle's got the right idea, life's better here on the street, fuck them all, my father, the lot . . .' He called Aminadab, and told her to dance with Dr Lavo, a man of the law, embracing me: 'He's my friend.' I danced with Aminadab, we drank beer behind the market and got into an old boat that rented berths for clients of the Recanto. We went back to the Castanhola in the early morning; Aminadab went to await the crew of an Italian ship. Mundo and Daiana Cleide danced in the middle of the street, and she sang: 'Hold me tight, in the middle of the night,' and the other women joined in the chorus and clapped. When he staggered, he was grabbed by Daiana, and the two of them began to dance again, tottering around. Suddenly Mundo stopped short, raised his head up and shouted in a hoarse voice: 'Do you know who Trajano Mattoso is?'

Daiana Cleide looked at her friends; no one knew, so she had a guess: 'A singer?'

Mundo fell to his knees, laughing: 'A singer, Lavo. What can he sing with that falsetto voice?'

The women laughed too, and Aminadab said: 'What does he sing? Samba? Bolero? Who is this Trajano?'

'He sings for his supper at Colonel Zanda's, you can say that again. D'you know who Zanda is? Don't you know?

He's a bastard, never stops persecuting me. It was him, Lavo
. . . he was the one gave the order . . .'

'Order? What order?'

'It was him, I know . . . He gave the order for me to be
left alone; they all abandoned me, and I was left for more
than twenty hours lost in the jungle. Ask your uncle if it
wasn't him . . .'

I asked the owner of the Recanto for Mundo's knapsack.
It was late to be going to Arana's house. If he was found
drunk at the college, he'd be disciplined, or expelled.

'They're around here . . . hiding. Both of them, Lavo . . .
Zanda and my father.'

The singers and the owner of the Recanto helped me to
drag him to the Amazonas Hotel. We went in a taxi to the
Vila da Ópera, and in the street he began to shout: 'Jano, a
singer . . . that's a good one. Let's go to the General Osório
Square.'

'You'll wake my aunt,' I said, trying to cover his mouth.

'Ramira, the singer . . . They could be a duet . . .'

Aunt Ramira appeared in her nightdress with a look of
disbelief, her eyes on Mundo, and then on me.

'Dona Ramira, do you by any chance sing?'

'But what's this? What's that friend of yours . . .?'

'He's going to sleep,' I said.

'It's almost four o'clock . . . What will the neighbours . . . ?
Why doesn't he go to sleep in his own home?'

'Mundo's going to sleep here in the front room,' I said.

'Isn't there any drink here?' asked Mundo.

'He talks just like your uncle.'

'Lie down there, on Uncle Ran's mat.'

'Castanhola . . . let's go there,' he groaned. He began to

belch and then moaned again. 'Fuck, no one's laughing, no one's singing . . . That colonel son of a bitch . . . he ordered . . . gave the instructions to the commander . . . alone in the jungle.'

Ramira backed away in fright, and disappeared into her bedroom. For some moments Mundo sat there mumbling; then his tired face turned to sewing materials in the front room and to the ceiling. He sat down on the mat, leant back against the partition, his head slumped forwards. His mouth was trembling, and he was trying to say something, his eyes almost shut. I put the knapsack down near the mat and stuck around, afraid he might try to escape. A dead weight, he leant to one side, then fell down. I left the door of my room open, and slept badly; I got up before nine and found Mundo in the kitchen. With his uniform on, he was drinking coffee and eating fried bananas with cinnamon.

'I've apologised to your aunt,' he said, chewing. 'She's gone to Mass, but she ironed my trousers before she left. She's good at ironing – she still uses an iron filled with charcoal.'

Uncle Ran's sarcasm was in his voice; he yawned, and grunted. 'Good at ironing, and a good person too. She said that Jano liked her . . . she piously believes that. Your aunt wants me to give up the drink, I think she's going to pray for me.' He gave a little laugh and went on. 'I asked her to pray for my father, for peace between us . . . Father and son . . . She was moved, Lavo. I've found someone who's moved.'

'With so much hypocrisy around you'll end up being friends with Ramira,' I said.

'How much did my father pay for her to make my uniform, eh? D'you think he's generous?' Mundo asked.

121

'How much did he pay?' I enquired.

'That I don't know. When it's a question of money, he doesn't mention figures. But at home he said that your aunt's work is worth the price of a friendship.'

He looked at me and raised his eyebrows: 'Has complicity got a price?'

Then I remembered Jano's hand holding the envelope full of banknotes . . . the voice, the bribe . . . had Jano touched on the subject? He might have lied, told his son I'd accepted the offer. I didn't reply, or look away from Mundo's face.

'You know what my father's capable of doing,' he murmured. He put his beret on – he was going to the college.

Wasn't he going by the studio?

'I've got to write the report on the last training exercise,' he said.

The college had impelled him into Manaus's nightlife in places I was unaware of. Uncle Ran found him in bars in the Cidade das Palhas, Cachoeirinha and the Morro da Liberdade. He went from one shack to another, talking to people who'd just arrived in the city, sitting at the table with locals, offering them beer and sometimes paying the bill, as he did in the Castanhola.

One afternoon, when we were crossing the iron bridge of the Manaus creek to go to the Eden cinema, someone shouted: 'Hey there, cadet!'

Mundo turned his head, slowly approached the dumpy, fat man and held out his hand. The other man made to reply with the same gesture, but he was forcibly pushed and jammed against the bridge parapet. Mundo grabbed him by his shirt, tearing it, picked the guy up and threatened to chuck him into the creek. The man fell on the pavement, without understanding what had happened.

'I'm going to lodge a complaint to the officer in charge,' he muttered.

'If you open your gob, I'll break you in two,' Mundo threatened.

He was a cook at the Military School, who'd met him in the Recanto and called him cadet. Why had Mundo got so furious?

'I mistrust them all: from the cooks to the director. Those bastards want the skin off my back,' he said, looking back. 'They know whose son I am, they get money from my mother, but they want more, they want everything.'

We didn't go to the cinema; he preferred to take a walk. The strong sun dissolved the outlines of the landscape. At the end of the bridge, a queue was growing at the entrance to the Eden: the white building, now greying, had just opened its doors. Behind the State Capitol, a dark stain moved slowly by the banks of the river. Vultures, dozens of them, were pecking at debris left by the river as it receded. A gap opened in the fluttering wings, and in it appeared ragged men and children. 'Our city . . .' Mundo said.

We went up the streets of Educandos. On Beira-Rio Avenue we saw, below, the empty space near the Escadaria harbour which before had been occupied by a group of shanties built out over the water.

'Do you know where they've gone?' asked Mundo.

'Who d'you mean, they?' I asked.

'The people who lived by the edge of the river. They were pushed out and sent to the other side of the city. They stripped the area of jungle, built some houses . . . All that was left was a rubber tree. That's to say, the trunk and a few branches . . . a carcass.'

We went into the Horizonte to have a beer. In the bay, a raft loaded with tree trunks was approaching a sawmill in the Educandos. Mundo asked for a piece of wrapping paper and began to draw and write.

'Cará's family was moved as well. Before the last training exercise he took me to see the little house and the new neighbourhood. My father's friends will open it with some pompous ceremonial.'

He returned to his drawing, while I drank, looking at the Rio Negro. On the pavement, children carrying jars of milk and vendors' trays were coming back from the Panair market; one boy stopped near the bar steps and offered peach palm and bunches of star apples for sale. Mundo threw two coins on to his tray and gave a strange laugh: 'That's enough now, leave us to have a drink in peace.' The boy picked the coins up, crossed the avenue and went down the ravine. Others were coming back from the fair, shouting: 'Milk from the Careiro, fresh milk from the Careiro.'

'What's the point of so much nature? Star apples and peach palm for fifty centavos . . .' said Mundo, letting out a hot, stinking belch. Now he had a serious look on his face, turned towards the river and the jungle, his sweaty hands on the wrapping paper. He put the pencil on the table, and emptied the bottle; he was drinking out of urgent need rather than pleasure.

Was it the housing estate they were building? The New Eldorado?

'Yes, you'll see what a wonderful Eldorado that is . . .' said Mundo. 'Even Fogo wouldn't want to live there.'

A low-pitched siren sounded from the bay. A white ship was moving towards the River Amazon: *The World Mistery*, with a band of blue lettering – 'Journey to the indigenous villages on the High Solimões'.

'Arana's clients,' he muttered.

The passengers were throwing objects into the canoes that approached the ship. It was getting dark, weren't we going to go by the studio?

'I arranged to meet Arana in the Three Stars. Lately, he's got into preaching sermons. He knows I'm drinking. He thinks it'll be the end of me and my work. What's it got to do with him? He should look after his assistants better. Either that, or chuck the lot of them in the river.'

He folded his drawing up and put it in his trouser pocket.

'Arana takes against my work,' he went on. 'He takes against just about everything and couldn't give a toss about what's burning me up inside. He doesn't know my father, and doesn't want to understand who he is. Now all he talks about is prudence, and all he thinks about is the friendships he's made in Brasília . . . Prudence, for him, is a way of getting money and prestige. He's frightened of what I want to do, and says it might harm my studies and infuriate my father. Twenty months in that college, and he asks me to be prudent . . . Not even my mother talks that way.'

'Uncle Ran said he's an impostor . . . he's played one trick after another . . . But I think you don't want to believe . . .'

'Ranulfo's spoken to me too. Loads of times, and we've even had fights about it. I didn't want to believe him, because my father thinks the same things about Arana, and my father's always thought the opposite from me.'

'The story of the bones . . . How did Arana manage to do that?'

'When I fell ill in the studio, he didn't want me to sleep there. I heard what you were saying about that horrific picture . . . I said he should put the picture inside the cage and set it alight. He was furious, and said I was drunk.'

He drank two more glasses and got up: 'Now I'm going to show Arana the sketch I made. I want to see his reaction.'

We went down a dark alleyway in the Educandos as far as the edge of the creek. In a workshop, an old man was dozing in a hammock; a lamp lit the little floating shed; two mangy dogs lay asleep amongst bits of motors and twisted propellers.

'Are there any boatmen around?' asked Mundo. 'I'm in a hurry; I want a canoe with a motor.'

The old man lifted his face, with his eyes shut; the dogs began to snarl. A red plastic curtain opened, heads and arms emerged, and someone came out: a thin boy, his bony face marked with white spots. Now the animals were barking and jumping by the hammock. His eyes still closed, the old man grumbled: 'Raimundinho, get the canoe with the motor and take these two.'

'Another namesake,' said Mundo, throwing a piece of oakum at the dogs. Other sounds of barking came from the houses around, and when the canoe moved away from the workshop, the creek banks shone with so many eyes. The whole neighbourhood seemed to growl and bark in the night. Mundo let out a fierce howl and shouted to the boy: 'Moor the boat over there, Mundinho. In that house with the light on.'

It was the Three Stars, a floating bar at the mouth of São

Raimundo creek. A fat woman, with a short skirt and a tight T-shirt, met us at the mooring-place: did we want a table on the veranda or inside? Mundo didn't want to sit down; he went looking for Arana on the veranda, and I went to drink beer at the bar. I looked around at the room full of girls; one or two were dancing on their own, waiting for a partner. In the semi-darkness I saw the outline of a bloated figure, half hidden by a curtain of glass beads. I waved to my friend and pointed to the end of the bar. Arana was alone at the table; girls of thirteen or fourteen were dancing around. Mundo pulled the curtain aside and stood in front of him.

'Already?' said the artist, looking at his watch. He gave a forced smile, wondering why I was there. He offered whisky and pulled up a chair; I sat beside Mundo. The bar owner appeared with three girls and winked at Arana: 'They came yesterday from upriver.'

'Not today, Dalva. Today I'm going to talk about this young artist's big idea.' And the affected voice asked, as if he were talking to a child: 'What is the idea? What is this *Field of Crosses*?'

Dalva and the three girls went back to the main room. Mundo took the piece of paper from his pocket and showed the drawing: he wanted to stick a burnt wooden cross in front of every house in New Eldorado; eighty crosses, all told. Then he was going to hang black rags on the branches of the rubber tree in the middle of the wasteland . . .

'The idea is to burn the tree trunk too,' he added.

Arana looked attentively at the drawing, then picked up the piece of paper and hesitated: why had he chosen New Eldorado?

Mundo explained that in the college he had nightmares of scorched landscapes: the devastated forest to the north of Manaus. He had visited the unfinished houses of New Eldorado and walked along the muddy streets: houses with no septic tanks and a fearful stench. The inhabitants complained: they had to pay to live in awful conditions, far from the centre, far from everything . . . They wanted to return to a place near the river. Some had brought canoes, oars, fishing nets, harpoons; the kitchens were tiny and hot; for that reason, they took a brazier out into the unpaved street and made their food right there. He'd slept in Cará's family's house. The afternoon sun heated the walls, the bedroom was an oven, worse than the dormitory in the college. The inhabitants of New Eldorado were prisoners in their own city. Didn't that justify his choice?

'I know that estate is an urban crime,' said Arana. 'But it's Zanda's first big project, and he's your father's idol. He's been appointed prefect and wants to be seen doing something. I think you should use your revolt for other things, Mundo. A burnt tree trunk with a load of crosses . . . That's not art, it's nothing at all.'

Mundo took a sip of whisky, slowly turned round to me and imitated Arana's voice. 'That's not art, it's nothing at all. Hear that, Lavo?'

'You've already drunk a lot,' Arana remarked, plainly uncomfortable. 'It's not art, it really is nothing at all. Mere provocation. They'll persecute you . . .'

'And what if they do? What if I'm arrested? Are they going to work me over, kill me? Fuck them!'

'Fuck them? How long have you been coming to my studio? Everyone knows that, your father was the first one to know. You want to get your own back on him, don't

128

you? But this *Field of Crosses* isn't the way you're going to do it . . . not with my help. I'm not putting my name to that, never!'

Mundo thumped the table with his fist: 'That's the artist for you!'

Arana had been about to say something, but the shock pulled him up short.

'Now he's shitting himself because he's my friend,' Mundo went on. 'The Eldorado isn't just an urban crime. Cará died in the last training exercise, others died too . . . they're dying, here, all over the place.'

With a sudden impulse, he got up, turned his face to the room and began to shout, beside himself with rage: 'D'you know the greatest artist in Amazonas? He sells pictures for a small fortune and pays small change to deflower those girls.'

Looking Arana straight in the face, he asked: 'Isn't that what your art's for?'

'Dalva,' Arana shouted.

The bar owner ran to our table, and a man came after her, put his arm round Mundo's neck, and dragged him down to the moorings. Some other men jumped out of a motor boat and surrounded him.

'Don't hit him, he's drunk, that's all . . . drunk,' Arana said, over and over.

'Get him out of here,' the bar owner said to the namesake.

'Mundo,' Arana shouted, 'we'll talk about this . . . at my place.'

My friend didn't hear, or didn't want to answer: he was lying down in the bottom of the boat, with his mouth open, his head resting on a plank.

'Have they hurt you?' I asked.

'Three Stars,' he said. 'The owner's a madam; she sells girls from the interior. They could be in Vila Amazônia, grating manioc. It's better here, they get a bit of amusement, a few bits of small change from Arana . . .'

He picked up an oar and nudged the boatman in the back: 'Hey, namesake. Stop for a moment and turn the motor off.'

'Here, in the middle of the river?'

Mundo crouched, then suddenly jumped and dived in.

'He's nuts,' said the namesake.

He surfaced a few yards away, swam around in circles, dived again and reappeared near the prow. He came up, stretched himself and sighed.

'Look, Lavo, what a sky. What a huge moon. Those girls, Arana's clients . . . before they die they'll remember nights like these.'

'We'll get off at the mooring at the Aparecida,' I said to the boatman.

'No, we're going to the Municipal Market,' said Mundo.

At the little harbour, he called an employee of a kiosk over and asked for two beers.

'Where are we going to drink?' I asked.

He looked at me and said he'd changed his mind: he wanted to drink alone, in the canoe.

'My namesake's my guide,' he laughed. Then, seriously, he said: 'I've got rid of the hangover, Lavo. Before dawn I'm going to Arana's place. I'm not going to take what he said lying down. What's got to be settled is between us two.'

They were both still young girls – the elder was eleven, the younger eight – when they came to live in a whitewashed wooden house with a tiled roof, much more comfortable and solid than the straw-roofed shacks put up by North-Easterners fleeing from the rubber plantations. A tall thin man with brown face and arms arrived in a big aluminium boat with a sad-looking woman and the two children. He took his shirt off, and we saw the mark the sun had left on his skin: a bi-coloured body. He engaged a dock-worker who lived at the end of the unpaved street, and the two of them went to the boat and brought in a bundle of clothes, hammocks, a brazier, a blackboard, a table, three stools and a fridge run on kerosene, small and blue, the first we'd seen in the neighbourhood. Then the man, the woman and the children went into the whitewashed house protected by a wooden fence. He spent the whole day between the house and the street, and from time to time shouted a name – Ozélia – and the woman came over, he gesticulated, and she went to do something. He bought fruit, a bag of manioc and slabs of dried pirarucu in the Saúva bar, and took everything into the house. In the evening, he got into the boat, and the locals crowded on the top of the bank to watch him starting the motor and see the boat slip down the river. A powerful motor it was, all black with the make in gold lettering, which not even my brother-in-law recognised. For a month he didn't reappear, and the girls only left the house holding hands with the woman: they walked to the end of the ravine, where they stood looking at the river and the far-off city. They went back to the dark house, and no one saw them again. My brother-in-law Jonas said Ozélia was an Indian, because she didn't speak Portuguese and sometimes wore only a skirt, her breasts naked, and sat with her back leaning on the wooden fence and drank caiçuma out of a gourd, and that she, Ozélia, had come from a long way off, maybe from the High Solimões, but my brother-in-law wasn't sure. She planted manioc and pineapples behind the house, and with the older girl built a clay oven to roast flour. Some friends and I went into the forest at the back of the house just to watch them grating and squeezing the manioc, and later making flour. I looked at the legs and face of the younger sister, your mother, and I couldn't keep my eyes off her. I asked my brother-in-law why he didn't give a litre or even a basketful of flour to the woman, and he said she liked grating manioc, it was her custom, but that if she asked for it he'd give it to her. I remember that on a Monday morning the man came back and from then on visited them three times a week. He brought packets of macaroni, biscuits, coffee and sugar, and with him was a well-dressed woman, really smart, her cheeks shining with so much rouge, her lips so thin and red they looked like a thin line of blood, her hair rolled and caught in a bun, where two greyish locks shone, just the colour of zinc. She walked like a seriema along the unpaved road, balancing on her high-heeled shoes, her arms so stiff they hardly moved. She spent the day teaching the young girls on the little open-air patio, between the fence and the sitting-room doorway. The blackboard, a map of Brazil and a cane were hanging on the partition by the door, and the girls sat on the stools and wrote in an exercise book leaning on a slate resting on their knees. During the lessons, a small group of men stood on a box to watch the teacher speak and then write numbers and letters with a piece of chalk on the blackboard and wait for the girls to answer her questions. When their attention wandered or they stayed silent for too long, the teacher took the cane and walked round the table, giving tiny slaps on her own thighs or backside. My brother-in-law recounted how the older girl trembled with fear and cried before she even felt the first blow, and screamed and writhed after it, and the woman gripped the girl's hand and held it open until the end of the punishment. Then she did the same thing on the other hand. A puddle of urine collected on the earth below, and the teacher interrupted the lesson and ordered the girl to go and change her clothes and wipe the stool. The other, the younger, didn't cry or scream; her body trembled and gave a jerk, her gaze fixed on the cane descending on the open hand. The teacher also showed the two sisters how to eat with cutlery: she put plates on the table, took one of the girls by the hand and pretended she was cutting something with a knife, and with the other hand the fork went up to the mouth, and she ordered the girl to chew slowly, making no noise, sitting up straight, and so they cut, chewed and swallowed the air, without opening their mouths, as if they were dolls being watched over by a mannequin with a cane hanging from her wrist by a piece of string. My brother-in-law and other men who spied on the lessons from on top of boxes thought that she – the mannequin – was mad or going mad and that the girls would go mad too with those lessons. Ozélia would go and sit in the street and wasn't allowed back in the house before the woman finished her lessons. The scene was repeated every day, except Sundays, and one afternoon, when I was coming back from the school in São Jorge, I disobeyed my brother-in-law, got up on to a box and saw the teacher speaking, writing and then hitting with the cane, and I didn't understand why the girls didn't study in my school or any other school for that matter. Many children didn't study, wandered round all day amusing themselves, swimming in the river and climbing the trees in the Castanhal and hunting with a catapult, and I only went to school because my older sister, Lavo's mother, forced me to study. When I was thirteen or fourteen I watched some of the open-air classes, even the one where they ate the air. The older girl no longer cried or screamed, and reacted to the cane just like her sister: her body gave a jump as if she'd had an electric shock, and then she looked up and saw the teacher's face – her red lips pressed together, her skin sweaty, and her nostrils so wide you could have put a pitomba inside. I told my brother-in-law that I and a couple of friends could stop the classes with a few sharp blows on the teacher's backside. He said: 'Don't you dare, the man'll send for the police and they'll arrest the three of you, and me for good measure.' It was around that time that the man wanted to give money for Father Tadeu to buy the pulpit and the stained-glass windows for St Francis's chapel, but the priest wouldn't accept the offer. Then the man suggested the chapel should be enlarged, he'd buy the materials and pay the workmen; again, the priest refused. And one Sunday, soon after Father Tadeu celebrated the first Mass on the Morro in an improvised pulpit, my brother-in-law heard a conversation in the chapel doorway. The priest said in a friendly but firm voice: 'It's not right to mistreat children, it's against God's commandments.' Then the man said in an angry outburst: 'Don't be meddling in my children's education, you filthy atheist.' The priest said nothing, and on the Monday morning, before the teacher and the man arrived, my brother-in-law went into the jungle and entered the house by the back, took the cane and the blackboard and buried them in the Castanhal. When the teacher arrived, the younger girl, crouching down between two stools, was looking at the sky. 'Has your sister disappeared?' The girl didn't reply, and then the woman noticed the blackboard and the cane were missing, and her thin red lips trembled; she went to the partition, tore down the map of Brazil and began to roll it up. The elder daughter appeared in the doorway, and threw the contents of a gourd at her head, and we all saw the woman's bun unrolling, and her hair covered her face and shoulders. She dropped the map on the ground and left the house, shouting at the man that she wasn't going to teach those two she-devils another thing; she was flinging her arms around so much, she tripped and fell, then she picked up her shoes and went down the ravine barefoot; she got into the boat and sat there screaming that she wanted to get out of that place. She never came back. And the man started coming only on Sundays: he brought a box with cans of food in it and gave it to Ozélia. He didn't stay long inside the house, took the girls for a trip in the boat, going round in circles on the river – it lasted about ten or fifteen minutes. When the boat moored up again, your mother jumped on to the bank and ran home, but her sister wanted to stay behind, clung to the man, begging him to take her back, without saying where it was she wanted to go. We heard her shouts, the weeping, tremulous voice of an aggrieved, wounded child. The man carried her to the house in his arms, and we didn't know what they said or what they did. Then he went back to the city. My brother-in-law Jonas thought the man was foreign, but I found out he was Brazilian, the grandson of an old family, the Dalemers. I also found out that he had inherited several bits of land in that area, and that he intended to sell them as soon as the war was over. Jonas wanted to know if the girls were his daughters, or Ozélia's, or both of theirs, and the man got really angry; shouting, he threatened to call the police, so my brother-in-law dropped the subject. So no one ever found out. Neither your mother nor Algisa had a birth certificate; they were nobodies, just two beings here in this world, living with an Indian woman who had nothing either. That's to say, they had first names, and the locals gave them the surname Dalemer, and that's the way it stayed. Then, in August 1944, the man disappeared too. My brother-in-law gave Ozélia a paca or a chicken from time to time, and she would make a stew with manioc and green bananas. She herself would bring a portion of the food to our house: she gave my brother-in-law a tin plate and left without saying a word; when he came back from up-country, he gave Ozélia some fish she salted, dried on the washing line, and then wrapped in banana leaves. Sitting in the street, she drank caiçuma, silent, staring at the horizon with a fearful look of nostalgia. Sometimes, in the heat of the early afternoon, we saw her copper-coloured face looking into the sultry heat, her body leaning against the trunk of the

135

flowering jambeiro, *her hands trailing on the ground. I felt a horrible sadness, just looking at her. The elder girl — Algisa was about fourteen — washed clothes, tore branches off the trees and cut bits of wood in the Castanhal forest to use in the brazier and the flour oven. The younger one asked for leftovers from the bigger houses, and a little sugar and coffee in the Saúva bar, and one day, at lunchtime, she came into our house and stood there, on one leg, looking at the pans and plates on the table. My brother-in-law asked if she wanted to eat. She didn't answer: she went to the table, stuck her hand into a pan, took a piece of fish and began to eat it, taking the bones out with her teeth and putting them into the other hand. Ramira got up and left the table. Your mother sat down and went on eating with her hands, using Ramira's plate, and when Raimunda gave her a knife and fork, she used them, as if that was natural to her too. From then on, she began to eat at our house, not every day, but when she wanted to. Your mother . . . Her fleshy, half-open lips had a wavy outline, and her dark eyes, the colour of her hair, seemed to light up her angular features. But I hadn't yet realised the full beauty of her face, and her body. What I did see was her impudence, which exasperated Ramira: she tried on the clothes Ramira made, and one day the seamstress asked if your mother was the Indian Ozélia's daughter, and your mother gave Ramira such an aggressive look that my brother-in-law intervened so the two of them didn't slap each other in the face. My other sister, Raimunda, liked your mother, and they became friends in spite of the difference in age. The two of them used to go with my brother-in-law Jonas to the centre of town, and then we found out your mother didn't know Manaus, or only in passing, because she'd come from the interior directly to the Jardim dos Barés. They say she ran round the squares and read out loud the names of cinemas and everything she saw written on signs and shop-fronts, and went into the shops like a madwoman, wanting to lay hold of everything, to which my sister said 'no'. Then my brother-in-law bought her a dress, two pairs of panties and a pair of shoes, and it was this first dress — blue cotton, with red butterflies and a white collar — that she wore on the unpaved street when I started to see her with a young man's eyes. And she, your mother, wearing the dress that only went halfway down her thighs, asked me to take her to town. The two times we went to the centre, she went into a shop and wanted to take a lipstick and an oval mirror with a gilded frame; I didn't let her. She seemed possessed by the mirror, looking at her own face smiling and grimacing, and she made me promise I'd give her one. I went back to the shop on my own and stole two lipsticks, the oval mirror and a flask of eau-de-Cologne, and gave them to your mother as a present. When she came into the house, scented and with red lips, Jonas dragged me into the Castanhal and gave me a dressing-down: I was never to steal anything again, not even a lollipop. And that was the way it was until he and my sister Raimunda died, in a shipwreck in which our family lost everything. That's to say, all I stole was the linen dress Ramira had made, but that was domestic theft, which Jonas put up with because Alícia returned the dress, after she'd used it on that September night. He, Jonas, gave me money, and I went to buy presents for your mother, and started to spoil her . . . she was beautiful, and stayed that way till the end. When I was called up, they sent me far off, to the frontier with Colombia. I was supposed to spend a year there, and at the end of the fifth month, I wrote to my brother-in-law telling him I was going to desert. He managed to get me transferred to the barracks of the Jungle Infantry Battalion, near the Morro. I already liked your mother a lot, and when she saw me in uniform, looking like a recruit, she didn't look at me with a girl's eyes any more. My sister Raimunda had taught her a lot of women's things, and Alícia was interested in everything in the city: she wanted to see the traditional* clubs and even found a single relative, a cousin of the man who had brought her here with her sister – neither she nor Algisa knew if he was their father. This Dalemer hardly spoke to your mother: he treated her like a gatecrasher and said: 'You've nothing to do with my family, not a drop of my blood, and your surname's false.' After the party at the Bosque Club your mother stopped chasing him. I still didn't know that all she could think about was how to get out of our neighbourhood; some people do everything they can to get out of where they are, and sometimes they go too far. Our love affair began one evening, when it was already dark in the Castanhola forest. Alícia learnt everything with me, and not with Jano, who was a virgin, as she told me years later, laughing, telling me her husband didn't know what to do on the first night, two months or so before the wedding. She told me only to make me more jealous: 'I had to take Jano's underpants off . . . he made love with his eyes closed, dying of shame.' They say he was never naked, not even undressed down to his underpants in front of your mother. And to think he was your father . . . Raimunda had taught your mother certain things and warned her: 'Ranulfo's already been with whores, he's been around.' And she learnt quickly, as eager as could be, she wanted to make love in the forest, in the hammock, in the canoe, even in my house, much to Ramira's horror – she shut the door of the little room where she did her sewing, turned the radio on and wouldn't speak to me for days; she blamed my brother-in-law and Raimunda for allowing such debauchery in the house. We made love too on the trips in the Fé em Deus: Lavo's parents used to go selling things in the area near Manaus, and Raimunda invited your mother to go with us; we made love at every stop: Cacau Pirera, Catalão, Rio Preto da Eva, Itacoatiara. We stayed in the hold, lying on boxes and bags of sugar, wheat flour and bars of soap. My brother-in-law allowed it; he only complained when your mother and I, after the convulsions of lovemaking, came up on deck with our faces and arms covered in flour. Ramira stayed alone at the back of the house on the Morro da Catita, sewing and brooding over it; all she needed was to put burning needles through her tongue. Jonas put up with these attacks of jealousy; he brought home fresh fish and meat and gave Ramira cuts of cloth. Raimunda said to her: 'Sister, get yourself a boyfriend; there's lots of men in the city sleeping alone.' But the city, for Ramira, was a place for her to find clients, and so keep her eyes fixed on her sewing and work more. Your mother and I spent four years having a good time. Algisa and Ozélia didn't get on with anyone, communicated by gestures, and the new inhabitants of the area thought they were deaf-mutes; sitting on the dirt street, they drank pineapple caiçuma out of the same gourd, and then went together to look at the city at the end of the afternoon; they came back home at nightfall and went into the Castanhal to get pieces of wood. They didn't go to the church festivals or St John's Night parties, and if it hadn't been for my brother-in-law's help, I don't know how they'd have got hold of food and clothing. Your mother would invite Algisa to take a walk down to the port or around other neighbourhoods; she never went, and only opened her mouth to say: 'I'm waiting for my father to come and see us.'

10

A T THE END of October I was taken on as a trainee in the firm of a professor of criminal law; I was most interested in cases which were judged summarily, with no due legal process or right to a defence. These crimes hardly ever appeared in the press; I read about them in the quasi-clandestine reports of the Law Association. The motto of the bulletins from Rio de Janeiro was: 'Fearless in the face of censorship and arbitrary justice.' Now, when I look through these old papers, I remember Mundo's angry reaction to fear.

The last time I saw him in uniform was at the entrance to the Vila da Ópera, his hands nervously tapping on his legs. He had been let out before the weekend, he didn't say why; I asked how the night had ended: had he talked to Arana again?

He took his beret off, stuck it into his trouser pocket and gave me a strange look.

'He's changed,' he said harshly. 'In fact, none of us are the same any more, Lavo. His studio is a factory of pictures and sculptures. Arana even disowned that burnt cage full of bones and dry grass . . . He said it was very critical, but now he thinks that's futile. It was an experimental phase, and he's past that now . . . That's what he said, and he laughed as well. Arana's turned into a vulgar art salesman. He wanted me to repeat everything I'd said about my project. So why was the *Field of Crosses* no more than a provocative gesture? He didn't answer. He's too scared. Now he decorates offices, sends presents to officers and politicians . . . And he can't forgive your uncle. Go to the studio . . . He doesn't hide his hatred for Ranulfo.'

He went to the door of our house and stopped, with a mysterious look in his eye, but no hostility. A neighbour, who was gathering washing from a line, laughed; Mundo took offence: 'What's the matter?' The woman stopped laughing, and he went over to the fence. 'What's going on?'

With the clothes rolled up in her hands, she said: 'Calm down, soldier, I was just looking . . .'

I pulled him back, suggesting he come and have a *guaraná*; he stayed there, crouched down, his fingers scrabbling in the dark soil. There was the sound of footsteps in the entrance to the Vila; then he got up, wiped his hands on his trousers, and went to greet the new arrival.

Mundo had fixed a meeting with Uncle Ran.

They went in. Though it wasn't a secret rendezvous – it looked more like a family meeting – they ignored my aunt and excluded me from the conversation. I wandered aimlessly from the bedroom to the kitchen and back, stopping in the sitting room, pretending to be interested in the black masks and capes of the Bats' carnival club. The two of them made no secret of what they were talking about, but they spoke in low voices. My friend, the more urgent of the two, refused Uncle Ran's advice, because he'd already decided to construct his work in New Eldorado. Would Ranulfo help him? He knows the people there . . . he could persuade them to take part, they'd all protest, it would be a collective work of art. So?

'Your mother thinks it's better to put it off till after you graduate.' Uncle Ran wiped his mouth with his hand and shut his eyes. 'You should always respect a mother's fear.'

'Fear . . .' Mundo repeated impatiently. 'That's all anyone talks about . . . Every sentence brings it in. With so much fear, you might as well die.'

'She just asked you to put it off . . . In fact, that was the only thing she asked me for.'

'There's going to be no graduation party, no diploma,' said Mundo, pulling a knife from the top of his boot. Ranulfo stayed on the alert, with his eye on the blade. Mundo took his beret out of his pocket and began furiously stabbing and slashing it. Bits of red felt were falling on the ground, but my uncle didn't move.

'No more berets, no more uniforms.'

'But that wasn't what we agreed,' Uncle Ran reminded him. 'Jano is hand in glove with the prefect and the director of the Military School. If anything happens, he'll blame Alícia . . .'

'Do you know where the last training exercise for jungle operations is going to be? They want to take us to the Colombian frontier. When my mother finds out, she'll change her mind.'

Ranulfo looked at my friend as if he was looking at Alícia. He even smiled, perhaps thinking of the past, or even imagining future scenes . . . The noise of the sewing machine brought him back to the present; he sighed, looked angrily at his sister: why couldn't she stop pedalling that pile of junk?

Ramira repaid him with another angry look: 'If I take my foot off the pedal, I'll have to turn the fridge off.'

She became nervous: she'd been humiliated in front of Jano's son. She crouched over her work, like a hunchback, pretending to be busying herself. Mundo wanted to leave: he'd talk to me later.

He and my uncle were so in tune with one another that I felt betrayed by both of them; I was jealous. What was up with the two of them? More than friendship, I suspected. They were planning something and excluding me, I thought, when I saw them together, Ranulfo's hand grasping my friend's shoulder in an affectionate embrace I'd never seen before.

My aunt was waiting anxiously for Jano's return – he'd gone to Vila Amazônia. He wanted to give a Christmas present to the workers there: clothes, a lot of clothes, made of cheap cloth Ramira bought from travelling salesmen. She told us this news after lunch, in Ranulfo's presence. She suspected something: her brother was perfumed, his hair was combed back, he'd not eaten much and hadn't laid down on the mat for his siesta. He went out into the street and back, whistling nervously. Then she said, in an unctuous voice, that Jano was a rich man with a kind heart: he'd already given her money to buy the cloth. The clothes were simple, modern-looking, smart and with no patches. She was worried by the quantity; she wasn't going to be able to sew all the garments, she might employ an assistant. Uncle Ran stopped whistling: he knew some excellent assistants, more than fifty local girls who'd do the work for free.

'I'm not joking, sister. If you fill a big pan with charity soup and manioc, I'll fill this street with hardworking seamstresses. In less than a month we'll have clothes for all the poor of Vila Amazônia . . . for the whole of Brazil.'

He didn't say this in a mocking tone, but in the look he fixed on his sister there was the same rancorous glint I'd seen when he put the live turtle in boiling water.

'I'll do without your girls, and manage everything on my own,' said Ramira. 'And don't get on my nerves. Get on with your little job at the Booth Line . . . if you don't look out, you'll lose it.'

'Lose it? I don't depend on any little job.'

'You're expecting a lot from that woman . . .'

'I'm waiting for her, as a matter of fact. She'll be here in a short while.'

'And why are you so nervous? Something to do with the son?'

Uncle Ran looked at his watch and then at me. I knew why he was in a tight spot: he'd promised Alícia he'd persuade Mundo to put off the installation of his artwork in Eldorado. Ranulfo couldn't satisfy the wishes of both mother and son, and the divided loyalties were sending him round the bend. Delay exasperated my uncle. I remember it was a brief visit, and the last one she made to the Vila da Ópera. Alícia asked him why Mundo was avoiding her and where he was.

'I think that big lad of yours is away on training exercises,' he lied.

'Training?' Alícia's voice rose. 'And what's that idiot Macau doing? He gets more than a sergeant's wages to make my son's life easier.'

Her face darkened, and she challenged Ranulfo with a domineering look. 'Are you sure? Has my son been chucked into the jungle again?'

Uncle Ran got confused: he wasn't sure, it was only a hypothesis, but Mundo was already back in Manaus, which was all that mattered.

'You're not hiding anything from me, are you?' Alícia asked, in a threatening tone that made him tremble.

My aunt tried pathetically to come to her brother's aid, stammering out his name twice. Alícia ignored these outbursts, and slowly went over to the workroom. Ramira took the needles out of her mouth and tried to say something conciliatory. Alícia went up the step, and her tall woman's body, mature and attractive, loomed in the doorway. With her back to Ranulfo, she gave Aunt Ramira a cold smile: 'The clothes Jano ordered aren't a Christmas present, they're to celebrate Mundo's graduation at Vila Amazônia. Jano wants to see them all in new clothes, and he's going to hire a boat just for the guests from Manaus. You'll get an invitation, Ramira.'

The seamstress thanked her with a guttural laugh, but Alícia had already turned her back and was leaving in a hurry. I saw my uncle running after her and trying to grab her. She angrily pushed him away, and Ranulfo stumbled and fell in the street. The neighbours' laughter irritated him; he sat there, humiliated by his fall. Then he left and didn't come back home.

The order for the clothes had excited Ramira, and the invitation to Vila Amazônia moved her. She even turned the little radio on, and I, when I came back from my classes, heard her tuneless, energetic crooning, and saw her head, immersed in alpaca and thick cotton cloth. She bought more books for me, and for weeks she sewed and hummed, so happy it was horrible to see.

On the Day of the Dead, we went to the Colina cemetery to visit our parents' graves: hers and mine. We came back sad, Aunt Ramira much more than I; hardly had we got into the house than she forgot the Colina and its dead, and a breath of happiness lit up her face, aged by years bent over her sewing. It was no more than a breath, for 1973 ended in a series of misfortunes, and a departure.

I beached the canoe some twenty yards from the house, next to a rubber dinghy. Arana greeted me without enthusiasm; he opened all the doors and windows, and the warm wind aired the studio; he himself started being more open at the same time, until he seemed as happy as Aunt Ramira. The artist had also had a commission, not from Jano or Alícia, but from a Japanese executive in charge of one of the new factories in Manaus. He said the request had given him a lot of work. I didn't ask what it was about: all I had to do was look at the colour photos of macaws on one of the walls. Two of them, with their wings open, were taking shape on a canvas, and were ready to fly off in the golden sky lighting up the forest.

Arana said that the Japanese and Korean executives couldn't even speak Portuguese, but they put a high value on art: they bought pictures without haggling, which was rare in our city. He became serious again: almost at the same moment our eyes fell on a green bag with Mundo's initials, forgotten or abandoned under the stairs.

'He woke me up on the morning after that encounter in the Three Stars. He appeared with his clothes wet, but his head was still burning,' Arana complained. 'I thought he was going to launch straight back into our conversation from the bar. But no. He read out some ideas he had written down in a notebook. He said he was going to invent new monsters and bury our natural surroundings once and for all. He praised the two artists he'd met in Rio. One lives in New York, the other in Berlin. When I said anything, he made fun of it, walking hither and thither with an aggressive demeanour. He disparaged my pictures and objects, called me a little jungle painter. I disagreed. A brat like him sticking two fingers up to me! He saw everything here, learnt everything with me, perspective, light . . . At the beginning, he took an interest in our region; he saw that Amazonia wasn't just anywhere. But gradually he moved away from all that . . .'

'Nowhere is just anywhere,' I said.

'But it doesn't belong to us. What you mean is . . .'

He stopped talking when we heard the sound of voices and steps: children were carrying jute sacks down to the edge of the river, getting into the canoes and rowing quickly away.

'They leave the remains of nature that I use for my work, and take food away,' Arana said, justifying himself.

'But the party won't last long,' I said.

He knitted his hands together and then opened his arms, in a theatrical gesture: 'Mundo always detested that. He attacked me when he saw the kids carrying sacks of food. He said I was giving carrion to vultures. I managed to say a whole sentence, from beginning to end: "Your mother married a wealthy man; that's why you can't bear to see these poor kids carrying food." That offended him more than the criticism he'd got from me in the Three Stars. *Field of Crosses*! What guilt can do . . . guilt, that Jano . . . and your uncle.'

'Ranulfo encourages Mundo's work, he always helped . . .'

Arana frowned with disapproval. 'Some encouragement. They're going to ask the inhabitants of that place to lie down on the ground beside a cross, as if they were dead bodies. Mundo hasn't learnt that from me. He must have got it from Ranulfo, that pervert . . .'

'What happened between you? Why . . .'

He interrupted me, beating his chest and saying 'a pervert' over and over.

My uncle's name angered him, made him lose his temper. He's been waiting a long time to get it off his chest, I thought. I realised I should go when he tied an apron round his waist and started painting a picture again. The green-and-yellow dome of the Opera House reached up towards marble clouds full of animals and birds. The picture had surrealist pretensions – it was almost comic. It was the only time Arana kept quiet in front of his own work. His hatred and resentment against Mundo and Ranulfo joined up with his conceit. Something wider than his artistic work seemed to exasperate him.

He gave me my friend's knapsack and said, in a tone more nervous than irritated: 'Only that blustering uncle of yours can stop Mundo doing something really stupid.'

The next week, when I was getting ready for my criminal law exams, I didn't see either Uncle Ran or my friend. When I was up in the early morning studying, I saw my aunt's tired eyes, her body bent over her machine. One night, I heard her muffled voice: 'I dreamt of Ranulfo . . . buried on the Morro.'

I looked at Ramira: she looked as if she was made of cloth. She stopped her machine, picked up some scissors, made a small indent in the alpaca and went on cutting it manually: the tearing noise gave me a scare.

'Uncle Ran buried on the Morro? What d'you mean?' I asked early next morning. Ramira didn't answer. She was half asleep amidst the trousers and shirts she'd skilfully and carefully sewn by herself and hung on wires. Her face was swollen, even. She only rested after she'd counted the forty-two pieces of clothing over and over again – eight more than the number required. More than that, she had a surprise for Jano: a shirt, made with the leftovers of a piece of cloth a client had bought in the Silk Corner shop, previously Au Bon Marché. At that time in Manaus, almost everything could be imported, and one of my aunt's pleasures was to admire, in the full afternoon sun, the shop windows full of pieces of Swiss organdie and silk from the East and from Italy. She showed me the white shirt, made of Irish linen, with Jano's initials embroidered on the pocket; she smoothed the cloth out, smelt it as if it was a rare flower, with the serenity that the break in her work gave her.

On the Sunday she put on the dress she wore to Mass, and before ten a porter loaded all the clothes on to a cart. She went on foot, with short, hasty steps, and carrying her black bag; she didn't go into the church, and just crossed herself. I'd never seen her so determined, she looked as if she was carrying out the greatest mission in her life. She'd left signs of happiness behind at home – music on the radio, lunch prepared in the early morning, and an affectionate note, unpunctuated and in spidery handwriting: 'Dear Nephew when I return we'll have a party just the two of us at lunch.'

Had the euphoria made her forget her ominous dream about her brother? I heard the church bell chime eleven times. I was fed up with studying law, reading boring case-histories about various sorts of crime. I remembered Uncle Ran's jibes: 'All this law for nothing! The military have chucked all these laws in the bin.'

'The military government's more ephemeral than the laws,' I said, with a shred of hope that my uncle didn't share. He might come to lunch with Corel and Chiquilito: it was Republic Day. I heard some shouting, and went to see if it was them. I came upon some red slices piled on a tray. The watermelon seller, lame and toothless, was a familiar figure in the Vila da Ópera. He stuck his head through the window: had the mistress gone to church? His hands trembling, he lowered the tray, put some juicy slices on a piece of paper, and asked me to give them to my aunt. He looked an immortal street-vendor, another one that survived one more Fifteenth of November in the history of Brazil. I gave him a few bits of change and off he went, limping into the hot afternoon.

Uncle Ran didn't come to lunch. Nobody came. I shut the fat tome on criminal law and remembered Mundo's green rucksack. I found in it a copy of *Manual for Survival in the Jungle*, the *MSJ*, with notes in the margin and observations on hunting and fishing, instructions on how to identify animals' footprints, camouflage, compass use, roots and plants that contain drinking water. In a notebook, the sketches of the work he wanted to do at New Eldorado and the project for a future work: *Seven Drawings: Father–Son–Vila Amazônia–History*. Two caricatures: one of a certain General J. F. d'Aisselle – a chubby face, deep-set, glassy eyes, a chest stuck out like a turkey's, hung with medals and corpses; the other showed the fatuous, pockmarked face of Lieutenant N. Trevo, who 'after contracting malaria, trembled and spoke in a thin, shrill voice'. There were also excerpts from a diary:

Lieutenant Trevo saw subversives in the trees, heard a noise in the leaves and fired furiously in that direction. When he was lucky, he killed a monkey. He detested these inoffensive animals; the shrieks of the howler-monkeys at night sent him mad. Nature set traps for him all the time . . . He was an idiot in the forest. All this because of the 1967 guerrilla war. The lieutenant swore that a general of the Amazonia Military Command would be president of Brazil . . . The majority of the pupils from the Military School are guinea pigs. They haven't messed with me yet; my father's well known in High Command. With the others it's different. Cará was treated like an animal; they made fun of him the whole time. When it rained, he had to raise the flag in the middle of the patio, and he had to help with the cleaning. There's no rest for the poor . . . The poor sons of low-rank officers who serve on the frontiers, kids who do the hard work and will never make it into the Preparatory School for Cadets, much less into a Military Academy, and can't even aspire to be an officer. A sergeant at the outside, or an assistant to an instructor on courses on jungle operations. But Cará knew the jungle like no one else. 'They can abandon me anywhere, without a knife, water, or anything; I can survive for months,' he said. 'You're weaklings, you'd not stick it for three days.' Cará was courageous . . . He'd cross a river with his rucksack on his back, sleep in the wet, climb up palm trees covered with spines . . . He'd hunt out maggots in the nuts of the *buriti* palm, fill his mouth with the raw larvae, chew and swallow the gooey material without vomiting; when he ate the flesh of a sick *paca*, he died of the infection.

Beneath this were the fingerprints of five fingers and these words: 'I took this impression with red ink taken from *annatto* seeds. Cará was already dead.'

In the early afternoon I went out to look for Aunt Ramira. I went to Jano's house: the doors and windows were shut. There were ashes in the air; I smelt smoke. No one replied to my knocking.

Ranulfo buried on the Morro. I don't know why these words brought my friend to mind as well. Where was I to find them on an almost deserted holiday afternoon? My uncle prided himself on not sleeping for more than two weeks together under the same roof. While I was looking for Mundo, Ramira's voice began to echo in my imagination. In the Castanhola, there weren't many people at the open-air party. Daiana Cleide recognised me: 'And isn't the little soldier coming?' She pinched me on the chin and winked, pouting in the direction of the square. She realised I didn't want to go with her, and then pointed towards the iron kiosk. 'Feel like some baked fish for tea?' I gave her the money for the meal; she went away and kept her eye on the Port Authority building. On that Fifteenth of November the Castanhola was just a place where a few sad bands kept playing; Mundo hadn't passed that way, nor by the bars in the Educandos. I took a canoe to the Three Stars; from a distance I recognised the red-striped boat. Arana was gesticulating between two men. The three of them, dressed in ties with the river and the forest in the background, looked like members of a brotherhood plotting something together.

I returned to the Vila da Ópera without finding any trace of my friend. I went hungrily into the house, and Aunt Ramira was stock-still next to the table: her hands were on her head, her fingers stuck in her hair, her silk blouse stuck to her sweaty skin. When she saw me, she picked that day's paper off the floor and threw it at me, as if I was to blame for her misfortune. I saw Mundo's photo, and was going to read the report, when Ramira distracted me, saying that Macau hadn't wanted to let the carter who was delivering the clothes in Jano's house. Then she gave some shouts, and the idiot opened the gate. She saw a pile of books and papers on the patio. She didn't understand. She looked at the kitchen veranda, and Jano was there, with his arms crossed. He gave the chauffeur an envelope and whispered something. It was the money for the clothes. Macau spoke sharply to the carter, and the two of them put clothes on top of the books and papers, then Macau threw kerosene over them and set them alight. All those new clothes burning . . . turning to ash.

'All my work . . . all that effort,' she wailed. 'I was so dizzy I forgot to give him the shirt I'd made for him, I left it all there . . . Jano didn't take his eyes off the fire. I don't understand. The chauffeur took me outside and said: "Read the paper, Dona Ramira." I bought the paper and read the news item. That friend of yours, the son of that woman . . . Wonderful friendship that is. Your uncle didn't come for lunch, I bet that dream I had . . .'

She refused to say any more. In the kitchen, Ranulfo's table setting was untouched. I devoured the fish stuffed with *farofa*; sideways, I looked at Ramira: she was carefully counting the money. Now she seemed less shocked or upset. The fire had devoured the clothes, some of Arana's books and all Mundo's books and drawings. My friend's artwork, in the New Eldorado, had also ended in ashes. In the newspaper photo, you could see the trunk and the dry branches of a single tree, covered in black rags, and a row of wooden crosses stuck into the unpaved streets. The title and subtitle of the report had doubtless scandalised his father: '*Field of Crosses* – Tycoon's son unveils macabre "work of art".'

The story, for the most part a glowing summary of Jano's biography, commented ironically on Mundo's pretensions: 'a rebel son, failed student and dandy in uniform who wanted to create contemporary art in a poor neighbourhood, where almost everyone is illiterate.' In one of the photos, he was between a man and a woman, the parents of Cará, Mundo's dead friend; in the background was the forest.

Very early the following day I went to New Eldorado. The *Field of Crosses* had been destroyed by the police on the afternoon of the day of the holiday. The sight of the ruins underlined the sadness of the place. Scorched wooden crosses covered an area of wasteland; the trunk of the rubber tree had been cut down and its roots ripped up; dead branches stuck in burnt rags looked like charred carcasses. In the unpaved streets, women were collecting bits of the crosses to make a bonfire. Around eight o'clock, the council employees threw the remains into the back of a lorry, leaving only the felled tree behind.

I crossed the wasteland and walked slowly to the other end of the neighbourhood. Mundo hadn't exaggerated:

there were no trees; the place had no shade at all. I showed one of the inhabitants the photo of my friend between Cará's parents, and asked if he knew them. He pointed me to the last house, about a hundred yards before the forest.

I told them I was Mundo's friend. They were still shocked by what had happened the previous day. The father had a strip of black cloth on his pocket, and the mother pointed at the picture of her son with the uniform of the Military School: he'd wanted to be a soldier since he was a child, and dreamt of the Jungle Infantry Battalion. She brought a caricature of Cará made by Mundo: a high forehead, large eyes and ears that stuck out; he was in uniform, knife in hand, and one of his boots standing on a peccary's head.

'He was very courageous,' she said. 'After the funeral a lieutenant came here, and left a little box with a medal . . . He said they're going to set up a football tournament named after my son.'

She complained about New Eldorado: there were shortages of electricity and water, the bathroom had no septic tank, the inhabitants chucked their waste away near the jungle, and the animals came to eat in the filth they left.

I asked if she and her husband had seen my friend's work.

'The smoke? That man who went around with him . . . Ranulfo . . . he climbed on to a branch of the rubber tree and said some things. Then the people of the neighbourhood burnt the crosses and the tree . . . I invited Mundo to lunch here, but his friend looked depressed, and didn't want to. Then they went away . . . They say they're related. Father and son, are they?'

Before she disappeared into the city, Algisa gave us two surprises.
The first was at the festival of the patron saint of the Morro, when I'd
just arrived from my service with the frontier battalion. We were all
going to the celebrations. There were people from other neighbour-
hoods, and some soldiers on leave were wandering through the streets.
Suddenly, Algisa tore herself away from Ozélia and took her clothes
off at the edge of the ravine, and we all saw the beauty of her slender
body in the middle of the afternoon. At that moment, I shuddered to
imagine what your mother must be like. Chiquilito was going to run
to grab Algisa, but Corel tripped him up, and held him in a half
nelson. Defeated, Chiquilito decided to turn his back on the ravine.
She went up a few steps of the ladder, jumped into the river like an
arrow and only emerged by the opposite bank. She swam the rest of
the afternoon, and each stroke she took increased Father Tadeu's
despair – he implored the faithful to come back to the sweet stalls.
Not even my brother-in-law, as respectful as he was, failed to look at
the dark-skinned body coming and going. My sister Raimunda was
impressed by the rapidity of her strokes and the long dives, and
Ramira commented maliciously: 'She'll go a long way.' Then your
mother said: 'Algisa was always half crazy.' In the evening, Ozélia
threw the swimmer's clothes into the river, and she dressed herself in
the water, but when she stood at the water's edge she looked even
more naked. Algisa looked at no one and said nothing: she went into
the house, where a solitary, unlit night awaited her. A year later, she
buried once and for all her reputation for timidity. Ozélia appeared
at the back of the house and gave us to understand that Algisa was in
trouble. She stretched her arm out, pointing at the farthest point of
the Castanhal, and my brother-in-law asked if Algisa had got lost in
the forest. She shook her head. Some beast, some animal? She
nodded. Jonas and I ran to the Castanhal, to the edge of the military
area, where today there's housing for the junior officers. Jonas was the

156

first to see her. She was astride the thick, high branch of a jatobá, holding a machete; her unblinking eyes cast downwards, her body rigid. We looked for the dangerous animal that was threatening her, and found him camouflaged by the green of the forest. Squatting down, with his head raised, a private soldier was masturbating. He was so possessed by the pleasurable trance he was in, and by the vision of the woman, that he had no time to react to the hard kick Jonas gave him in the backside. He fell over, rolled in the leaves and sat down, with his active hand still stuck in his trousers: his open mouth gave him an expression like an asthmatic. He crawled backwards, and we had to hold Algisa to stop her castrating him with the machete: even so, she managed to spit in her aggressor's face and insulted him with all the swear-words she knew. Jonas promised Algisa he'd report the soldier to a friend in the Army – she ignored the promise and said: 'If that son of a bitch comes anywhere near our house, I'll cut him to pieces.' I never forgot the threat, especially in the five months we slept in separate hammocks in the humid basement in Vila Amazônia. My brother-in-law waited for the recruit to disappear into the foliage like a timid chameleon, and Algisa decided to go back to the Jardim dos Barés alone. We followed her at a distance, watching her cut branches off with blows of her machete, and when we were close to the houses my brother-in-law whispered a prophecy: 'Whoever lives with that woman is going to have to bite his tongue, day and night.' And, some six months later, Algisa and Ozélia got into a river-peddler's canoe, and went downriver saying neither where they were going nor when they'd be back. Your mother asked everyone: 'Where's that madwoman gone?' Then I went after the two of them with my brother-in-law, but we couldn't find them. The police began to look for them, and as there were no photos of Algisa, their solution was to show your mother to the policemen and say: 'She looks just like her, only a little less pretty, not quite so tall and about three years older.' After a week's search, a civilian policeman told Jonas that Algisa had been interned in the asylum at Flores for having harassed and grabbed hold of a man at the harbour that she said was her father; the man had denied it with a laugh, had been scratched in the face, and had accused her of being a dangerous madwoman. My brother-in-law talked to the asylum director and found out she'd been brought there by mistake and that she'd be handed over as a vagrant to the Brazilian Legion of Charity. Jonas explained that Algisa lived in the Jardim dos Barés, and that he'd brought her sister, Alícia, as witness. The director asked why she had no identification document. 'Half the population hasn't got one,' Jonas replied. Algisa was sitting on the grass shaded by a red ocotea tree, admiring the head of a clay saint that Pai Jobel was sculpting. She said she wasn't mad and she was only looking for a man, her father, after Ozélia had left for the interior, leaving her alone. 'Interior? What interior?' your mother demanded. 'There, where we were born,' said Algisa. 'You don't remember, but I remember when the man appeared and talked to Ozélia, and the three of us got into a boat and travelled for three days and two nights, and I remember our house on the riverbank . . .' Your mother was first ashamed, then furious. She said: 'We haven't got a father, that man's nothing to us.' But Alícia didn't know, she wasn't certain about it. Then Algisa said she wanted to stay in the asylum; there she ate, walked round the garden and talked to other people. She stayed seated where she was, looking at Jobel's hands. Then we dragged her away by force. She kicked out: 'Let go of me, I want to stay here,' and cried all the way to São Raimundo harbour, and told us, sobbing, that a man had abused her in a pension where she wanted to sleep but had no money. She'd struggled with him, scratched his nose with her nails, then she'd run away and slept on a bench in Cathedral Square. My brother-in-law wanted the police to arrest the man, but Algisa didn't reveal who he was nor where the pension was. 'Stop bothering me with nonsense about going to the police,' she said to Jonas, putting an end to the matter. She lost the habit of drinking caiçuma and looking at the river at the end of the afternoon. Sometimes she went out at sunset and only came back the next day, with new clothes, earrings and leather shoes, and politely greeted the neighbours. She was less unsociable, almost friendly with us, and even smiled. But no one could ask her where she slept on the nights she spent away from the Morro.

11

O N THE AFTERNOON Mundo's artwork was unveiled, Colonel Zanda informed Jano immediately. In New Eldorado, Jano saw a horizon of charred crosses and asked what the hell it was: why had they built the houses in a cemetery? Where was his son's work? Laughing, the prefect said: 'Right in front of your eyes, Trajano. Your son's daring: he's made a cemetery of the whole neighbourhood. He's done well. But we'll destroy all his rubbish in no time. One day we'll really give him a fright. Now come to the headquarters of the Military School Command, the director wants a word with you.'

In General Osório Square, Jano took his time getting out of the car: he feared his meeting with the director, and feared what Macau would later pass on to Naiá. The chauffeur waited for him on the pavement outside the college, between the two cannons pointing at the river. He exchanged a few words with the sentinels, looking at the dark wooden staircase his boss had just gone up. He didn't wait for long: Jano came out looking smaller, walking slowly, holding his hands in front of his eyes against the light. In the car, you could hear his panting breath and the clicks of his tongue. On Epaminondas Avenue, Jano murmured that he was thirsty; the chauffeur bought a bottle of mineral water at a bar. He wetted his face, eagerly drank the water, and rested for a few minutes. He wanted to go by the office before going home, but on Marshal Deodoro he changed his mind: he wouldn't be able to go up the stairs. He was shaking, pale with fear or anger, and looked as if he was suffocating. On the way home, Macau heard his boss recount, in a weak voice, how he'd been humiliated. Straight away, Jano had seen the look of annoyance on the director's face; he greeted him coldly. He'd tried to hide his feelings, looking at the Duke of Caxias's bust on the wall, and the photographs of the latest presidents in uniform. Silently, he looked at them one by one, feeling uneasy in the presence of their serious faces, and he remembered two of them, whom he'd met when they came through the city. Now they looked threatening, even the one who was dead. That was what he'd thought when the colonel, whom he'd thought of as a friend, pronounced this severe sentence: 'You don't make a mockery of your father, or of an institution.' Then Jano found out that Mundo had tricked them all, even the director. He had taken a letter from his father, complete with falsified signature, and in which Jano asked for two weeks' leave for his son to accompany him to Rio de Janeiro. The soldier revealed a tangle of lies, all of them surrounding Jano's illness; he realised that Mundo had protested, in subversive language, at the accidental death of a student during a survival exercise in the jungle, and that on Fridays he asked permission to go and see his father, who was in hospital. Jano saw and signed the last report on Mundo: failed, to all intents and purposes – he wouldn't get his diploma. Apart from that, his escape or flight from the college was a grave transgression against discipline. This insubordination was graver still. How could he have done this? A student, inciting a whole neighbourhood to protest against the city's prefect, an officer of the Armed Forces! Mundo could be arrested, along with a vagabond, a certain Ranulfo. Two idiots. The colonel cited the Law of Military Education: the case had been passed on to the Amazonia Military Command, and they'd decided to expel Mundo.

Macau couldn't believe it: expel the boy?

'He's no longer a boy,' Jano said in a hoarse voice. 'He's a man . . . a delinquent.'

At home, Jano felt dizzy, began to sweat and fell on to the bed; Naiá helped him put his pyjamas on and made a rice broth with pieces of beef. Jano had already taken his dose of insulin, and didn't want a doctor to be called. He implored the maid to convince his wife to come and sleep beside him. Alícia was reluctant. Naiá reacted like an indignant friend: she took her mistress to the room, and, looking at the sad, pale man lying there, she threatened: 'If you don't sleep here, I'm leaving this house.'

Alícia only went to bed in the early morning, half drunk, wanting to know where Mundo was. Later that morning, Macau was reading the papers when he saw Jano coming out on to the patio. Still pale, he walked slowly, hands in pockets, thoughtful. He said good morning and walked round the palm trees, stopping to pick leaves off the ground and pull worm-eaten guavas off the trees, trying to occupy himself. Suddenly, he turned round and asked him: 'What's the matter, Macau? Why've you got that face on?'

The chauffeur's hands began to shake; he stammered, shook his head, got confused, unable to say anything, gave his boss the papers and crouched down next to the car. Jano leafed through them one by one, and his eyes fixed on his son's photograph. He folded the papers, lifted his head, and seeing Naiá on the kitchen veranda, called her.

'Macau's going to help me with a job,' he said. 'And I want to give Alícia a surprise. Go to the Avenida cake shop and get some pastries to have with coffee.'

He waited for Naiá to go out and coldly put his decision into practice: he went into Mundo's room with the chauffeur. Macau carried the books, magazines and drawings out on to the cement patio. When the maid came back, she realised what had happened. She found Alícia sleeping on the floor, curled up, with the previous day's clothes still on. Naiá waited before waking her mistress; she only managed to drag her out of the couple's bedroom after eleven. The patio was covered with ashes; sheets of paper and charred rags were blowing around the garden.

'It's a wonder you didn't hear the shouting,' Naiá had told Ramira. 'The boss was afraid he might get a thrashing and called Macau . . . I was afraid too . . . even Macau got a fright. She let loose with some swear-words, opened her hands and advanced on Jano, shouting at him, telling him he was a coward. When she got close to her husband, she tripped on the step, got dizzy and vomited on the wall and over us, holding on to the banister so as not to fall. She scratched the wood and the wall with her nails – a horrible squealing noise. She got up on her own, and Jano ran out of the room. Then she pulled the photograph of Vila Amazônia off the wall and threw it at the crystal cabinet. She picked up the toy soldiers and weapons and threw them on the ground covered in vomit and bits of glass. Then she picked up all her clothes and shoes and took them to the boy's room. I think the boss is going to die before his time.'

★　　★　　★

Alícia moved into Mundo's bedroom for good. She'd never thought Jano capable of burning things that were so important to their son. She treated him coldly and distantly, Macau too, and said to Naiá that the chauffeur was a sly customer, an arsonist in the service of his boss, she'd not give another penny to the bootlicker, and from now on he could eat in the same hole he slept in. She only spoke to Naiá, who, as well as looking after the house, also kept an eye on her husband. The doctor came by once a week to see Jano, and when he was feeling unwell, a nurse accompanied him to the office.

Even at a distance, Aunt Ramira slowly penetrated and involved herself in the world inside the mansion she'd always dreamt of getting to know; she was so caught up in the life of the Mattosos that she seemed a new woman on the mornings of her trips to the market. She heard from Naiá what Jano had told Macau about his meeting with the director of the Military School, and listened to a tense conversation between Jano and Albino Palha. Jano couldn't resign himself to the very sudden fall in the price of jute and *malva*. Palha had suggested to his friend that he change direction: he should construct houses and apartment blocks, export metal ore or expensive hardwoods, or take a role in some Asian electronics industry – lots of people from the south of Brazil were doing that in Manaus.

'Anything, except jute and Brazil nuts, Trajano.'

His friend waited for an answer, but Jano didn't say a thing, stroking Fogo's ears and looking at the photograph of Vila Amazônia. When Palha asked about Mundo, he got up, said goodbye with a cold handshake, as if he'd not heard the question, as if the other man was just a visitor like any other.

That same day, he asked Naiá to give him an insulin injection. He'd almost never done that: he didn't like to do so, he was ashamed, but now he felt weak and nervous. The maid wiped some cotton soaked in alcohol on his thigh, and saw the marks of the needle, dark pricks on his reddened muscle. Like a pigeon's thigh, poor thing! She stuck the needle in, and her boss didn't groan; he leant his head back on the red back of the chair, his eyes shut, and his head sweaty. He told her he was in agony, and there was no cure for his pain. Then he asked to be left alone, he wanted to have a siesta. Naiá listened to his complaints: 'I should've burnt other things as well . . . Alícia deserves to inherit nothing, not a single canoe.'

My aunt recounted all these conversations in a sad voice. She plucked up courage and told Naiá she'd sewn a shirt for Jano. Pure Irish linen! A week later, during supper, she took a postcard out of her bra, and read to me the message written by the man she venerated. Jano was sorry about what he'd done with the shirt. All said and done, he was sorry to be alive. Aunt Ramira sobbed and put the postcard away as if it was a relic. On the 7th of December, her birthday, Naiá gave her a bouquet of flowers with some affectionate words from Jano. Ramira fell into an ecstatic trance. The only bouquet a man had sent her in almost half a century of life. She began to brood over the illusion of something like love. Then she sewed a pair of navy-blue trousers for him, taking enormous care over the cut and the finish. I asked if she shouldn't take the measurements of his height and waist. 'Of course not,' my aunt replied. 'A good seamstress doesn't have to take the measurements of some-one she admires.'

She decided to go to the late Sunday afternoon Mass; Jano might be in the church of St Sebastian. She asked me to go with her, all she wanted to do was thank him for the flowers and give him the trousers; she was shy of going alone: people would whisper, gossip, invent stories. I stood near the door, surrounded by the poor in the congregation. Jano, alone, was kneeling in the front pew. He and my aunt prayed, and looked at one another. I didn't wait for the end of the homily, and I don't know what other communion there was between the two of them. At seven I had supper in the kitchen, from where I could see the twinkle of sequins on carnival costumes. Ramira was late back, and when she got back she didn't want to work or eat: she was exhausted, and only wanted to sleep. Had she talked to Jano?

She smiled: 'I talked . . . a great deal. What a man!'

Nevertheless, her brother's prolonged disappearance got her worried. It hadn't happened since Ranulfo had run away from Vila Amazônia. Ramira imagined him drowned or knifed, gasping his last breath. She came into my room and accused me: 'You're only thinking about your friend. What about your uncle, why don't you go and look for him?'

The next day she was in a better mood, and busied herself with the stiff, reddish capsules of wild flowers. She'd planted them in a clay pot shaped like a shell, and didn't want to see the green stems wilt. She was divided by two strong feelings, thinking of Jano and Uncle Ran, while exhausting herself to finish her end-of-year orders.

In the last days of December I'd gone out in a chaotic search for Mundo, counting simply on chance and good fortune. His only friend from the Military School was dead. There was no one else, apart from my uncle and Alícia.

Naiá saw me at the back door, stopped putting out the clothes to bleach in the sun, and waved for me to come in. She told Macau it was time to go and fetch the boss.

'The wife doesn't come down at all,' she said. 'The owners of the house are like guests, not a married couple. I'll tell her you want to talk to her.'

I stayed for some minutes in the room, peering at the record collection, the library, and some broken toy soldiers. Enough wars, books and music for a lifetime. The owner of all this hated his son's art; maybe he hated his son and art. In the glass cabinet was a photo of Fogo, still a puppy, in Jano's arms. How he'd grown! Fat, sad and very old, he no longer jumped up in the way that used to irritate Mundo, but he had the smell of a spoilt animal, petted and fed on the family's food. His faded eyes looked up from the red sofa; I stroked his muzzle and he came closer. He let out a weak snarl when he saw Naiá on the staircase: I could go up, Alícia was waiting for me.

I found her sitting on a wicker chair, her legs crossed, the same chair and the same pose as years later, when I saw her in the sitting room of an apartment in Rio. She apologised for receiving me in her bedroom. She was scented and had put her make-up on, not to see me, but to talk about her son and maybe about my uncle. 'Look what that bastard of a husband of mine did,' she said, her glance sweeping over the marks of rectangles and squares on the walls. 'The drawings, the objects . . . all gone. Jano knows how to get at Mundo, only this time he got at me too.'

Dried leaves and seeds, bits of wood, boxes of pencils and tubes of paint had all disappeared. The empty room spoke of the violence of his father's act. Only one thin thread hung from the ceiling.

'A pair of wings or blades, I don't know which,' said Alícia, 'It was ripped down and burnt. Mundo was given it by an artist in Rio. He'll go berserk when he finds out.'

I told her I'd not seen my friend: did she know whereabouts he was?

'He must be well hidden,' she said, hurriedly. Then she dissimulated: 'Your uncle didn't manage to persuade my son to put off this . . . I don't know what to call it . . . that thing they did in New Eldorado. Ranulfo hasn't the least idea what's happened in this house.'

Jano had planned a huge party in Vila Amazônia to celebrate his son's graduation, with musicians from Parintins and any amount of food and drink. He was going to hire a pleasure boat to take the students, teachers and guests to the property. She wasn't going to go, but it was all her husband talked about. He was going to lay out an enormous amount because of Mundo; he'd already hired a photographer and a cinematographer – he wanted to show his son with his uniform on, with his fellow graduates in the Military School. The Archbishop of Manaus would say Mass. Jano knew that jute had no future, but he was laying bets on his son's future. It was his dream. Also, the prefecture was going to buy jute from Vila Amazônia. Zanda would do that to help him, and the two were in negotiations. Palha was giving advice, suggesting prices and mediating. But Zanda had distanced himself and was going to cancel the deal.

In her voice there was the fear of a threat. She picked up a card pack, and her hands opened and closed a fan of cards. The gold and the stones of her rings shone as she moved her arm; with a gloomy look, she stared at the walls. 'Your uncle went too far, too . . . Jano was always very fond of me. What could I do? A woman can do what she likes when she's got a man who's in love with her. Ranulfo never wanted to accept . . .'

She threw the pack on the bed, and seemed embarrassed by what she had just said, or hadn't said. I heard barking, and feared Jano was coming.

'Hungry . . . he wants lunch,' said Alícia. 'Fogo's the only one that eats at the right time. But he's not worried about me any more. Before, when a man came in the house, he snarled a little, out of jealousy. Now I can walk naked down the corridor and he doesn't even come to sniff.'

She looked at me sideways, saw I was going to ask about Mundo again and began to say that the Cornos creek didn't used to be as filthy as it was now. She used to swim and canoe there with my uncle, but they fought a lot. He would say: 'I wasn't born to sit on a school bench. I stopped being stupid when I read good books.' Books and girlfriends did the trick.

'He never talked about anyone else,' I said. 'I know he married your sister.'

'Algisa got in with your uncle and insisted she was determined to marry him. She said she was going to tame the lion, but your uncle never lost his urgency, he wanted the two of us, and even that wasn't enough. Then I thought of Vila Amazônia. Ranulfo could make a good adminis-trator, and the property would save us all: me, him, my sister . . . and my marriage. But when Mundo was born, he was furious; then he became attached to the child, and I let him . . .'

Proud, and still pretty; her legs crossed: firm legs, like a ballet-dancer's; biggish eyes, like a knowing cat. Did her soft voice hide a pent-up anger? She asked me to stay for lunch, just me and Jano, alone. She no longer sat at table with her husband.

'He admires you, Lavo. An orphan brought up by a poor aunt . . . You're going to be a lawyer; you might be a judge, a doctor of laws . . . Another one who's risen from the depths! Jano thinks Mundo degenerated. He's afraid of his artist son. Why don't you lunch with him? The words of an orphan are worth more than mine.'

With a forced insouciance, she added: 'I swore I'm only coming down for Christmas dinner. They'll all be at the table, from the dog to Macau.'

I refused the invitation, so she insisted I came back after Christmas.

She got up to say goodbye; her whole body, which Uncle Ran knew every inch of and still desired, clung to me in an embrace. I remembered the morning I saw her close to, wet, climbing the steps of the Pedro II, with the pupils whistling at the woman who was marching resolutely towards the headmaster's door; then she reappeared, smiling, and crossed the corridor under a hail of whistles and gallantries. She never made an effort to look attractive. But now something, beyond her inhibited speech and interrupted laughter, veiled her spontaneity. I had the impression Alícia knew where Mundo and my uncle were hidden.

'The mistress is strange, isn't she?' said Naiá, opening the garage door. 'Your aunt too. Ramira was in seventh heaven, now she's in a bitchy frame of mind, angry with everyone. What's got into her?'

We saw Jano's car coming up to the mansion.

'And the boss, eh? He's hardly eating, seems a bit mad, and spends all his time chatting away to himself.'

She told me she was sad to see him so mortified, with no appetite for anything. He didn't even touch his favourite dish: marinated *tucunaré* with mashed manioc. He hadn't the energy to walk Fogo, or pick guavas off the trees as he walked round the garden. In the last few days, she'd even been helping him to eat, for Jano, like a baby, pushed the fork away from his mouth and the food dribbled down his chin.

'But Alícia asked me to have lunch with him,' I said.

'Have lunch with the living dead?' Naiá answered. 'Sometimes he's more alive than dead, but that's not usually the way things are.'

What Naiá had said about my aunt was true. One rainy Saturday, Ramira came back exhausted from the market: not saying much, and with an angry look that took time to wear off. She spread a piece of cloth out on the table and began to cut the material; the open scissors, hooked on her fingers, looked like a weapon.

'Naiá's lying to me,' she said, without moving.

The hand gripping the scissors turned and fell: 'Lying or hiding something, it doesn't matter which. I don't like people who are false, like chameleons. In the market, she told me she'd heard a bit of conversation between her boss and Macau. I asked her if Ranulfo's name hadn't cropped up. She pretended she was deaf. She touched the eye of one fish, then another . . . but she didn't choose either. Then she went to buy *maxixe* and okra in the stalls owned by the

Japanese: she said she was going to make a stew for your friend's mother.'

She didn't even utter Alícia's name, and only stopped griping about Naiá when an important customer appeared: Dona Santita Biró, who was the mother of twins, both of them débutantes. She had so much perfume on that Ramira left the door open. Santita showed her the photograph of a tall, blonde princess: she wanted her daughters' dresses to be exactly the same. My aunt hesitated, and looking at the photo, blinked, began to frown, somewhat irritated: 'But your daughters haven't got the height . . .'

'So what? Aren't I paying for the design?'

Hardly had she gone, Aunt Ramira grumbled: that customer spends her days looking at photographs of princesses . . .

She got mixed up in her sewing, lost a pattern, got the cut of an armpit wrong, and openly swore at Naiá and my friend's mother. A secret thought, maybe about Jano and her brother, distracted her from her work, and she got behind with her orders; she hated mess, weakness and doubt.

On Christmas Eve, we sat at the breakfast table, on the little patio at the back of the house; we listened to the birds singing in the mango trees and palms of the Calvado mansion. The monotonous sounds of the fountain and the waterfall were blotted out by the sound of diving and swimming.

She gave me a hard look: 'How are your crimes going?'

'Other people's crimes, you mean.'

'Your internship in the professor's firm. Are you earning anything yet? Or am I going to have to spend the rest of my life sewing for princesses and pirates?'

She put her cup down on the table, and looked with disgust at a chameleon devouring insects on the climbing plant on the fence. The reptile disappeared through a crack, and reappeared in the Calvados' garden.

'There'll be no shortage of cases for you, Lavo. There are thieves and robbers everywhere.'

Later, someone knocked at the door. In the middle of the window there appeared a half-Indian face: two large staring eyes looked at us with the bleakness of exhaustion.

'I've come to pick up the ensemble,' said the boy, underlining his pronunciation of the French word. He didn't want to come in, and his eyes grew even larger and looked at everything: the inside of the house, me and my aunt. He took the package, paid and went out in a hurry.

'He's the illegitimate son of a family from the Rua dos Barés,' said Ramira.

At lunchtime, Corel and Chiquilito came unexpectedly; they seemed not so much drunk as dazed: Chiquilito, who was the more agitated of the two, was stammering, couldn't string words together, and his breath was hot, his nostrils flared as if he were a horse.

'What do you want? My brother hasn't set foot in this house for more than a month,' my aunt said.

Corel wiped his face: 'That's why we're here. They've caught Ranulfo.'

'Caught?! What do you mean, caught?' my aunt asked, bending a needle.

'They've found him . . . some thugs . . . or police, no one knows. They gave your brother a good drubbing. He's in the Portuguese Beneficent hospital.'

Ramira rushed past between them and set off for the hospital. She took short steps as she ran, her grey nightdress billowed out, and her grey hair was scattered over her back; near to the hospital garden, she left her worn-out sandals and disappeared into the entrance of the mortuary chapel, perhaps to shorten the distance. On the flower-beds on Getúlio Vargas Avenue armed men made me fall back. I heard shouts, bells ringing, the hum of motors: it was a convoy of lorries full of fat men, all dressed in red and with caps, their cotton beards drenched in sweat. They were ringing little bells, throwing plastic balls and sweets to a crowd of children who stood in their bare feet on the asphalt. The convoy came from distant parts of the city, and now it was circulating round the centre, celebrating the opening of a chain of shops. I followed the figures in fancy dress and saw that they each had a cardboard mouth, smiling and brightly coloured, covering half of their faces. At the corner of the alleyway, a tall figure stood out: Mundo, with no shirt, his arms and shoulders scratched, barefoot, his trousers rolled up; there were dishevelled clumps of hair instead of the crew cut. Frightened, he looked as if he was in a trance, and his body seemed about to advance on the convoy. Suddenly, he opened his arms, made obscene gestures, tried to climb up into a lorry-cab; he was pushed away by security men and taken to the pavement. He lifted his fists and went on gesticulating furiously, until he turned his back on the crowd and disappeared up the alley.

The head of the convoy was already at Seventh of September Avenue, but that mass of laughter was still parading in front of me. It took me some minutes to decide whether to visit Uncle Ran or follow Mundo. Christmas with the family, from the dog to Macau, everyone together, Alícia had said. My friend would arrive unexpectedly, in rags and with the face of an animal, to frighten his father; he would burst out laughing, or shut himself up with his mother, in her room, in secret whispers. There was the sound of rockets, bells and shouts; Christmas music and a strident voice announcing: 'Everything from Taiwan and Panama at low, low prices.' I ran to the chapel, but there was no one I knew. I thought of my uncle lying in his room and Mundo disappearing up the alley. I went round the side of the hospital, and, near the steps at the entrance, I moved away. I remembered Corel's words when he told us about the attack on Uncle Ran: 'thugs . . . or police'. Mundo might be facing something worse still, I thought, as I went up the alley. Up there, I could only see the windows of the hospital, above the tops of the mango trees. The door of Jano's house was open, I passed under the arbour and on the veranda I heard shouts and barking. When I came into the room, the first thing I saw was Mundo saying to his father: 'Why don't you take your belt off now? Why don't you shut me in the basement?'

Standing up, and his hands spread out on his chest, Jano began to fall back when his son advanced on him. I ran, but before I could grab Mundo round the waist, he thrust his hands into his father's shirt and gave him a violent shove.

'Out of here, Lavo, our conversation's not over yet,' he shouted, in his desire to get at the body on the ground.

I grabbed him by the arms, and his furious eyes faced me; I thought he was going to advance on me. He wouldn't stop shouting: 'He's not the man for my mother,' while I dragged him towards the door. He wouldn't listen, and, threatening me with his fist, he yelled: 'Let me go, you bastard. Go over there with that coward. Aren't you the son he wanted?' With a jerk, he pulled himself free and slowly went out, looking at the sitting-room floor, where his father had fallen.

I carried Jano to the sofa. His eyes, half-open, turned towards the ceiling, frightened me. Cotton wool, a flask of alcohol and two broken glass ampoules stood on the central table. I went up to the rooms. There was no one. I looked for Macau at the back of the house, and couldn't see the DKW. When I came back, Fogo was sniffing at his master's head. He whined, and lifted his tired, yellow eyes to me. I took Jano's wrist and felt a slow, weak beating. I don't know how long I stayed there, listening to howls, next to the two of them: four eyes that could no longer meet.

It seemed as if a whole epoch had lain down and died.

12

NAIÁ AND THE DOCTOR got out of a taxi, but only the doctor went inside: she didn't want to see Jano, and stayed on the pavement, asking me with her eyes if he'd died, and my silence made her more nervous. She said he'd woken up in an anxious state, and hadn't taken his medicines or eaten anything. At mid-morning a strange character appeared wanting to talk to him. The two of them had a conversation, and the boss smiled when the man said Ranulfo was done for; then the man said I don't know what – Naiá couldn't make it out. After that Jano got irritated, sent the man away, but Alícia managed to stop him by the door and tried to force him to say where her son was. He didn't know, he'd not found Mundo. 'Your son's got away,' he said. Then she went back into the sitting room; she stood looking straight at her husband, without saying a word. That was worse; Jano wanted to hear her voice, but Alícia looked at him with hatred and went out with Macau. Naiá stayed with her master, half dead with fear.

'I still struggled to make him eat something, but he didn't hear what I was saying,' the maid went on. 'He treated me as a stranger, sat down on the sofa and shut his eyes; he didn't even manage to stroke Fogo. An embittered man, it looked as if he wanted to die.'

I asked where Alícia had gone, and Naiá answered with a question: had Mundo been around?

'He insulted his father . . . he went to hit him,' I said.

'So they only managed to catch Ranulfo . . .'

'And Alícia?' I pressed her.

'They must have battered your uncle,' said Naiá, disdaining to answer my question.

I was going to say I was going to the hospital, when the doctor called her. I waited on the pavement, and when Naiá appeared in the doorway, I gathered Jano was dead.

Dead or dying, Jano aroused no pity in me; but I felt no anger towards him, nor aversion, I didn't even despise him, something Mundo had noticed since the beginning of our friendship. What I felt for Jano was fear . . .

Ramira saw me on the pavement in front of the hospital: she was going to change and bring food for her brother. She grasped my hands, as if she felt something in the air: 'Have you seen a ghost or something?'

'I'm worried about Ranulfo,' I said.

'Just about him? What's happened? Why've you been so long?'

'I went looking for my friend . . . that's all.'

She still tried to see in my eyes the words I was hiding from her. And, as if she'd already found them, she looked sad, and in a weak voice simply informed me: 'Go on up, he's in number 102.'

The door was open. Corel seemed to be recounting something important. Then Chiquilito got angry: 'No one knows how the thugs found his hiding-place . . . Some altar boy . . . or the church cook . . .'

'No, it was no bleeding altar boy . . . much less a cook . . .

It doesn't matter. What I want to know is where Mundo's hidden.'

I recognised my uncle's voice and went in. They changed the subject. Corel tapped the plaster on Ranulfo's leg and gave a little laugh: 'Our hero's had a fall! Now here's a little legal case for you to solve.'

'A criminal case, Doctor Lavo,' Chiquilito added.

Uncle Ran had been properly done over: his lips were swollen, there were purple marks on his face, stitches near his nose. His left leg was in plaster; his toenails were long and dirty, like a tramp's. The two friends went out into the corridor. Next to the bed, I held Ranulfo's arm; he made a gesture with his fingers: water. He took a few sips through a straw, swallowing with difficulty. He spoke in a falsetto, his voice half choked: 'Mundo's managed to escape. Where is he?'

'I've just come from Jano's house,' I said.

He tried to clench his fists and groaned: 'That son of a bitch . . .'

I went over to the window: two nuns in black were walking towards the mortuary chapel. Jano's house was shut. The leaves on the trees in the hospital garden fluttered, and the nuns' habits spread out like black wings. The wind presaged heavy rain. I went back to the bed.

'I think he's dead,' I said. 'He was alone in the house . . . him and Fogo.'

Ranulfo tried to lift his head, with his eyes wide open: a slow, evil smile deformed his face even more.

I said goodbye as soon as the friends came back. Immobilised like that, my uncle looked useless. Tomorrow or the next day he'd go back to the house in the Vila da Ópera, go on eating and drinking at his sister's expense, putting up with her peevishness and resentment.

In the early evening I went to the wake in the Portuguese Beneficent hospital. The dead make way for one another, but Jano's wake wasn't in the chapel in the garden: he deserved a higher position, a few steps above the morning's dead body, and there were Heaven knows how many acts of homage. The coffin, between the flags of Brazil and the state of Amazonas, lay in the hospital's great hall. The room smelt of flowers and sweat, and the Archbishop of Manaus was there, with nuns and members of the hospital board, employees of Jano's company and relatives of the Japanese in Vila Amazônia now living in Manaus.

Alícia wore a grey dress; her plunging neckline attracted more attention than the pearl necklace, and the hair, combed back, revealed her whole face, with its unceasing beauty. She accepted condolences, arm in arm with Naiá, both of them elegantly dressed; the maid's eyes, red, were turned towards her boss's face. Either as a coincidence or some perverse intent, he was wearing the navy-blue trousers sewn by Ramira, which were loose and too long – and the same leather belt he'd beaten Mundo with.

Behind the two women, leaning against the wall, Macau stared at the ground. At times Alícia looked round, searching for her son. The murmur of the crowd was drowned by a growing patter of boots. Aquiles Zanda appeared at the head of the group of men. I recognised two or three of the partners at cards at Alícia's house; each player looked at the dead man, crossed himself and went to embrace the widow.

A little later, Albino Palha emerged from a circle of military men, and was the only one to spend some time at her side; they exchanged whispers, and he nodded with his big head with its slicked-back hair. Then the archbishop opened his arms in front of the dead man, and began to chant in Latin; the others echoed him in a loud, deep voice. It was the most solemn moment of the wake. Even the colonel-prefect seemed uplifted by the melody of the church Latin, despite not understanding a single word. The only person absent was Mundo.

When I went to give my condolences to Alícia, I had the impression that the dried-up tears on her wet cheeks came from a mixture of sadness, relief and an urge to be free; or maybe they hid some secret. I asked about Mundo, and she whispered in my ear: 'He must be up there with your uncle. I heard Ranulfo can't walk, but he's full of life.'

She saw the shock these words had on me and held her hand out to some of her husband's old acquaintances: two butchers from the Canto do Quintela and a group of poor Japanese, smallholders from the area around Manaus. I embraced Naiá, who sobbed and murmured twice over: 'I liked Jano . . .' Macau said nothing, and just held out his hand. He ended up holding out both, as if we were near relatives of the deceased. The commanding officer's kepi he was holding under his arm fell. Then I hurried up to the first floor of the hospital. Ranulfo was asleep, and Mundo wasn't in the room. Ramira was stooped over and still in a chair, her face yellowed by light coming through a lampshade. She really was sad and shrunken, more of a widow than the other one, the real one. She didn't say a thing; her watery eyes were fixed on her brother's immobilised leg.

That night, before I went back to the Vila da Ópera, I passed by the mansion. I knocked on the door, and stood waiting on the veranda. Not a sign of Mundo, or Fogo. Nothing. Later, at home, I found the sewing room without the woman sitting at the machine. Unfinished uniforms and carnival costumes gave the quiet atmosphere a strange aspect.

The forecast downpour hadn't materialised, and the partitions in my room were still warm; I opened the window and turned on the ceiling fan: the buzzing of the motor and the blades was annoying, but it did disperse the heat. A few more months and I'm out of here, I thought. The two of them'll be fighting every day, Ramira'll call him a thief and a parasite; she'll lock food and money away in the wardrobe, shoo Corel and Chiquilito away. The air gets thicker and warmer when the rain doesn't fall; when I'm lying on my bed, I can see flies out there; the neighbours throw fish remains into the street, the cats come and eat them and fight over them, mewing all night.

I took a while to get to sleep, and the vision of Jano and Fogo, together on the sofa, made more of an impression on me than the dead man in the hospital's great hall. I re-membered the whispers at the wake: 'Why hasn't the son come?' 'He didn't want to see his dead father!' 'Is the mother to blame?' 'They say he's a layabout, wanted to be an artist . . .' At some time in the night, I saw in a dream the image of harlequins, corsairs, débutantes and students from the Mili-tary School. Half in carnival costume, they were all having a fine time in the main room at Vila Amazônia. Mundo appeared in a magistrate's gown, later in a cadet's uniform, and his father changed expression with each costume, but laughed all the time. He looked like a man at peace. During the graduation ball, my friend reappeared dressed as a harlequin surrounded by cadets and officers; the musicians stopped playing, excitement spread through the room, Alícia's body spun round and couldn't stop Jano's advance; his hand held a gun, and he shot his son in the face. There was a loud noise, then the sound of screaming and panic. Mundo was on the floor . . .

I woke up in a sweat; the fan was silent in the dark; early morning shouts came from the Calvado mansion; then I heard women talking and noises in the swimming pool. When dawn came, the heavy rain swamped the street and dripped into my room. It was the 25th of December. I went to the sewing room and covered the pieces of cloth and the patterns over with plastic. The stone slabs on the kitchen roof stopped the water coming in. I hooked up my hammock there and went to sleep again, in the ugly morning on which Jano went down into the earth.

13

AFTER JANO'S DEATH, I only talked to Mundo once, because the second and last meeting was a brief farewell at the airport, where my friend, his mother and Naiá said goodbye to the city. They left in a hurry, like fugitives. Alícia refused to celebrate Mass on the seventh day; she did precisely as she had promised, leaving the inventory and the sale of the properties and all the possessions in the hands of Albino Palha.

On the Monday, Mundo was not in the mansion. Naiá suggested that on the following day, at the end of the afternoon, I went to the Horizon bar, on the Beira-Rio Avenue. Out of the corner of my eye, I saw shapes covered in white sheets. Alícia, in her urgent desire to get away, was emptying the house. I missed Fogo and asked about him. Naiá wiped her eyes with her hand, went silent, and entered the house.

On the Tuesday afternoon I went on foot to the Municipal Market and took a boat to the Baixa da Égua; I got to the Horizon bar before six. The light of the setting sun was spread over the waters of the Rio Negro, and market sellers were coming down to the ravine to get their boats back to the villages upriver.

I was getting impatient with Mundo's delay. A single light lit the place, and from the kitchen came a smell of frying, bananas and fish. I turned my head to ask for the bill and suddenly saw him, hidden at the last table. Still in the half darkness, he looked like a wolf. He must have come in through the back, I thought; he's spent all that time observing, drinking, chewing things over. Elusive as always. He waved, shaking a piece of paper; he showed me a drawing of the inside of the bar with a view of the bay.

'My last view of this river,' he said, giving me the drawing. 'It was Naiá who told you I was coming, wasn't it? She never fails.'

He was thinner, his hair was all tangled. I saw no expression of sadness on his face: only fatigue. I said how sorry I was about what had happened at New Eldorado, and the burning of all his things . . .

'My father took his inspiration from *Field of Crosses*. He even burnt the cheap clothes your aunt sewed, didn't he? That's the man that wanted to civilise Amazonia.'

He greedily swallowed a glass of beer, and wiped his mouth, cleaning off the froth and the saliva. He said he'd got to know my neighbourhood: 'The alleys, the hideouts, the gardens, the people, and the hill where you grew up.' I asked about Uncle Ran: what had the two of them hatched up? Why had they hidden on the Morro? Who had beaten up my uncle?

'Your uncle helped me put *Field of Crosses* up; we spent months planning the work. He detested the plan for cheap public housing. "Holes for animals", he'd say. Your uncle had a real grudge against Zanda. He told me he'd been persecuted by him . . . revenge over a woman . . . He didn't tell me any more . . . and I don't know if my mother was involved in it. Ranulfo mixed revenge and politics, and got enthused with my idea. I wanted to douse the crosses in kerosene and light them before daybreak, but the local inhabitants were afraid, and wouldn't agree to it. Ranulfo stole offcuts from your aunt and dyed everything black. We went to New Eldorado several times. He got some five families together and said: "You've been tricked; they promised everything, and look what a miserable place it is . . . miserable, and miles from the harbour area . . ."'

'Did he help you just to get at your father?'

'He helped me because he likes me.'

'One time my uncle and aunt were quarrelling, and Ramira asked Uncle Ran to tell me a secret. She said you were a part of the story . . .'

My friend bent his head over a little and revealed in an undertone: 'Ranulfo was always crazy about my mother, Lavo. I tried to find out more, but neither of them would open their mouths. I argued with her and had the courage to ask if I might be his son. She jumped up and said I wasn't even to think about it. I don't know . . . What I know is that he risked his life and didn't give in to Alícia's requests. We hid for more than a month, near São Francisco church. Your uncle knows everyone in the neighbourhood, from the priest to the street urchins . . . he knows the old families, the owners of houses and the people who sell stakes in the *jogo do bicho*. The Morro was his home. Now it's an ant-hill, one neighbourhood piled on top of another. We slept in a wooden shack at the back of the priest's house. The area was full of trees, there was fruit everywhere. Sometimes Ranulfo went out at daybreak and came back with money and drink – I don't know how he got hold of it. A friend of his, Américo, brought food from the market, the cook prepared the fish and in the morning brought coffee with tapioca and fried banana. The days were long . . . We played dominoes; Father Tadeu lent novels and history books, and gave me paper and pencils. I drew and read all day, but just before Christmas the calm period ended. Some strange people were prowling round the church. The priest wanted to take us to another area of the city, but Ranulfo wouldn't have it. Then I dug a hole in the garden, a pit to keep the hammocks, our clothes and the drawings; I covered it with leaves and branches, your uncle laughed . . . but the pit saved us from Jano's henchmen . . . some characters from the police, with links to the prefect. On the first sortie they entered the church, inspected everything . . . We heard their talk, the questions they asked, their steps. They invaded the empty hut, and came close to our pit; your uncle was trembling with hatred, he wanted to go out and fight, be the big tough guy. He got more and more irritated, and went out looking for my mother, dying for a sniff of her skirts . . . he couldn't stand it any longer. He must have told her everything, in exchange for some promise . . . But she didn't give us away; it must have been one of the neighbours . . . They gave a big fat bribe to someone on the Morro. The men came back in the early morning. The dogs started barking – that was our first warning. Then there was shouting in the priest's house, and your mad uncle emerged from our hiding-place and shouted . . . he went to face the thugs. Out of instinct, I climbed into a mango tree and stayed up there, keeping quiet. I heard the howls and the blows – they destroyed the hut; found the chamber pot in the garden and threw the shit in your uncle's face; there were lots of them; they only stopped when the priest arrived with some of the local people; three or four cops were still prowling round with a light; they wanted to give me a fright . . . I think they were going to crush my hands. One of the cops was asking about the artist . . . It wasn't Macau, I know his voice. Macau wouldn't betray me. It must have been some bastard under the orders of my father or Zanda. I spent the rest of the night sitting on the branch of the mango tree. Before the dawn came, Father Tadeu came with the cook, Américo and some poor kids, altar boys . . . They looked for me, rummaged all through the garden, woke the neighbours . . .'

Mundo smiled ironically: 'They forgot to look up . . . I picked a mango and threw it down. Even then they didn't see! When I got down, they looked at me as if I was a devil. I slept a little, drank some coffee and ate. I met some of the local people, who were coming to try their luck in the *jogo do bicho*. People from the Jardim dos Barés and the Cidade das Palhas, a new neighbourhood, just shacks made out of bits of wood and cardboard. And I got to know the house where my mother lived with her sister. Ranulfo said the house had been much smaller; people who lived there later renovated and extended it. My mother never took me to the Morro, she spent her life wanting to forget the place she came from. When I asked to visit the house, she said it was no longer there, it had been knocked down. At the end of the morning I went to get my revenge. It was Christmas Eve. I kicked the door open, went into the house and said my piece; I said it all out loud. Man to man, the way he always wanted. I touched on his fear, and he heard things he never expected to hear; that he was impotent in soul and body . . . Vila Amazônia was bust, only he didn't see it.'

He pointed his bent finger at my chest: 'I've not finished yet. I want to make a work of art about Vila Amazônia . . .

There's still the revenge of the imagination, the revenge of the artist, Lavo. I'm going to play merry hell with his face, with his cruelty and madness . . .'

'*Your* madness, Mundo.'

A pair of lovers began to dance between the tables. One was bent over the other, and they swung together, slowly. Silently, we looked at the dancers in the bar, in the poor part of our city.

On the Friday afternoon, in the old airport of Ponta Pelada, he left his mother and Naiá, left the departure lounge and gave me an embrace. Then the silvery Electra took off: after Jano's death, she'd never come back to Manaus . . . But I still had hopes of seeing Mundo again.

In the eighth month of pregnancy, your mother asked Jano to put off a trip to Vila Amazônia. Alícia didn't exert undue pressure on him, she only wanted her husband to wait until she gave birth. It was only a quick trip, Jano said. His father, Mattosão, wanted to say goodbye to his property before going back to Portugal for good. Jano, who worshipped his father, didn't want to disappoint him: he went in the Santa Maria. Your mother took against Vila Amazônia after that trip. Because she never forgave him, maybe she wanted to give birth in his absence. That was what happened, and she didn't even send him a message by the Voice of the Amazon radio station. And while Jano was at the property — he was going only for a few days, and stayed three weeks with his father — you were born prematurely in the Portuguese Beneficent hospital, and I got to know you on the second day of your life. Macau appeared on the Morro to bring the news. My brother-in-law, Raimunda and I came into the maternity ward and saw a baby with all the features of your mother, not a single one of your father: not the ears, the fingers, nothing. We spent the afternoon with her, and I kissed her while you were suckling, I kissed and licked her face in the presence of Jonas, Raimunda and the little girl who was going to look after you: Naiá. On the next day she went back to the mansion, and my sister, who was pregnant, went to visit her every day. She said your mother was going to christen you Raimundo, and three months later, when I saw you with Alícia and Naiá in the square, I came over and called you Mundo and lifted you on to my lap. She said that Jano was happy to have a Mattoso heir, a male, and talked about nothing else, and then your mother saw that he was proud not about his son, but about the heir, until one day they had a fight about the word 'heir', which she could no longer bear to hear, as if you weren't a baby, but a man in charge of Vila Amazônia. Jano said: 'It's what my father wanted, a grandson . . . an heir, that's why he gave you so many jewels before he went back to Portugal: jewels belonging to my late mother. If it had been a girl, I don't know . . .' When Lavo was born, my sister and Alícia used to meet to drink tacacá in front of the Odeon cinema, Raimunda stayed with Lavo, Naiá with you, and your mother and I went into the dark cinema, and hugged and kissed in the back row like two adolescents and we came out before the end of the film: we did that several times at the early evening showing in other cinemas, while your father was working for the heir. As soon as he came home he'd ask: 'Where's the heir?' Your mother would say: 'Our son's got a name: Raimundo, Mundo.' Then the disaster happened. Jano wanted to celebrate your first birthday at Vila Amazônia, and the newspapers reported that he'd hired a Portuguese film-maker and a German photographer who worked for the wealthiest families in Manaus. To your mother's despair, the headline read: 'Vila Amazônia celebrates the first birthday of the Mattoso heir.' On the afternoon of the party Jano distributed provisions to the employees who came to wish you well and pose for the cameras on the veranda of the house. In the ruined shed of the old kaikan they stuffed themselves with so much food and guaraná, but Jano had forbidden music, dancing and alcohol. A week later, the press began to publish news items and some of the photographs: you, at the age of one, sitting on a pile of Brazil nuts; standing between bales of jute; lying in a rubber dinghy floating in the swimming pool; in Doctor Kazuma's lap; dressed in white with a little bow-tie, being blessed by the archbishop inside the cathedral at Parintins; with your parents and Naiá in the drawing-room of the house, a big photo in which Alícia held you in her lap and Jano was pointing at your head. You spent a month there, and your mother only found out about the tragedy when she came back to the city. She was exhausted and alarmed by all the absurd scenes she had to witness and hearing Jano say to every visitor that you would be the biggest exporter in the area.

When I told Alícia about the wreck of the Fé em Deus near the Eva branch of the river, she fell to weeping and trembling, which surprised me, because she was strong, she had iron in her soul. Not even when she was in the clinic did she cry so much – in fact, she didn't cry at all then, so certain was she you were going to live. She said my sister Raimunda was her only friend, almost a mother for her. She always asked me: 'How's Lavo?' She wanted you to be friends. Ramira thought I stole the toys and books I gave Lavo, but I bought them with money from Alícia, the money Jano gave your mother; then my sister suspected something and wouldn't accept any more, she swore she'd kill herself working to educate her nephew, and when Lavo was a child and lived on the Morro, she never let him out of her sight, took him to the primary school, and forbade him to go to the centre on his own; that was why Lavo became your friend only after they moved to the Vila da Ópera. Ramira never wanted that either. From the time I began going out with your mother, she didn't like our meetings at home and in the settlements on the Morro; she envied our expeditions and fishing trips; she always envied Alícia's laugh, and took against you even before you were born. She even disapproved of your name: 'I don't know why that woman christened her son Raimundo, the masculine form of my dead sister's name,' she'd say. Ramira was certain that you were going to despise me, she always hoped you would, but she lost her bet: you and I were father and son . . . I saw you were going to be an artist when your mother showed me the drawings you made on rainy days, alone, shut up in the mansion basement. Once, I asked about the origin of a scar on your right hand, you went quiet and then said: 'My mother's never told me how it happened . . .'

14

W HEN I LEFT the Vila da Ópera to live in a house near
the Manaus creek, Uncle Ran was already taking his
first steps: he leant on a forked stick, hobbled and jumped,
pretending to suffer horrible pain so his sister would act as a
crutch. Ramira protected him, gave him both her arms, and,
for good measure, her religious maunderings. She prayed for
Jano's soul, while Ranulfo waited for letters from Alícia.
When my uncle bragged that he was going to live like a
nabob in Rio, his drinking acquaintances and domino
partners in the square made fun of him: 'Where's the widow
Alícia Dalemer Mattoso?' 'When are you off to live in
Copacabana?' 'Ranulfo's going to inherit the turtles in Vila
Amazônia . . .'

Ramira swore he'd never even got a note from Rio, or a
telegram. Nothing. However, I thought my uncle was in
secret communication with Alícia or Naiá; he kept quiet
about these contacts, and little by little I began to realise that
Ranulfo and I got news about Mundo which coincided, but
was both incomplete and contradictory. To this day I'm not
certain who engineered this confusion.

I kept up a strange correspondence with my friend: he
didn't comment on the subjects I broached in my letters. He
wanted to spend six months in Rio with his mother and
Naiá, but he'd brought his trip to Europe forward because

he'd been arrested during a protest against censorship in front of the National Library:

I was arrested, then interned in an asylum, Lavo . . . I was sedated, tied up . . . when Alícia saw me that way, she said it was better for me to travel and further my artistic career in Europe. I don't like seeing her playing cards and drinking until dawn on Sundays . . . with bags under her eyes . . . The widow that loses most at cards . . . she even loses her beauty . . . At night her look changes, and her hung-over eyes light up, avid for the night to come, exhausted again the next dawn. She wakes up after lunch, sits alone, in a state of anguish, drinking, desperate for the next card game . . . Naiá and I wanted to take her to the Arpoador, to the Botanical Garden, to the Urca, to the Largo da Carioca, to the area of small shops near the centre of the city, even to Petrópolis, but she won't set foot outside the Labourdett. The apartment drawing-room has become a casino, Naiá serves dinner to the players and offers them coffee and drinks as the dawn's breaking. And she still has the time and the inclination to spoil me, she comes into my room and puts a plateful of tapioca with butter on my bed, as she did in Manaus. I see my mother filling out cheques, the money from the sale of the properties is going to disappear in these late-night sessions. When I was arrested and interned, she and Naiá visited me. My mother didn't want to understand what had happened. She said I'd been arrested because I was a drug-addict, that I was going to become a delinquent, that the shame I'd submitted her to in Manaus, where the press had rubbished her, was enough. I saw she was hung over and furious at having to get out of bed. I must be a burden in her life, I thought, after she'd asked, in the asylum: 'Where are your clothes? Where did you get that face like an Egyptian mummy from?' I said I was going to go to West Berlin with a little money . . . I was going to live in Alex Fleming's studio. She admired my pluck and even encouraged me: 'You can walk on your own,' she said.

Mundo wrote that he missed me and my uncle, and that he was doing sketches for a sequence of pictures entitled *A Jungle Capital*, 'pictures of the pavement outside the Castanhola, portraits of women and girls I won't see, hear or touch for a while'.

I asked Uncle Ran if he knew Mundo had been arrested and interned. He reacted like a wounded animal: 'Of course I know.'

'I phoned several times, but no one answers at the Labourdett,' I said.

'There's no point in ringing the Labourdett,' he said, as if he was party to some secret. 'Mundo's imprisonment is Zanda's revenge . . . That bastard of a prefect has pals in Rio, and he can persecute and punish whoever he wants.'

Far from Alícia and her son, Ranulfo seemed possessed by a sensation of powerlessness that upset him even more. Mundo's absence left a hole that neither Uncle Ran nor I had felt before. I felt miserable when I visited the various places in the city we'd frequented together. Even though they were far away, Mundo and Alícia were still present in our lives and in the conversations in the Vila da Ópera, where I went to see my uncle and aunt and pick up my friend's letters.

What was new was the position of the sewing machine: now my aunt worked with her back to the street and facing the little patio, which she'd filled with maidenhair ferns and caladiums. That way she avoided coming face to face with her brother every time he crossed the room or went out.

'Are you still fighting a lot?'

'Without looking at each other,' she answered, not batting an eyelid.

When I got there, she left her needles and bits of cloth, and gave me Brazil-nut tart and *guaraná*. She drooled over me, and turned into a saint for the nephew who, before he left, left a few notes on the table laden with bits of fabric. I suspected she was losing customers when she asked me, rather embarrassed: 'In your office or in the courts . . . the lawyers . . . gentlemen and ladies . . . is there anyone wants a suit, a toga, a little outfit?'

Ramira let slip that Ranulfo took part of my money and went to burn it in nocturnal revelries at the Ingleses nightclub, where he tried to make up for the absence of the woman he loved. When he saw me, he pretended he was busy, walking up and down, taking short paces, watched by my aunt: one eye on her needle, the other on her brother. The blows he'd received from Jano's thugs had marked his arms with long, thin scars; and a thick ridge, near his nose, made him look like an irascible, frightened man. Even so, he'd not lost his insolent, mean way of addressing others, and me: 'And how's legal chicanery these days? Begun applying the law yet?'

I didn't reply, and he went on: 'There's no such fucking thing as the law, my lad. It all depends on circumstances: either the accused has money or he doesn't. A friend in the system's useful too. That's the law for you, the beginning and end of every sentence that's handed down.'

These words gave a certain dignity to Uncle Ran: the stature of a rebel. I don't know if he spoke from mere resentment, or just to humiliate me. Maybe that was what he really thought about my profession and the whole of humanity.

My room, which he now occupied, was a stinking mess. Ranulfo left everything on the floor, like a child, and on the little table where I'd read and studied so much law and so many legal codes, I saw a block of letter paper, some crumpled sheets and a photo in which he and Alícia were kissing on the deck of the *Fé em Deus*. On the back, written in pencil: 'Last trip to the Eva branch of the river, May 1951.'

'More than twenty years later and he's still dreaming about that woman,' said Ramira, when I told her I'd seen the photo. 'Jano was right to suspect all the men who came to play cards at that house. Only the dog . . .'

She slowly got up out of her chair, picked up a rag and blew her nose.

'Only the dog . . .' she repeated.

She stretched out a cut of black linen, trying to disguise her fury. She began to recount that in the morning, when she passed in front of the mansion, she'd seen the sign of a demolition company. 'And you know who was on the pavement? That giant Palha . . . He was talking to three men, not from here, from the South, either that or they were foreigners. They were pointing at those horrible buildings in the centre, near the Opera House. When they'd gone, I went in. I'd never set foot in that garden. The climbing plant had dried up, and the azaleas. They've taken down the trellised arch. What a shame! When I went by before I could smell the scent . . . I used to stop to smell the calla lilies. From down there you could see the walls and the bedroom ceiling. I know Jano slept alone, him and the dog. That traitor Naiá told me things like that. The front garden – good God! – full of debris, the grass was dead. I looked at the entrance to the house and I couldn't believe it. The poor animal was there, with his legs stretched out, wanting to go in . . . It was just Fogo's skeleton . . . his skin was yellow and dry . . . Poor thing! I think they chucked him out into the forest, and he came back; he died on the threshold, missing his master . . .'

I went to look for Fogo's carcass, but it wasn't there. Another, much bigger skeleton was being destroyed and turning into ruin. Jano's mansion had already lost its roof tiles, and the windows and doors had been ripped out. For the last time, I saw *The Glorification of the Arts in Amazonia* on the ceiling of the drawing-room: the workmen had set about destroying it with hammers and chisels. The stucco fell and smashed like eggshells; on the floor lay bits of muses, easels and lyres, which the men were sweeping up, putting into sacks and throwing out into the garden full of debris; I asked one of the demolishers for a bit of the painting representing a paintbrush. 'You can take all this rubbish if you want,' he said, coughing in the dust.

I only picked up the paintbrush with De Angelis's signature, as a souvenir. Then I went on to the Law Courts. As I was going up Eduardo Ribeiro Avenue, Arana, in suit and tie, came walking in my direction, measuring his steps like a tight-rope walker; he stopped under an *oitizeiro* and threw some coins at the beggars lying on the pavement. About ten yards away from me, he opened his long fat arms. 'Great doctor and magistrate,' he shouted in a reverential voice, knowing how descriptions like that irritated me. Then he started taking a drawing and an envelope out of his pocket. 'Our cosmopolitan friend has remembered old Arana,' he said. He showed a letter from Cologne and a drawing: 'Doesn't this look like one of my works? That series of Brazilian cycles of paintings I sold to a French collector?'

'What if it does?' I asked. 'Everything looks like something.'

'I'm not saying it's just imitation. I mean, at some moment in his life, a young man imitates a great artist.'

I looked at the drawing and shook my head, impatient. Arana thought I'd agreed. Then I mentioned an appeal at the Law Courts: I had to be there on time, and I was in a hurry.

We walked onwards. He continued: 'Do you know what he says in the letter? That he's going to exhibitions in Germany, visiting museums, getting to know artists.'

'Mundo's turned into a well-travelled snob,' I said, laughing.

He looked at me, trying to decipher my laugh.

We stopped in front of the courts. From the shade of the *oitizeiro*, there crawled an old woman; she crouched at Arana's feet and pulled the hem of his trousers. He kicked the old woman's arm, and she fell on her back. She lifted her head up: 'Doctor shit.'

'It's hell! They won't leave me alone,' he said, with his eyes on the ground. 'Every Sunday folks from the neighbourhood come to forage for food at my studio. I don't feel

I'm to blame for so much misery. When Mundo came to say goodbye, he wasn't pleased to hear that . . .'

'Did he come by the studio?'

'Spent a whole morning . . . I listened to his accusations on Christmas Day. I didn't want to argue out of respect for the dead. Jano was being buried . . .'

He turned his head: he'd felt the shadow of the woman at his feet, and he pulled me over to the wall; he took a note out of his wallet, folded it and threw it at the tree trunk. He looked at the group of beggars and gave a grimace of disgust: lepers. He wiped his mouth with a handkerchief.

'Mundo told me how he hid with your uncle and how he faced Jano down. He apologised about the burnt books. His father . . . that madman . . . God rest his soul. But Mundo seemed to feel blame for something much more serious. His father's dead, but his mother . . . He won't be able to stay away from her for long.'

He peered at the bodies near the *oitizeiro*. The woman was feeling her bruised arm with her hand. In the dark, eight eyes were fixed on Arana's face.

'Well, you're in a hurry. I've got a meeting with my clients too. But one thing I'll guarantee, Dr Lavo: Mundo won't be long, in less than a year he'll be back.'

He was certain that Mundo would come back to Manaus to see him, and that left me confused. My friend had been living in Europe for more than two years, and in no letter had he said anything about coming back. Maybe he wasn't living off his father's inheritance, for he said he was washing dishes in a Latin American bar in Berlin, and was buying paint and paper with the money from the sale of his works in bars and restaurants. He was living for free in Alex Fleming's studio in Kreuzberg, and in summer went to swim in a public swimming pool in Charlottenberg, in splendid art deco, with warm water and paintings on the ceiling; either that, or in the Spreewald, near the studio. When Alex sold some pictures, he was able to spend a week in Brazil. But not him: 'Brazil's beginning to seem distant, Lavo. And the Amazon's only a memory.' With a postcard, he attached a drawing, a caricature of Arana, lying in a hammock, surrounded by poor children. 'The impostor's siesta,' he wrote by the side.

Now Arana was transforming mahogany logs into enormous animals, which didn't inspire fear, or surprise, or any emotion at all. His canvases, of landscapes with natives and naked Indians, with copper-coloured skin and self-satisfied smiles, were poor imitations of Gauguin and the paintings in the grand foyer of the Opera House. The technique was as impeccable as the exoticism. In one of the paintings, an audience of ecstatic Indians was present at an opera.

I was looking at these works at the time when Mundo was moving to London. One Sunday morning, I was looking at the papers of a lawsuit, at home, when Arana appeared out of the blue, with the insouciance of an old friend: he was wearing a pair of green Bermudas and a loose shirt, with colours like a parrot, which hid his paunch. He dragged me to his studio.

A blue launch was awaiting us in Manaus Harbour. On either side of the curving prow was the name of the boat in white lettering: *The Island Artist.* We went rapidly along the bay, and then entered the São Raimundo creek. He wanted to show me the shed at the bottom of his garden, and the work he'd had done on the house. Now the tools and the machines were in the new studio. The sitting room had grown on one side, and ended in a swimming pool in the shape of a clover leaf; the refraction of the light and the water from an artificial waterfall gave mass and movement to the mosaic of Amazonian animals at the bottom. Further on, a path with bamboo on either side led to the shed. I smelt fresh wood and benzine; and the smell of earth, leaves and dampness. In the middle of the area a small transplanted forest, isolated by sheets of glass and with an opening to the sky, mixed with the garden trees. Arana invited me in. The greatest novelty came from above: stuffed animals, immense and sad, were tied by strands of yellow *tucum*-palm fibre to the steel beams. They floated, enclosed in boxes also of glass, like beings who'd been kidnapped from the forest and immobilised for ever. For a moment we stood still, listening to the song of some intrusive bird that plunged into the vegetation and escaped through the opening. Something made me uncomfortable, and then I saw that there, in the centre, all the animals were looking at us. The light refracted from the glass sheets lit up their eyes, which shone in the semi-dark. There's something gruesome about this, I thought; it's just a macabre decorative scheme, nothing else. I heard a devilish little laugh and then his voice: 'When it rains, they're enchanted. They come into my forest and feel they're in paradise.'

'Who d'you mean, they?'

'The visitors . . . tourists. They're coming in the middle of the afternoon.'

When I heard that, I hastened to look at the pictures Arana was so proud of. Four on each side wall: eight panels of an 'Amazonian sequence'.

He explained that the panels were exhibited on Sundays, when the visitors chose the model they wanted, which would then be packed up and sent to them. He was thinking of painting a series he'd call *The Rediscovery of Paradise*, based on the idea that the origin and the future of Brazil were to be found in Amazonia.

'The problem is that the painting of the panels is work I have to do on my own,' he complained. 'The lads help me in cutting and finishing the sculptured objects. But painting . . . only I can do it. The motifs are mine, and the choice of colours, the brush-strokes, the luminosity and the perspective, everything depends on a single individual: the artist.'

The shed was like a hothouse; I felt the throbbing of a headache, and couldn't stand Arana's voice or the sight of the forest and the artificial fauna. In the room, he turned on the air-conditioning and showed me some sketches that Mundo thought he'd lost. I remember that in several periods when he was on leave from boarding school my friend had worked on these things. He'd first sketched a map of the Amazon region dating from 1889 on a canvas and had written a lot of indigenous names on it, with a cross beside each tribe; then, in the centre of the canvas, he'd made a large circle with green and yellow seeds, cut into with dry leaves and bird bones. Arana, delighted by the circle, had exclaimed: 'The eye of the Amazon.'

'No. The idol of Brazil,' Mundo corrected him.

'I helped your friend to put the work together,' said Arana, holding the sheaves of paper. 'I helped with ideas and with my hands. When we finished it, he destroyed it all. He was furious, he ripped the canvas, kicked the bones and the seeds. Then he scarpered.'

'Mundo was always an angry critic of his own work . . .' I observed.

'If that was all it was, it'd have been OK,' said Arana. 'For some months before Jano's death, he wouldn't stop criticising everything *I* did. Once, in fun, I asked him if he wanted to be the author of works that had been destroyed. You know what he answered? "That's what a real artist is."'

I looked at the muddy, dirty water in the creek, at the shacks and the poor people living on the riverbank, and thought of my friend in Berlin.

It was already after two in the afternoon, and my head was still throbbing. I didn't take up his offer of a lift back. I called a boatman, and when I got into the canoe, Arana stepped on the plank at the prow and bent over: 'D'you know Mundo's skint?'

With a gesture, I said no: he'd not told me.

'He's struggling to live in Europe . . . His mother must be broke.'

He held on to the oar, trying to make me stay a little longer. 'A good lawyer must know a good place to change dollars,' he said, in a conspiratorial voice. 'I want to send money to your friend. An experienced money-changer would do that for me. I've not got the address, Lavo. The scoundrel doesn't want to know me any more. Pride . . . or the arrogance of a young artist. It doesn't matter. The important thing is for the money to reach him.'

He didn't wait for my question.

'You must tell him the money's yours. You're Mundo's only friend in this town. Your uncle doesn't count, he's a lunatic. Mundo doesn't write to anyone. I never asked you for anything, Dr Lavo. Send that money . . .'

He turned his head towards the muddy water, and you could see he was really worried.

'Mundo's in a confused state . . . I think he's been laid low . . . he's done for,' he said, with sadness.

Laid low? Was it some illness?

He undid the rope, put his hand in his pocket and gave me an envelope. I insisted: why was he done for? How had he got to know?

Arana came into the water, gave the canoe a good push and looked at me with a serious expression. More than half his body was immersed in the dirty water. Only his head looked free of the pollution: his austere, ambitious head, in front of the house and his employees.

How come Arana knew about Mundo's situation? It might be just one more of his ruses. When I opened the envelope, I was shocked by the amount of the cheque; the boatman saw and stopped rowing. I turned to look at the island: Arana was on the riverbank, looking at the canoe, as if he knew what my reaction was. Maybe he wanted to pay for Mundo to come back to Manaus, or to pay debts I knew nothing of. The stink of the water and the riverside latrines was unbearable, and that sum was an aberration in this devastated landscape. What would Mundo think? That his friend the orphan had become a lawyer for foreign firms wanting to keep close relationships with government bureaucrats? More than my friend's moral disapproval, I feared Arana was playing an underhand trick on me.

15

I CONSULTED MONEY-CHANGERS; there'd be no difficulty sending the money. I decided to tear up the cheque and return it to Arana. I sent a boatman to take the envelope to the 'island artist', and enclosed a note saying: 'Mundo's disappeared without trace.'

I did this after I'd read, in the Vila da Ópera, a letter that Mundo had sent from Dover: the exhibition he'd been about to put on in Berlin had been cancelled, and he'd had to leave Germany, for fear of being arrested or deported. He said that for five days he'd worked on the mounting of his show in Die Ursache, a little gallery in Kreuzberg, where he'd been going to finish some of the works to be exhibited; he was talking for six or seven hours at a time to his mother; sometimes he went to sleep with the phone on his chest; the employees found him talking Portuguese when they came in in the morning, and heard the same language when they left.

I spoke to Brazil for more than thirty hours, that's to say, I talked and my mother listened: a monologue. I didn't hear a single affectionate word, Lavo. Not a breath of love . . . what they call *Liebeshauch* here. My mother put the phone down, and I rang back. When the dawn was breaking in Berlin, she was already drunk, in the middle of the night, in Rio . . .

He had to give part of his work to the gallery, to pay the telephone bill; still, he tried to make free calls by installing illegal connections or putting counterfeit coins into public telephones. He knew his mother was depressed, given over to drink and gambling:

She's putting an end to herself, I think both of us are . . . Even so, I'm going to England. I managed to sell three paintings out of five of the *Jungle Capital* sequence. Two faces of the same woman in a boarding-house bedroom in the Marapatá pension, and in the cabin of a boat, aground for good in the Educandos. The third picture is the mysterious face of my mother . . . I'm writing from Dover, on my way to London.

I no longer had any doubts about what my uncle had said so many times on the subject of Arana. Nevertheless, Ranulfo might have exaggerated, for there was rivalry between the two, a conflict of character and social standing; Arana had gone several steps up the ladder, while my uncle had done nothing but go down, and was still going in the same direction.

I'd hardly finished reading the letter when my uncle jumped over to me, half stumbling, and waved the newspaper in my face: 'Didn't I tell you? Some revolutionary artist he is! A scoundrel, that's what he is!'

He crushed the pages together and kicked the ball of paper against the wall; I heard Ramira pedalling firmly on the sewing machine; then the metallic humming stopped, and Ranulfo filled the room with a gust of hatred, impotence and despair.

'Still, he's a man who provides for himself,' my aunt whispered.

'A man! For you, Jano was an example of a man too,' said Ranulfo. 'Tell our lawyer nephew who Arana is.'

They were no longer fighting in silence; they were sharpening themselves for a real quarrel. Alive again, I thought.

'You're the one who's really close to that waste of space,' she shouted accusingly, as if her tongue was going to come loose. 'Tell Lavo, in my presence . . . now the widow's not got a penny left and wants nothing to do with you. She's never written you a line.'

Ranulfo's look could nearly have knocked his sister over; she got up and raised her eyebrows. He didn't react: he crumbled, looking submissive, with his chin on his chest; Aunt Ramira rummaged on the table, picked out a pair of trousers and threw them on the ground, near him.

'Put them on,' she ordered, inspecting him up and down. 'You're a bundle of rags . . . ugly and skinny.'

He obeyed; he went into the bedroom and reappeared in new clothes, loose and ill-fitting on his thin body, still with the same shoes as ever. He went out without saying a word to us.

'He'll come back to eat,' said Aunt Ramira. 'He only spends money on drink. He's saving up . . . He's got it into his head that the widow's waiting for him in Rio.'

'That's not what I want to talk about. I want to know the story Uncle Ran didn't tell.'

'Oh . . . I don't know everything, and you'll find nothing in the old newspapers.'

I left some money on the table with its bits of cloth. She stuck her neck out, eager to see the notes.

'What waste of space were you talking about?' I asked, impatiently.

'There's no reason to hide what I know . . .'

I picked up the crumpled newspaper and stood near the door.

'All this filth has to do with your friend,' said Ramira. 'One day he'll find out about it.'

She took a step backwards, smiling maliciously at my face, which was bursting with curiosity.

'It's not a certainty, Lavo. Just an intuition . . .'

She looked at the stamps on the envelope I was holding and went on, with the same fierce serenity. 'Is he in England now? Burning the money from Vila Amazônia in Europe . . . That's a real son . . .'

If she'd been less prudish, she'd have said 'a real son of a bitch', but the snarl in her voice and her hard expression were more offensive than any swear-word she might have used.

'You've been living on your own for some time. Why does your friend only send letters here? Maybe he just misses your uncle, not you. Now I've got to get back to my rags.'

I don't know how many letters I sent to Alex Fleming's studio in the Oranienstrasse. Long letters, in which I asked a lot of questions about life in Europe, reminisced about times in the Pedro II, and sent news about the political situation in Brazil and the chaos in Manaus. When he went on short trips to visit a museum, he began like this:

209

I'm writing from Madrid: Goya and Velázquez . . . Francis
Bacon holds up a distorting mirror to Velázquez . . .
Tomorrow I'm going to Toledo; I want to see the El
Grecos . . . I'm writing to you from Barcelona: Miró . . . I
went to a wonderful show by Els Comediants in the Plaza
de Catalunya.

Since he'd left Brazil, he'd made no mention of my letters.
But that day, when I sat on a bench in São Sebastião Square,
between the Opera House and the Casa Africana, I really
wanted him to answer the letter I'd sent to his address in
London. Looking at the bronze ships on the monument,
where I'd seen Mundo drawing a ship cut loose and heeling
in the wind, I read in a paper the item that had so exasperated
Ranulfo. Next to the text was a photograph of Arana, with a
guy who'd just come back from exile. Older people knew
the illustrious biography of the 'exile'; a politician excluded
from politics in 1964 by the military government, not for his
ideas, but because of his sudden, huge and inexplicable
wealth. In the photo, his arms were open in a gesture of
triumph; half the page was taken up with the voracious,
threatening laugh on his swollen face. Arana had given him a
painting with the flag of Amazonas on it. 'A painting of our
future, with the brush-strokes of hope and freedom. An
artistic message to the youth of our homeland,' he'd said.

It wasn't just this warm reception for a crook that had
infuriated my uncle, but the mention of Mundo's name. At
the end of the item Arana had said that his ex-disciple would
come to Brazil in December: he was going to exhibit in a
gallery in Rio and then in the 'studio on the island', in
Manaus.

What did Arana mean by such an absurd statement? Two weeks later, I thought of confronting the impostor, and showing him the postcard Mundo had sent me from London:

I'll not be back in Brazil any time soon. I'm doing boring, stupid work to survive, but I've got a roof over my head in a working-class area, in south-east London. Mrs Holly Hern's classes in her house in the Vila Municipal have turned out useful. I've got plans and news, and I promise one day I'll write a letter telling you all.

He sent me two postcards in the same envelope, dated June and September, one from the National Gallery, the other from the Tate. He'd met Francis Bacon in a pub and had the intention of visiting his studio. On one of the postcards he wrote:

Arana tried to inject my head with the poison of an 'authentic, pure Amazonian art', but now I'm immune to all his lectures. Nothing is pure, authentic or original . . . I'm planning to organise a work about Vila Amazônia. I want to use my father's clothes and his cast-offs. An idea I had in Berlin, when I was wandering round the Tiergarten . . .

Jano's clothes and his cast-offs? What did Mundo mean by that? In October I got his last letter from Europe . . .

16

D AMN THESE BITS of paper, Lavo! And damn the words I
can't budge, sentences all snarled up . . . Drawing's my
destiny, and writing's torture . . . What's it like for lawyers?
Who draws up the papers for a case: you or the clerks? If I
don't start scribbling now, I never will . . . I'll write one drop
at a time, half a page a day. Europe: three years here and only
two friends, maybe three, if I count Mona. My solitude's not
the result of geography, but life would be harder if it weren't
for certain coincidences, without friends and without memory. In April, when I got off the train at King's Cross, I was
lost; I had no idea where to go. It all began the night when I
said goodbye in Berlin, Alex and I were drinking in the
studio on Oranienstrasse: Paris, Poitiers, Lyon, Arles, Mont-
pellier, Aix-en-Provence . . . I seemed happy, and it wasn't
just brought on by my daily snifter of brandy: France and its
galleries were opening their doors to the Brazilian artist from
Kreuzberg. Alex said I could go on living in the studio. 'You
can use as much paint, brushes, paper and canvas as you
want, but don't use the phone to insult your mother,' he
said, throwing a duplicate key into my lap. I gave him the
key back and said right off: 'Alex, I'm going to live in

London. I've failed on the continent, who knows if on the island . . . I'm going by train to Ostend, and I'll get a ferry to Dover.' I already owed Alex more than 800 marks, but he wasn't looking at me as if he wanted the money back – you could see he was going to miss me: he realised I wouldn't come back, and in his face his happiness gave way to doubt and fear, the expression the same as that on the disorientated, wandering figures on his paintings and collages. 'In London, you can stay in the house of a great friend of mine,' he said. 'Mona and I took part in a show in the same gallery that threw you out, the Ursache.' Alex offered me another brandy and wrote down Mona's address on a scrap of paper I lost; I only realised I'd lost it at King's Cross. Brixton: the only word that stuck in my memory from that blasted piece of paper. With no money to go back and no Alex Fleming under an April sky, I found out that Brixton was far off, south of the Thames. Then I made my first bus journey in London, and that was only the beginning of a discovery, because from the top of the bus the city looked infinite to me. I next got a number 2 on Charing Cross Road, and the big red monster crossed the Thames by Westminster and went on to Stockwell. I got off in Brixton, on the corner of Atlantic Road, and wandered round, pulling my case with a rope. I went along dark, sad streets which led to a park where there were Africans and Caribbeans lying around with their children, and others were singing or talking or kicking a ball around. I climbed a hillock and saw a building which looked like a huge medieval dungeon. I left the park, went up Brixton Road, and an hour later stopped in front of a red building like the Manaus Customs House, and wondered if I'd been that way before. I was on Atlantic Road again, and there was no sign of Mona. Then I thought of the Avenida Atlântica and my mother on the balcony of the Labourdett, and I felt the melancholy of the ferry journey mixed with the sensation of yet another defeat. Hungry, and gasping for a drink, I went into a pub for the first time. I devoured a plateful of mince and mashed potatoes, slaked my thirst with a beer, and counted the six pounds I had left. Right there, I opened my case and took out two drawings of the women at the Castanhola. I looked at the face of each of the singers of the open-air cabaret, and remembered the afternoons and nights that seemed to belong to another period in history. Is the Castanhola still there? I went from table to table, trying to sell the drawings: nothing doing. Six pounds in my pocket, and frightened to the marrow of my bones . . . Alex Fleming traipsing round France . . . If I could have done, I'd have gone straight to the airport and flown to Brazil; that was what I thought at the time. Going back would be giving in. If only I could remember Mona's surname . . . I came out of the pub and followed a group of African immigrants as far as the corner of Brixton Road, and went on following them without knowing why, either that or knowing they were lost too. I joined them, and we went on side by side for a few minutes; when we entered a noisy street, the group moved away from me and I went on alone. Then I felt, for the first time in London, something close to me: a smell that only the hot and humid port known in childhood can give off. A piece of the West Indies, Africa and Amazonia could be felt round the little shops and mini-markets selling okra, manioc flour, *dendê* oil, watermelons . . . On the other side of the street a tall, striking woman was selling slices of a fruit with a green rind. She was holding the fruit, cut in two. I went across: where was she from? 'Georgetown, Guiana'; she smiled. I looked into her dark eyes, and breathed in the smell of the inside of the fruit, and I saw Naiá's body with a glass of *graviola* juice on the afternoons when we were alone in Manaus and I always asked for my mother and Naiá answered: 'She's gone on a visit, she'll be back soon,' but Alícia only came back a bit before my father, went to the bathroom, and came to talk to me with a towel round her, happiness in her face, and her voice asking: 'Did Naiá bring your *graviola* juice?' I stayed around that area, looking at the people, smelling familiar fruit, till I started walking again and coming up against a street name that brought back the image of my father: Villa Road. Elegant houses, in a Georgian style . . . Nothing like the big house at Vila Amazônia, but that name, Villa Road, was like a gunshot in my memory. I was drawn by some movement: a wall was being demolished, and wheelbarrows full of bricks and branches were lined up along the pavement. I stopped at the door of a house and stood looking at a thin guy, a bit hunchbacked, and pleasant-looking. He was carrying a cine-camera which looked like a toy. Despair was going to make me ask after Mona, but he focused on my face and said in English: 'Do what you want, say what you want . . .' With a tired voice, I said some words in Portuguese. Who would understand? The guy lowered the camera, and laughed: 'Brazilian? Adrian,' and held out his hand before saying: 'I speak Spantuguese,' and asking me questions, first with his eyes, then with words: was I looking for someone? 'Mona,' I said. 'An artist . . . a friend of Alex Fleming,' I tried to elucidate. He laughed again. 'If it's Mona, my neighbour, it's some coincidence! But she's not at home.' Adrian explained that the red-brick houses had been invaded more than a year before. Many houses had been occupied by artists, film-makers, writers, actors, and by immigrants, expatriates and exiles. 'Don't you need a Brazilian in the Villa?' I asked. Adrian invited me into the house which would be my London home; he got me a sandwich and some tea, and said I could lie down in the main room, he'd be back later: he was filming the destruction of the wall, and the people who lived there were going to make a collective garden. Adrian was a friend at first sight. He picked up his camera and went out. I ate, drank, lay down on the floor, half in a daze, feeling the same giddiness that had flattened me on a walk through the Tiergarten in Berlin and again on the ferry, near Dover. When my body gives way, I remember the giddiness, the headache and the fever that day in Arana's studio. Giddiness and itching, my skin full of blisters and scratches, and those awful training sessions in the jungle throb in my memory along with the names of the officers. Before I began this letter, I went to see the doctor; in a five-minute examination, he looked at the scratches from the itching and the scars, asked where I was from, how I was living in London, and without looking me in the eye, do you know what he said? 'Change your way of life.' It seemed as if my father was speaking, and it's him, Jano, who appears in my nightmares and in the sequence of three-dimensional pic-tures I'm doing. Only now have I got more time to dedicate to this work; in the last few months I had to do odd jobs to eat, pay for my bills and the hashish, because everything in Villa Road is shared. If it wasn't for Adrian, I'd have gone back to Brazil already. Mona is a surly woman: a smile on her face is a real event. She mistrusts her own shadow, and has the melancholy, ironic look of those exiled for ever. Only in June, when Alex told Mona on the telephone that we are friends, did she believe in the lost piece of paper, and then I realised my memory had lapsed once again, because, apart from the address, Alex had written: 'Take good care of him.' She herself told me that, giving me her monthly smile. We've been neighbours since June, and maybe friends, because she's told me she wants to film the inside of her body, so that the innards can appear on the screen. But it was Adrian who, in April, got some small jobs in the Brixton Labour Exchange and invited me to help him. My mother has no notion of what I've done to survive; she thinks I'm getting rich with my art. If she knew that the heir to Vila Amazônia has turned into an odd-job man . . . I remember Ranulfo told me to refuse boring, badly paid jobs. 'You should never work to be a slave,' he said. But that's what I've done all this time in Europe, and what I went on doing until last month. My first job in London was to count the number of cars, lorries, motorcycles and bicycles passing per minute over a pedestrian crossing in some of the busiest streets in Brixton; then I worked on redecorating flats here in this area. What gave me a bit of money, though, was a job as a driver's mate in the Wallpaper Centre. While Adrian drove the lorry, I did the heavy work, delivering wallpaper and tins of paint in the London suburbs and towns in the south of England. Hours and hours' driving in terrible traffic: sometimes our working day lasted some twelve hours, and Adrian drove like a madman. As he jolted up and down and jammed on the brakes, leaving me a nervous wreck, he hummed Bob Dylan songs and talked about Antonioni, Resnais and Fellini films, as if we were sitting in the Academy cinema or the Notting

Hill Electric, and I thought of the old cinemas in Manaus, which must have been demolished by the colonel-prefect by now. Further on, a tight curve would throw me against the door, and I'd shout: 'You're going to kill us like this,' and Adrian laughed: 'We'll die talking about the movies,' and the van screeched and jolted as we went into Southampton, where we stopped to have tea and eat a load of fried food, and talk to other drivers. I couldn't understand cockney, and I still can't – it excludes foreigners and even a lot of English people. During one of these sessions Adrian introduced me as a Brazilian artist, and I began to sell drawings to the shop managers and employees. As hard-faced as you like: 'Wouldn't you like to decorate your bedroom or living room with a drawing or a watercolour?' Some of them bought things, maybe out of pity, and I put five or ten pounds in my pocket and went to buy tubes of paint, paper and canvas. So I pushed drawings and watercolours on to the clients of the Wallpaper Centre or offered them in bars and restaurants, as I'd done in Germany. Lots of images of Vila Amazônia, of Manaus, Berlin and London are hanging on walls, or they've been thrown in the bin. I remembered the first time I saw Arana in the middle of a group of tourists on the pavement at Manaus Harbour, selling his objects for next to nothing. I felt angry that I was acting his farce out again, for I'm an artist of pavements and bars too, and I got about twenty-five pounds a week in the three months we went around, Adrian and I, delivering wallpaper with hideous patterns. I'd have nightmares if I lived in a room with repetitive patterns. God, Lavo, bad taste has taken charge of the planet; uniformity's going to kill the human soul. We went out at eight in the morning and only came back at night, desperate to drink and smoke hashish on Villa Road. At weekends Adrian would go to see several films, while I sketched out my visual memories. Mona saw the vacuum surrounding me, said I'd go mad shut up like that at weekends, and dragged me out to take part in performances in Notting Hill or the area around Hyde Park, where other artists met to provoke and then attract the tourists. These shows were almost always fun, apart from the odd aggressive or offensive remark from some wise guy who called us perverts, the same word my father uttered in front of the Indian and Japanese children in Vila Amazônia. All Jano's brutality was resurrected in Notting Hill and made me feel sick and angry. By the end of June, the freedom given by being driven round in the passenger seat of a van had worn off. We were coming back from a boring trip, Adrian and I both tired and headachy at the end of a rainy afternoon, desperate to get back to the wallpaper warehouse before the traffic got really chaotic. The space between a steel container on the pavement and a bus was too small, and Adrian put his foot on the accelerator, believing in his skill or luck. I hardly had time to shout: 'We're going to crash,' when the driver's door was torn by the bus, which was also accelerating. Adrian and I saw the terrified faces of the passengers looking at us. We broke the window glass and jumped down. A crowd on Kingston Road were looking at us accusingly. Adrian said I should go to Villa Road, a foreigner only complicates things. Later, at eleven at night, he told me he'd been sacked, but he was relieved. 'It's a relief for you too,' he said, knowing my body could hardly stand it and I could barely carry the rolls of paper. In August my friend's life changed, and I cadged a lift on that new life. Mona asked him to film a show by Street Action Live; Mona herself was going to put it on, with her contortionist's figure, in Hyde Park. Adrian got a prize in a Super 8 festival, and got a job in a film distribution firm, The Other Cinema, and for more than a month now I've been helping him to make contacts with cineastes and small producers from all over the world. Now I've got two afternoons free, and I can spend entire nights drawing and constructing objects for my memoirs. I thought of sending some rough sketches to Alícia, but she's only got eyes for playing cards, the sequences that end in the ace of spades, the royal flush of her nocturnal fantasies. Yesterday I managed to speak to Naiá: my mother's up to her ears in debt . . . She spends the whole day lying down, she says she's depressed. I asked if she doesn't get up at night for a round of poker. Naiá's more ashamed than her mistress. She wanted to know when I was coming back. Never, Lavo. I was on the point of telling her I'm weak, with a fever that won't go away. I'm scared of a stroke, and then there are these weeping blisters, my body's swollen and inflamed . . . Tomorrow I'm going to the hospital with Adrian. He and Mona helped me to cut bits of clothing and build the elements of my visual memoirs. Mona said I should exhibit the work in a gallery and then go to an art school, the Slade. I would so like to see you and your uncle. Ranulfo hasn't got a sou, but a lawyer can travel. Why don't you come to London? There's a place for you here, in Villa Road, where I've been sheltered for so long . . .

You were five. On rainy days you'd go out alone to play in the garden, or the alleyway, and your mother was worried about diseases: typhus, yellow fever, mumps . . . Jano feared other things. One morning when the rain was pouring down, Macau found you playing with some poor people from the slums built out over the river in the centre of the city. 'Mundo's only happy with poor kids,' your father'd say to Alícia. 'The neighbourhood children belong to respectable families, but he chases after savages.' Your mother tried to get you friendly with the lads from the area around the mansion, the children of important businessmen and magistrates. It was a disaster. You'd get stuck in your own bell-jar, bad-tempered and silent, with no time for toy planes, bears beating drums, roundabouts with coloured horses, and all the paraphernalia of electric toys bought by a smuggler acquaintance of Corel's. Your mother saw that your idea of fun was walking around in the rain and drawing was your greatest pleasure. And you wanted to be alone to do both. Then Jano forbade you to go out in the rain, shut you in the basement and sometimes delayed going out to work because he wanted to keep an eye on you, and on your mother, who'd let you out as soon as he'd gone. She told Jano there was no harm in playing in the street on rainy days, children loved it, but Jano didn't listen: that year, during the winter months, he'd send an employee to the mansion to see if you were still in the basement, and your mother threw him out yelling: 'Tell your boss my son's not an animal'; then Jano himself would come back to keep watch, and while your parents argued, you'd escape, and your mother laughed out loud from sheer nerves, and that idiot Jano thought she was making fun of him. Then Macau went after you, and your father shut you up in the basement again. You asked your mother why everything was so dark, and why you only heard the noise of the rain and the thunder, and why you had to eat on your own and were only let out at night to sleep in your

*bedroom, and she, your mother, didn't know what to say to you. I
wanted to confront your father, but Alícia said: 'No, that would set
the cat among the pigeons; it'd be the end,' and one day you drew
the face of a screaming child, and when I saw the drawing, I said to
your mother: 'Mundo's going to be an artist, you can forget all the
other professions'; either she didn't understand or thought it was such
an absurd idea as to be not worth thinking about. That was in
January 1958. Before he left for the office, your father ordered
Macau and Naiá to keep watch on you. He came back for lunch and
called you to eat at the table; during the meal you showed him the
drawings, and your father, without looking at the sheets of paper or
at your face, asked: 'Is that all he knows how to do?' Your mother
said: 'He's a child; he likes drawing, and plays and draws alone in
the basement.' Then your parents started arguing, and in the midst
of the shouting you started crying and ran to the basement, and your
mother went after you, and Jano said: 'Leave the child down there,
he's got used to it, now he's learnt he's not to play with ragamuffins
in the street.' And that same day – it was the end of the afternoon,
the sky was dark and overcast, and it was still drizzling – I was
having soup in the Luso restaurant when I saw a taxi stopped in the
street and your mother's wet face in the window. I dropped my
spoon, went to the car and heard: 'Mundo's broken the basement
window and escaped.' She'd already gone round the neighbours and
driven round the centre, and found nothing. 'Go back home, I'll go
after Mundo,' I said. I went from the Luso to the port, and walked
around in the area of Jano's mansion; a five-year-old boy couldn't be
that far from home. Then I went back to the port, going through the
same squares, but by different streets. The cathedral clock chimed
seven. Your father would be home already, and I remembered the toy
shops; when I crossed Marshal Deodoro, I saw a circle of men and
women and thought: some travelling salesman, a collapsed drunkard*

or an accident. I asked what was happening, and a man said: 'A lost child . . . he says he wants to show his father some drawings.' You were crying in the middle of the group and clutching a sheet of paper, and a cut on your right hand was still bleeding and smudging the paper. I carried you to Eduardo Ribeiro Avenue, and we took a taxi home, and you went on crying, wanting to show your father your drawings, and I was trying to stanch the blood with my shirt; at the front door of the house I asked the taxi-driver to take you into the sitting room. If I'd seen your father that night, I might have killed him. I was afraid he'd hit you or worse, but Alícia told me that Jano had approved of your daring, and had begun to say that his heir was already a courageous little lad, and when he saw the wound on your hand and the sheet of paper wet with blood, he said over and over: 'A courageous lad, he didn't even cry.' Then I said to Alícia: 'That madman's going to kill your son' – this time she understood what I meant, and it worried her. She knew that Jano's illness wasn't just in his body. If it had been, your mother wouldn't have begun to drink and gamble. At first it was just a pastime, later she began to gamble with the pleasure, greed and passion of an addict, winning and losing, and when she won a little more, she gave me part of the money and said: 'Help Lavo, buy books and clothes for my dead friend's son.' Drinking, winning, losing . . . and your father putting up with it all because he was infatuated with her, but he already feared that his son would stray from his destiny as an heir. Because after the punishment in the basement he forced you to go once a week to his office on Marshal Deodoro – you only returned at the end of the day. At home, Jano said he'd shown bills, credit notes and contracts to his son, and talked about jute production, and your mother said that nothing of that was of interest to you, and you were too young to understand things like that, and he said: 'I began working with my father when I was ten.' And the afternoon she came into the office, you were in old Mattoso's chair, pale and as quiet as a doll; Alícia asked the manager where Jano was, and he replied: 'He's gone out to vaccinate a dog he found this morning,' and she wanted to know what you were doing sitting there, and the manager said: 'He's being punished because he spent the whole time drawing and tore up a block of invoices.' She took you home, asked Naiá to stay with you, and I found out all about it three days or so later; she, your mother, shut herself in the basement and began to drink, and only late in the evening, Macau pushed the door in and found her unconscious beside a pool of vomit; he took her to hospital, and Jano hurried there, and when he saw her being injected with serum, he said: 'This is a punishment: you never went to Mass, and you didn't want our son to be baptised . . .' There, in front of your mother, a friend of his called Palha advised him not to punish you, and Jano said you spent all your days drawing, and this friend said: 'Let the child draw, one day he'll get interested in something else.' And it was Palha who suggested to your father that he buy an apartment in Rio, which Jano did, and spend holidays there with his family. But he only went once to Rio, and didn't want to go back. Before the holiday period at the end of the year, he said: 'First we'll go to Vila Amazônia, then you both can go to Rio,' and these periods at the plantation were torture for your mother. At that time — you were about nine — I remember we went out together for the first time, and you looked at me suspiciously during the boat trip to Chameleon Island. Later I'd pick you up at the school gate, and we'd go to Manaus Harbour and swim in the pool on the Hilary, the Booth Line ship which was making one of its last trips to the Amazon. Your mother gave me money, and I bought boxes of pencils and tubes of English and Swiss paints for you. I encouraged you to be an artist and do caricatures which embarrassed your father and made him ashamed. I said to Alícia that you'd be an artist and *not his successor at Vila Amazônia, and sometimes she supported you, but other times she was pressured by Jano, who interfered in your life. She herself told me her husband would threaten her just with his look . . . The greatest threat was the loss of the inheritance, and Alícia's fear grew with time. Our great disagreement was over your going into the Military School. I didn't want to see you going there as a boarder, but your mother said it was just a ruse to keep your father happy, and so she gave way once more to Jano's blackmail. But I didn't give up on the creation of the* Field of Crosses.

17

I'LL COME AND visit you one day in London, I wrote in my reply to the Brixton letter. I asked if he was thinking of coming to Brazil in December, for Arana had advertised an exhibition of his ex-disciple's work in the island studio. Once again, Mundo didn't reply. At the end of November I received four sketches with drawings of torn clothes and three little watercolour landscapes of Vila Amazônia. No letter, not even a card. What was stranger was the series of envelopes Mundo sent me soon after, all posted on the same date: in each of them was a blank sheet of paper, empty front and back. Was it a joke? Ramira asked: 'What's that lunatic friend of yours trying to say?'

I looked at the seven sheets, trying to find some sign. They were his last 'messages'. I stopped thinking about games and jokes. I decided to phone Rio. I recognised Naiá's voice; at the beginning, she was bucked up by the call, and little by little her voice became feebler, until she revealed that Mundo wasn't himself, he was so weak he was fainting . . .

Was he ill?

'A strange fever, with blotches on his body. I think it's exhaustion, or nostalgia for Brazil.'

I asked to speak to Alícia; I waited for a few seconds, and the same voice said: 'Lavo, the mistress is in London. She and the boy are coming back . . . But they still haven't said when.'

She didn't know Alícia's phone number in London. Maybe she was lying, but her tone made me discard that hypothesis. I gave Naiá my new address and asked her to send news.

'I'll tell you when the lad comes back. In January, I think he's going to spend a few days in Manaus.'

Naiá hung up, leaving the echo of a sad, distant voice in my memory.

Something of what Arana had told me and declared to the press might be true. But how had he found out? Had all Mundo's criticisms of the island artist been insincere? After all that had happened between the two of them, their differences about art and life, about how to look at Amazonia, Mundo was going to come back to the city, exhibit his works in Arana's studio and maybe stay at his house. He was going to capitulate, to go back to his youth, his naivety, his blindly enthusiastic belief in the island artist. What extraordinary message was there in the blank sheets of paper? While I waited for a call from Naiá, I trawled through the papers in search of some news of my friend. In a few years Manaus had grown so much that Mundo wouldn't recognise certain areas. He'd only seen the beginning of the destruction; he'd missed Colonel Zanda's 'urban reform', the squares in the centre, like the Ninth of November, being split in two by avenues, all their monuments pillaged. He didn't see his house knocked down, or the gigantic hotel that was built on the same spot. Arana, clever and shrewd, saw that mahogany was valuable in Brazil and the rest of the world, and allied the materials of his art to a dubious project: he began to export objects and furniture made of hardwood.

On the first Sunday in 1978, when I saw Ranulfo sitting

227

on the stairs leading up to my house, I thought: he's come to tell me about Arana's achievements, which everybody already knows about. The sawmill and the furniture factory which the artist was constructing on the sly had been opened with razzamatazz the previous afternoon. In the most widely publicised photo of the event, Arana appeared standing, his arms spread out between two mahogany logs, on a raft beached in a little harbour in the Educandos.

Ranulfo was holding a package, his head turned towards the men playing snooker and dominoes on the pavement in front of a small bar; then, towards the children playing football and flying kites on a wasteland between the street and the riverbank. He spat on the asphalt, nimbly came up the stairs and gave a glance at the living room: 'This home's too modest for a lawyer. Don't the local crimes provide for a string of sardines?'

I offered a drink: he waved his hands – he didn't want anything. A whiff of *cachaça* mixed in with the stench coming from the wet package. Uncle Ran unwrapped it, threw the newspaper pages on the ground, picked the fish up by its tail and left it in the kitchen; when he came back, he saw that I was looking at the previous day's news with annoyance.

'Our illustrious friend is now the mahogany man . . . an Amazonian visionary. That's Arana's great work, the only one that'll be remembered.'

He sat on the wicker chair, wiped the sweat from his forehead with his shirtsleeve and looked at the masses of legal cases and the books on the desk.

'Not even air-conditioned, Lavo! How can you read and write in this oven? Being a lawyer in this hell is a punishment in itself.'

His face was burning with so much alcohol. He picked up the

228

wet newspaper, squeezed it until a thick trickle of filthy water ran out, dirtying the floor. He got up, scribbled a number on a sheet from one of my lawsuits, and threw it in my face: 'I've come to pick up that money, Lavo, that's all. I have to go to Rio. A very important matter, you'll find out afterwards.'

He leant his thin body on the window jamb, balancing on his left foot. 'Mundo sent you some blank sheets, isn't that right? Your aunt told me . . . she loves to reveal other people's absurdities. Ramira and her fantasies . . . and Fogo's bones. Did you know she buried the skeleton in the patio? She's a good grave-digger, is our seamstress. She knows where to stick needles and bones. Faithful, even to the dog's carcass! Only she didn't keep faith with her brother. She had the brass neck to tear up some letters sent to me . . . That's why I stopped going to the Vila.'

'Letters?' I asked.

'I'll never ask for another fucking thing. Just that cheque . . .'

'What's happened in Rio?'

'I'm going to write part of that story,' he said, losing control of himself. He opened the window wide, whistled and burst out laughing: 'What a magnificent landscape, eh, lad? That creek full of healthy children, those lovely shanties built out over the water, a smell of rare perfumes in the sunset. And so lively, too! Dominoes, *cachaça*, snooker . . . What fun they're having on the seventh day!'

He stuck his head out, and spat on the staircase. He insisted again: 'Come on, give us it, Lavo. I want to go tomorrow.'

He went on looking at the sunset while I filled out the cheque. He mocks everyone, feels no shame, and demands money as if it was the payment of a debt. He put the cheque in his trouser pocket, without a word of thanks. He quickly went down the stairs and went towards Seventh of September Street. A journey to Rio. Very important matter. Liar! He'll be back two months from now to trample all over his sister and tell more lies.

Some days later I went by the Vila da Ópera, wanting to know if the seamstress really had buried Fogo's bones in the patio.

'Did Ranulfo tell you? I picked up the poor animal's body and brought it here. I couldn't bear to see the dog in that begging position. I buried it at the back, and your uncle saw. There's something on his mind. He made a scene in front of my clients, wouldn't let me get on with my work . . .'

'Uncle Ran spoke about some letters . . .' I said.

She picked out the pattern of a pair of trousers and turned to face me: 'I tore up the letters your friend sent him. That must be it.'

'Letters from Mundo?'

'Not many.'

I said that was a crime and asked if she wanted to destroy the friendship between the two of them.

Instead of answering, she said, without a trace of boasting: 'I know why Ranulfo went after you. Money, wasn't it? He must be in Rio . . . He'll get his marching orders from the widow. The idiot. A whole life of delusion! He doesn't know the woman who's destroyed him.'

She piled up green trousers and white shirts. She said nothing more. She'd torn Mundo's letters up with no guilt or remorse, as coldly as she sewed or cut a piece of cloth. She didn't even look at me again. Her body accompanied her hands as they went back and forth, her gaze fixed on the needle as it jabbed into the cloth. The meeting between Ranulfo and Alícia threatened Aunt Ramira.

I went to the little patio at the back. Kerosene cans with caladiums and maidenhair ferns. Next to the hedge, a mound of cement hid the dog's bones, and an acacia from the big house next door shadowed Fogo's grave and Jano's flowers. The stems, in a vase in the shape of a shell, were growing exuberantly, and the bunches of little red flowers were wet. The dog's grave and the shell, side by side, gave a little colour and emphasis to the place.

Later, at home, I took up my work again. It was Friday, the end of the afternoon. Outside, the excitement was growing: ugly voices and crashing noises came from the bar. From the window, I could see a snooker player leaning over the table; women in shorts, sitting on the pavement, were painting their toenails and peeling *tucumã* nuts with their teeth. A violent knock pushed the black ball against the red, and others were hit too. The white one was still rolling when a player stuck his cue in the ground and spat on the floor. A woman threw a fruit stone at the losing player. She shouted: 'You idiot, you don't know how to play or how to lose.' A furious altercation ensued. I went back to reading my lawsuit, and when I turned a page, I came upon the figure written by Uncle Ran. I looked at the floor stained by the dirty water he'd squeezed from the paper, and only then noticed an envelope the postman had pushed under the door. It was sealed, with no sender's address: it had been posted in Rio. I took out a folded page of a Rio newspaper. On the back was an advertisement; on the front, a report with a photograph of an Indian, with a headdress, standing in the entrance to a tunnel in Copacabana: thin face and chest, and his eyes bulging, glazed, staring upwards. He was carrying an oar and had been arrested because he was threatening drivers and passengers. With his mouth open, after giving vent to a shout or an insult, he holds on to the oar with his hands in handcuffs. A squalid warrior, adrift in Rio de Janeiro. The rebellious Indian said he was the son of the moon and was there, naked, at the mouth of the tunnel, to celebrate the decline of the military regime. Mundo? Why hadn't he told me he was back? Naiá hadn't phoned, and when I called the Labourdett apartment, no one answered.

I remembered Albino Palha. I hadn't seen him since Jano's funeral; I found him on the top floor of a building in the centre, where he ran a construction firm. The office was large and air-conditioned, with grey glass windows which darkened the river and the forest. I felt his cold hands when he shook mine. His look, distant and supercilious, avoided any intimacy. He asked his secretary for *guaraná* and coffee. He hadn't lost his habit of smiling coldly, for no reason; it was a sort of tic. He said he saw me from time to time around the Tribunal, and the civil and criminal courts; he asked me if I still lived in the Vila da Ópera and pointed at the model of a building on a pedestal. Was I looking for a new apartment?

I said I was looking for something else: Alícia's address. He leant back in his chair, and murmured: 'Alícia Dalemer Mattoso . . . She sold the apartment in the Labourdett building and she's living in a shack near Copacabana.'

He opened a notebook, copied the address on the back of a visiting card and said contemptuously: 'I mean, Alícia had to sell a huge apartment, and still had to ask me for help to buy a hovel. I ended up assisting her, just because of Trajano. She said she was going to London . . . she wanted to bring the artist back. She and her son spent all the inheritance in a few years.'

'But are they back in Brazil?' I asked, thinking of Ranulfo.

'I don't know,' he said. He got up and handed me the card. 'But I think the woman's after a lawyer.'

There was nothing in the office, no object or image, to record the friendship and business association with Jano. When I turned round, I saw the wall was covered with a huge panel with macaws painted on it. Huge, they were flying over a jumble of glass and concrete towers stretching to a bare horizon. The grotesque, hallucinatory vision of the forest, and perhaps of the future, shook me.

'Our company commissioned that picture from an artist . . . Arana,' said Palha. 'He's a talented painter.'

I still had the time to ask about Vila Amazônia.

'It's been sold to a businessman from Taiwan,' he said, hastily. 'But he couldn't stick it for long, abandoned the jute and opened a mining company. They say the government's taken all that area over to settle colonists from the region. The interior of Amazonas is a desert . . .'

Standing at the door, he seemed more flustered, dismissing me with an impatient look. As I walked through the afternoon heat, I remembered his cold eyes. 'The woman's after a lawyer': his monotone, neutral voice, as if he was transmitting noises to the grey windows.

I planned to go to Rio in the middle of February, during the recess at the Tribunal, but I decided to bring the journey forward, because I had an intuition that my uncle had found something out. Maybe he'd gone to meet Mundo and didn't want to tell me, I thought. More than once Ramira had insinuated that: her brother, incapable of seducing Alícia, would seduce Mundo.

18

TWO DAYS BEFORE my journey, I heard loud knocking at the front door. It was very early, before seven, and I was still lying in my hammock. The knocks surprised me, and when I opened the door, I got a shock when I saw Ranulfo crying and sobbing like a child. He couldn't speak, nor did he have to: I could read the tragic message on his devastated face. This impetuous, sarcastic man was overcome with grief. How had it happened? When? Why didn't he come out with it?

'He was pitifully thin. When he died, he wasn't much more than a skeleton.'

Choking, he struggled to stop crying; he said that Alícia wanted to see me, not straight away, not tomorrow, nor next year. One day . . .

'What does she want with me? Why *one day*?' I asked.

'She didn't say, she wouldn't say.'

Uncle Ran tried to escape, perhaps embarrassed by his own weeping. I grabbed him by the arms, shaking him, forcing him to sit down; he pulled himself free and shouted: 'I've not come to ask for money, only to say this: Mundo died shrivelled up, alone . . . In the final days they wouldn't let me in to the ward.'

I couldn't keep him for long; then he threw it in my face: why hadn't I gone to Rio? Why hadn't I gone to Rio? Why had I shown so little care or concern for my friend?

'You and your selfishness, your lawsuits,' he yelled, banging a bunch of papers on the table. 'The one that needed you most was your friend. You work just like Ramira: neither of you understand what's beyond all this . . . This is all show, it's all surface, it's a waste of time.'

He took time lighting a cigarette, burnt his fingers with the match, and his lips and hands were trembling; he blew out some smoke, and coughed. His body relaxed, and only his hands went on trembling; there was a vague expression on his face.

'Alícia doesn't want to see me any more . . . Mundo's death killed my hope. He wanted to come to Manaus; it was going to be a surprise. I tried to bring the body to be buried here . . . Alícia called me a madman . . . It was our last quarrel.'

Before he went away, he said he was writing an 'account of Mundo' and that, as soon as he finished, he'd give it to me. He left behind him a smell of cheap drink, but he wasn't out of his mind. Nothing had gone right in his time in Rio. I cancelled my trip and thought, guiltily, if I shouldn't have gone earlier, even without being certain that Mundo had come back. I also thought of the accusations Ranulfo had made: my selfishness, lack of concern for my friend, my so-called important work, professional blindness. Maybe they were the accusations of a desperate man, still shocked by death, and who'd lost the great bet of his life well before the end. It would be no good to tell him that Mundo had always been standoffish, even if he had confided in me about episodes from his childhood, describing his anguish at having to confront his father, in and out of the house, as if that confrontation was the motive for his life and his unfinished art. Mundo knew it wasn't likely I'd leave Manaus; in the letters I sent him, I underlined that, telling him my city was my curse, that I was afraid of leaving, and stronger than the fear was the desire to stay, isolated, tied up in the routine of work with no particular ambition. I declaimed, almost in play, the verses I'd learnt by heart in the Pedro II, which one night he pompously recited, drowning in drink and debauchery in the Castanhola: 'Ungrateful the man who loves not the land where first he saw the sun.' He laughed and teased me: 'I think I'm that son, even without wanting to be . . .'

After Mundo's death, Ranulfo avoided his sister; when Ramira went to see him on the Morro da Catita, he kept silent for most of the time; he was given shelter at the back of a stone building by Américo, the same one who'd taken him food in the days when he was a refugee on the Morro. On Sundays his sister invited him to lunch in the Vila da Ópera, but my uncle couldn't bear seeing her enslaved by her sewing machine, or listening to her pleas for him to come back.

I reminded Ranulfo of the message Alícia had sent, and asked him to speak to her, or at least tell me what she wanted to say. He swore he knew nothing, and once, when I insisted, he lost his rag and said: 'I wanted to know what the hell it's about, too. But you know what Alícia's answer was? "If you pulled my tongue out, I wouldn't tell you. It's for your nephew's ears, and he'll know when it's the right time."'

Had Ranulfo invented that? His dry, anguished voice made me even more curious. Alícia's message wouldn't get out of my head.

He spent a lot of time out of Manaus; he went up the Rio Negro as far as Barcelos, and, when the river was high, visited villages on the Rio Branco. These were long trips, lasting six or seven weeks; when he came back to Manaus, with a thick beard with just a few black hairs left in it, the locks of his grey hair falling over his shoulders like strings of onions made his eyes look smaller and hid his face. He brought objects of indigenous craft, brushes and brooms made of piassava, and bags of Brazil nuts to be sold in Américo's shop. But there was another, main reason for these trips.

One of his friends, Corel, was now exporting tropical fish. Uncle Ran was paid to draw up contracts and negotiate with the piassava growers of the Rio Negro. 'Coloured fish, Lavo,' he said. 'I earn cash travelling by boat and bringing thousands of cardinal-fish and angelfish. It's good fun, my lad. You've no idea how much trickery there is in those warm waters . . . clear and muddy.'

He went on living from the same game; sometimes I ran into him in the Panair harbour or the Baixa da Égua, where he kept an eye on men carrying polystyrene boxes from a boat to a tub. Bare-chested, in Bermudas and sandals, the bearded man with his burnt skin gave the porters orders with a strange urgency; then he paid the men and went down the ravine. On one occasion, when he was shopping in the Portuguese emporium in the Adolpho Lisboa market, he saw me and came over for a chat. We sat at the table of the Recanto bar, in the Castanhola; Ranulfo asked for beer and a plate of fried *pacu* fish with manioc flour. It was a weekday, but the dancers and singers were there.

'Mundo liked it here,' he said, in categorical tones, and pointed with his chin at the women surrounding us. 'Just look at our wonderful city.' He picked up a five-*cruzeiro* note, knotted it in his beard, right at the corner of his mouth, and called over a dark-skinned girl in blue shorts and a tight

T-shirt with a faded print of toucans and red stars. Small, in spite of her high heels, hands on waist, she leant on the table and threw me a long, curious look. I tried to think where I might have met her before.

Then she remembered: 'It was in the boat, pal. Hey, it was some time ago. Where's that bloke? Don't you remember? The two of you in the yacht . . . and me with the girls in the broken-down boat . . . in the Rebojal, it was.'

The trip to Vila Amazônia . . . the girl who'd danced with Mundo . . . She opened her little mouth, with its dirty, broken teeth. She didn't hide the scar that divided her stomach in two.

'What the hell's going on?' Uncle Ran grumbled. The green-and-yellow note twisted in his beard gave him a comic air. He grabbed the woman's thighs, and stuck out his tongue until it reached the note. She understood, and sat in his lap, kissing and caressing him, and then trying to pull the money out. She gripped the note with her teeth and went away, winking.

'Those girls work their asses off to fill their stomachs,' he said. 'And you waste your time defending fraudulent bastards. Now I want you to defend a pensioner, Lavo: a poor fisherman, a saint who tried to reproduce fish. Corel'll pay you, your uncle'll thank you, and God bless you.'

It was a court order releasing one of Corel's employees: Jesuíno Macedônio Caulim. He'd been arrested by a naval patrol in the port of Barcelos, where he was carrying boxes of tropical fish in a smuggler's boat. I looked at the case and discovered that Jesuíno had been arrested for showing disrespect for the authorities. I sent the initial appeal to the judge and managed to get the man freed; he'd been in prison for five months, waiting for the trial to come up.

In the old prison, the jailer pointed to a person slumped in the corner of a cell. Jesuíno got up. He had no shirt on, his cheeks were sunken and his body emaciated with ribs sticking out. I took a few seconds to recognise him.

'Macau,' I murmured in astonishment.

He looked at my face, and without lowering his head, came out of the cell; he stiffened, before he embraced me: 'Doctor Lavo, Macau's dead and buried; now I'm Jesuíno.'

I accompanied him to New Eldorado, where he lived in a house Jano had given him. The area had grown enormously, and was now a small city within Manaus's suburban sprawl. The streets had been asphalted, and a thin layer of cement, full of holes, tried to look like a pavement. There was no vestige of the *Field of Crosses*, and the wasteland had turned into a grassy area with a tree in the middle. On its trunk was a rusty sign with green letters: 'Colonel Aquiles Zanda Square.'

'The square's still nothing but a promise,' said Macau. 'Only the grass has grown . . . and that tree . . . They say it's a red laurel. It's not. It's a shit-laurel.'

Several houses were now stalls, small shops and booths, bars and tyre changers. At the far end of the area was a jumble of shacks with straw roofs in a cleared space. 'Land invaders,' he said. They burnt the jungle down and built their shacks at night. He picked up the key from a neighbour, and we went into the tiny front room. He opened the windows of the empty, dusty house: all there was was a grimy hammock on the floor. His neighbour brought two benches out on to the pavement, and we sat there. Macau rubbed his left leg, rolled his trouser leg up, and showed a purple wound. Had be been knifed?

'Illness . . . leishmaniasis. The insect pierces your skin like a drill. Right to the bone. They knocked the jungle down, and all kinds of plagues were let loose on us. Leishmaniasis, malaria, the lot . . .'

After Jano's death, Macau had shacked up with a girl who'd come to New Eldorado with a string of relatives. Brazilians from Maranhão . . . all of them poor, dressed in nothing but rags. She worked in a *babaçu* plantation. She came looking for plenty, and found nothing. Some months before he was arrested, the woman entered a religious sect and took almost everything from the house: the TV, the fridge and the stove.

'She went crazy with so much praying, so many halle-lujahs to the Lord Jesus. And she tried to convert me,' he said, giving vent to his feelings. 'She went looking for the little bit of money I had and gave it to the pastor. All smooth talk: Jesus saves . . . and wants to be paid for his services. She exchanged Jesuíno for Jesus, and there was nothing left for me, not even caresses. But she didn't take the house. It's in my name.'

He took a photograph from his trouser pocket: Jano and him on the bridge of the yacht. Looking at the image, he confessed what he'd done in Alícia's house: 'I did all kinds . . . I lied a lot. I've paid for it, three times over . . . In that jail, the Christian soul who wakes up alive crosses himself three times, and still doubts if God exists.'

Did he know Mundo was dead?

'Your uncle told me. He said Mundo died of a terrible illness. I still remember that month before the boss's death. Ranulfo and the boy did some loony art thing here in this neighbourhood and then hid. Jano gave the order to go after the boy, gave me a wad of money to spend on petrol and informants. If it had been twenty years ago, it'd have been easier, but in that year the city was already monstrous. Then I thought: the fox always goes to its lair. Ranulfo's lair was the Morro da Catita. I went there. Nobody opened their mouth: who was going to betray your uncle? But I found out: Saúva was an old hand from the Morro, accepted a few notes, and spilt the beans. But I said nothing; I'd have been ashamed . . . I always liked Ranulfo and Mundo a lot. I kept the boss's money and pretended I was still after the boy. I didn't know others were after them both as well. Then, on Christmas Eve, a policeman went to speak to the boss. He said four men had beaten Ranulfo up, broken his leg and even scarred his face with a knife. Jano burst out laughing till he coughed. I think he wasn't entirely in his right mind. Then he asked after his son, the policeman didn't answer, the boy had got away. The boss nearly swallowed his own tongue in his anger. He paid the policeman and threw him out. Naiá called me and I thought: the boss and the mistress are going to have another fight. But no. Alícia knocked him over with just one look. She looked at him up close, a hand's distance away. Alícia hardly spoke to me, but suddenly she called me, and shouted: "We're going out, Macau." He fell on to the sofa. And I obeyed: I got the car out of the garage and asked where she wanted to go. "Far out of the city," she said. I took the Bolivia Bridge road and drove for almost half an hour, slowly, as she wanted. Then she said: "Macau, take me to the Jardim dos Barés, I want to see the house I lived in." I turned round, and when we were going along the Flores road, she asked me to pull up at the asylum door, and stopped to look at the building and the grass. She said in a low voice: "My sister Algisa ended up here." Then I went on to São Jorge and into that neighbourhood. She didn't even know everything had changed. She asked: "Where's the Castanhal, the forest, the houses?" I didn't answer. I parked near the house and remembered the afternoon when I took her to the centre by boat, on the day she was married in the cathedral. She was crying a lot, she cried until she got into the limousine waiting for us at the Escadaria harbour. I remembered so many things . . . She and your uncle had good times . . . Then she tapped my shoulder: "Macau, let's go home. I don't feel right here."'

'Jano was already dead,' I said.

'It seems she had an intuition . . . She said she had a horrible sense of foreboding, and I put my foot on the accelerator. Naiá was waiting for the mistress; they hugged each other and went to see the dead man. Poor Jano. Father and son were tough nuts. But, look here, I was always sorry for the boy . . . I couldn't say that, the boss wouldn't have liked it. Jano never stopped attacking his son. A twisted father: he never carried the child in his arms. He had a strange resentment against his son. And Dona Alícia was lots of people . . . She wanted to be more than a wife all the time: a free woman, with no husband or son. But the more you live, the worse things you see.'

Embarrassed, Macau said he couldn't offer me a thing, not even coffee: tomorrow he'd go by the company office, and Corel would be able to help him.

In that month of August 1980, a fisherman passed by my house, and left some strings of fat sardines and a note with these words: 'With thanks from Jesuíno the fisherman.'

242

When I married Algisa, our plan was to spend two years in Vila Amazônia, but I didn't stick it even for six months. Your mother wanted me to work at all costs. After I was demobbed from the Army, she persuaded herself that I was never going to study again, and when the Fé em Deus *was wrecked, I lost not only my brother-in-law and my sister, but also any hope of getting anything from work. I still tried work on the radio, earning little and working a lot, because I had to write stories and read them out with an actor's voice. It was fun, but that didn't work out either. Then your mother and I set up the plan for the marriage and the job at Vila Amazônia. Jano believed in it. And I collaborated: I was an angel while I lived with Algisa in a false honeymoon in a little house on a plantation, pretending I was looking for a job but giving her total freedom to pick up tourists at the port. I already knew my wife a bit, her explosive temper, the congenital fear from which she gathered strength to confront any dangerous situation. It was a kind of false fear, which in no time would turn to ferocity. When she moved there, she disclosed to me that she didn't like to hear the voice of any man at all. She said: 'I don't like to hear masculine voices or to see blood.' I listened to her and said nothing, and that made our married life on the middle reaches of the Amazon easier. We communicated in short sentences, which time whittled down to monosyllables, or facial expressions and gestures. At the end of the fifth month, when the cook in the main house told Algisa I'd got a girl pregnant, she protested with insults, like a powerful matriarch, breaking our pact of silence, and cornering me in such a way that there was only one way out – flight. To be honest, I'd already escaped at other times, always in secret. They all believed I spent five months in Vila Amazônia without seeing your mother, but Naiá knew I came to Manaus every month and met your mother at the Recife pension – then I went back, and Algisa thought I'd been having a high old time in Santarém or Parintins.*

243

And when I abandoned Vila Amazônia without warning, I didn't go to Belém by the back country: I came to Manaus, hid in a backstreet near the Seringal Mirim, and asked a boatman to give a message to Naiá, a sign that Alícia knew. The same boatman took a message to Ramira ('Ranulfo's travelling down the lower Amazon, but he won't be long'), and in November 1955 I appeared on the Morro and invented a story for Ramira which I later recounted in several transmissions of the programme Midnight and Just the Two of Us, *and in each programme I invented, one way or another, a journey full of adventures and amorous encounters. These meetings with other women were in fact encounters with your mother in afternoons in the middle of the week — not in a luxury motel or on the sands of some distant bathing spot, but in the sordid cubicles of Tamandaré Street and Visconde de Mauá. 'Shall we take a plunge tomorrow afternoon?' That was the sign Alícia sent via her accomplice, Naiá. Macau got money for making up lies about you; Naiá got clothes, perfume, money and free evenings to let her hair down once a month in the parties at the Fast Club, the Olímpico, the Barés or the Sheik. Macau did good work for me too, because I'd promised that after Jano's death I'd get him a little job, which I did. He relayed to me all that went on in the mansion: Jano's almost revolting servility to Colonel Aquiles Zanda; the business deals between the two of them when the colonel became prefect; the greedy, insinuating looks that elephant Palha gave your mother; the dinners Naiá prepared for the military men and business leaders who supported the government, and the contempt your mother felt for all of them. Even so, when the addiction really made itself felt, she'd even have a few rubbers with those bastards. I remember the first time she announced she was separating from your father and told him to go to hell. She was in such a state of euphoria she even agreed to meet me one afternoon when there was a storm that left the city in the dark. It was in a large room in the Pension America. She arrived drenched, with no disguise: she didn't even have the black mantilla she normally wore to our hidden meetings; she undressed slowly and provocatively, as if she was on the stage of some cheap cabaret. Then she lit several candles on the dressing-table and by the bed. She sat on the bed, and I devoured her soaking wet body with my eyes. I asked if she'd had a gift from God. She said: 'More than that: I've got my freedom.' She took a handful of fresh notes from her pocket, spread them out with a single magical flick of her fingers, and waved the money in front of my nose. I smelt the smell of sweet temptation, and began to think of myself as a millionaire. She asked: 'Are you excited by love or money?' 'Both of them are on this soaking bed,' I said, 'but if I had to choose, I'd stick with love.' It was what your mother wanted to hear, but it was also what I felt. Then she told me about her afternoon of incredible luck in the Water Park in the Rio Negro Club, when the cards and the numbers fell from heaven every time she picked up a card. She didn't blink; there wasn't a trace of emotion on her face. Twice she got three aces, three flushes, and in the second-last game, when all the other players had been fleeced, she realised she had an ace-high straight in her hand. Her adversaries were professionals used to playing in the gambling paradises in the West Indies; even so, in the last game they were enveloped in a deathly silence and went away depressed, leaving very large cheques for your mother. That afternoon she'd laid the highest bet of her life. After our meeting in the Pension America, I went to look for a plot of land in the Educandos, facing the river, because I didn't want to live at the other end of the beach, which was infested with military men and politicians. Your mother suggested a radical change of place: 'Let's go and live in Rio de Janeiro, the Labourdett apartment's in my name.' I agreed with no hesitation. You never found out about it: you were obsessed with*

Arana's artistic chicanery, and I didn't have time to tell you, because three days later your mother lost all she'd won, to the same players. So, when other threats of a change of life, or of city, occurred, I got used to seeing them as just that: threats. Gambling was a powerful thing: a passionate addiction, a dissipation of the body and the soul. The illusion of good luck was counterbalanced by the disappointment when she lost. In the end, vultures feed off each other. From then on she lowered the size of her bets, but she won less than she lost, and the more she lost, the more she drank. One of the very few things I admired about your father was stopping her betting with money when she played at home. But my admiration didn't last long, because Jano's persistent weakness made him close his eyes to small bets after a dinner with his most intimate friends: Zanda, Palha and Maximino Lontra, otherwise known as Herodotus or Skullface. Jano allowed her to play in the drawing-room. He went up to bed, without realising that they were playing a different game. Naiá told me that Alícia played in silence, but suddenly she'd hear warnings from your mother, her speech loosened and excited by drink. Once, Alícia said to Colonel Zanda: 'There's no need to behave like a common politician, Aquiles. Gambling is serious entertainment.' The colonel was taken aback, because she'd seen him cheating when he dealt the cards. Another time, she said to the three of them, without addressing any one in particular: 'Act like men, not oafs: I'll be faithful to my love even after I'm dead.' She didn't say who her love was: they knew. Each one took vengeance on me in their own way: the colonel, by the campaign of persecution that led to our capture, in the hail of blows I got from his henchmen and the scar deforming my face. The agreement between your father and Zanda was to finish me off, but the colonel had political pretensions, and another murder might get in the way of his ambition. That elephant Palha, whose measured, refined gestures only underlined his falsity, *was the gentleman in Jano's circle. His greed and rapacity jump out of his eyes so eagerly they devour his own head. He robbed your mother after Jano's death, and spat on the dead man's name, with the self-confidence of a real con man. Palha and Arana, if you put them on a seesaw, would have balanced each other out perfectly. The first came from the upper reaches of society, the other from the lower, and both of them use all kinds of fantastic tricks to make doubtful business deals and a lot of money, all in the name of progress. Maximino Lontra used his influence to get me sacked from my job serving in the Booth Line shop, where I earned a few coppers when your mother was losing her last cent gambling. Skullface went even further: he managed to get rid of the commercial manager of the shop, my friend John Gladstone, who later opened the Casa Gladstone, known as the Englishmen's nightclub. John was his own first and last customer: he drank more than anyone, but he strictly controlled the age of his clients. I remember lots of girls used to celebrate their coming of age in the club, and for many years it was a riot of the sounds and rhythms of all kinds of places in the heart of the port area. Your mother was sorry she couldn't drink or dance in the Gladstone or any other club in the city, because she spent her evenings in frustration in the mansion, and Jano wouldn't set foot outside it, unless it was to go to some concert in the Opera House or a boring charity dinner, where Alícia embarrassed the ladies of the Women's Voluntary League for Progress. Your mother didn't dare go out at night even when Jano went to the Vila Amazônia on his own. I was mystified by this, and when I asked her why she hid herself away, she replied: 'For safety. Everyone goes out at night to have a good time, and I want to be the only one that only goes out in the daytime.' Sometimes I'd get an urgent note from Naiá and ran to the little room on Tamandaré Street, but for the most part her escapes were planned. So, each Tuesday and Thursday of the first and last* week of the month, Macau took your mother to the beauty parlour; then she got another taxi, driven by my friend Corel, and alighted in front of a narrow doorway next to the Heron's Flight bar; she went up the stairway accompanied by the girls who came from up-country to work as prostitutes in Manaus. I was already lying in the hammock of the little room, with open arms, and a bolero on the gramophone: 'las tardes que pasé contigo, son todos mis sueños y jamás olvido,' to which your mother listened to the end, before taking her clothes off and saying: 'Love', her hair smelling of lacquer and her dark glasses still on, the little window open so she could listen to the laughing and the invitations of the girls and then say: 'They're really lovely girls. Oh, if they were my daughters . . .' Later, Corel's taxi left her at the door of the same beauty parlour, and she went to the mansion with Macau. More than thirty years with your mother, Mundo. And what a lot of melodrama! I trained to be that kind of actor and to live that life . . . When your mother was living in Rio, Ramira said to me: 'You deserve that woman's contempt. You've dried up because she's forced you into a treacherous silence.' In truth, Alícia hadn't gone silent: she sent me letters to a post office box, saying she was trying to stop gambling and drinking. That she was waiting for you to come back. And that one day we'd all live together in Rio. Some three years of pretence in the little house in the Vila da Ópera, with Ramira believing your mother had abandoned me, and me, in the bedroom, writing and then ripping up and rewriting in secret love letters that were sent to Alícia, fooling my sister and Lavo. I pretended too that I'd left a son in Vila Amazônia and later pretended to get irritated when the subject was brought up. I wanted to end the marriage to Algisa and get her away from me for ever, because she was already talking about having a child and staying on at the plantation. I was terrified. Then I found a pregnant girl, whose lover had run away to Belém. I made an agreement with her; I offered her half my salary and said: 'Make believe that son is ours.' The girl agreed. Moreover, I asked Dr Kazuma to look after the mother-to-be. 'The child that's going to be born is mine,' I said to the doctor, knowing he would tell Jano and that that would infuriate your father. I acted out these farces to survive, and for some thirty years I only betrayed your mother on the nights and afternoons when I slept with Algisa. What I wanted your mother to see as sordid, half incestuous revenge, she saw as an almost infantile act of despair. 'My love, I know you look for my sister when you can't be with me,' she'd say. And it was true: the two of them were so much alike that at times I almost convinced myself that one could be the other. But it was only a passing impression, and I soon realised that it was only a superficial physical resemblance. No one could be your mother. And that was the only thing I couldn't feign . . .

19

L ESS THAN A YEAR later, I went to Rio to take part in a
series of debates in the Order of Advocates and see the
project for the creation of a school for magistrates. Macau's
case made me abandon the firm where I'd begun work as a
trainee; now I worked defending poor prisoners left to rot in
the prisons. The slow return to a properly constitutional state
with rule of law hadn't got rid of many privileges; Uncle
Ran was right about that.

I went without any call from Alícia, but I wanted to see
her, even if it was against her will. I stayed in a hotel in the
centre of town, and, after the debates, I wandered round
areas that Mundo had known well. The day before my
return to Manaus, I decided to go to the building where
Alícia lived, in Bittencourt Square. It's on the edge of
Copacabana, in Peixoto, a quiet, small neighbourhood, half
hidden away, nearer the mountains than the sea. In the
square, children were playing football and other games, old
men were playing dominoes and chatting under the mango
trees and acacias. The oldest man said: 'The military have had
it!' A hoarse voice said more doubtingly: 'And what comes
now?' On the pavement in front of a small hotel was a group
of young Americans who'd just got back from the beach. For
some time, I stood looking at the badly maintained façade,
with clothes hung out on the little verandas in front of the

living rooms, wondering what Mundo's life had been like in the short time he'd lived there, until he was arrested and then admitted to the clinic where he died. I went up to the third floor and knocked firmly on the door. When Naiá appeared, I was moved: I'd thought I'd never see her again. She embraced me, put her hands on my head and found the two lines of precocious baldness: 'Well, old friend, time isn't kind to any of us.'

In the sitting room, which I'd thought would be smaller, she asked me to take a seat on the sofa; then she disappeared down the dark corridor. When she came back, she said the mistress was getting herself ready.

'You know the way she is, she likes to spruce herself up.' She sat on a small bench, and told me no one had been to the apartment in a while. Her mistress hardly went out; sometimes Naiá dragged her out to walk along the beach or do a little shopping. She apologised for not having phoned me, because she had too much to do and no time to spare: 'When the two of them arrived from London, we moved here. I took care of the move, did everything. The worst moment was when the lad was arrested.'

She said the 'lad' had been arrested and then beaten up in a police station in Copacabana. 'That was at the end of January, the 25th of January 1978,' she remembered. 'We spent the whole night waiting for him, and we only found out about the arrest in the papers. Dona Alícia paid . . . gave some dollars to the police chief and a bit of money to his men. He got out then. He had dizzy spells, wasn't walking right, and fainted from time to time. But when he arrived from London, he talked only about Manaus. He wanted to see you, show his paintings . . . Two friends of his sent letters. Adrian drew and wrote just like a strip cartoon. I didn't understand a thing, just the word "London" repeated four times. The other one wrote in Portuguese, his name was Alex. He said he was waiting for Mundo in Berlin. That Alex is a bit touched, writing in little tiny lettering like ants, and drawing portraits on the page. The mistress didn't want to know, she didn't even write to say he'd died. But I wrote to the two of them, in my language. I smudged the words out with so much rubbing out and correcting, but I told everything. I said he'd died of sadness, during Carnival . . .'

She began to sob; her face, plumper now, was wet. She dried it with the edge of her skirt, and asked in a tearful voice: 'And our city? All we read here about it is scandals. Scandals and misfortunes.'

'It's grown, and a lot of poverty's come with that.'

'But I miss it so much . . . so much, Lavo. Dona Alícia doesn't want to go back. When I even touch on the subject, she gets really mad and says: "Off you go, on your own."'

'That's right: on your own. But now go and get a coffee ready for our visitor.' Alícia appeared from the dark corridor. Still proud, her make-up carefully put on, and the same spontaneous and detached way of giving me a kiss and a hug, and then sitting on the wicker chair she'd brought from Manaus: sitting upright, with her legs crossed and her hands clasped on her knee; on her lap was a Spanish fan.

'I knew you'd come and see me one day,' she said, with a Rio accent that was now perfectly unaffected, observing me from top to toe. I returned her inquisitive look and saw the difference between her body and her face: her make-up couldn't hide the suffering, there was much less light in her eyes, and less life in her voice.

'A long time, isn't it. And how many things have come to an end, Lavo!'

'The last time . . .'

'At my husband's funeral . . . the 24th of December,' she interrupted, cooling herself with her fan. 'I lied that night: I said Mundo was with Ranulfo, in the hospital ward. Then we saw each other at the airport. I'll never forget that Friday. Now it's over. I was left alone . . . with Naiá . . .'

In the sitting room, the glass cabinet was empty, without the photo of Fogo and his master, without the collection of toy soldiers and guns.

'Pay no attention, it's a very simple apartment,' she said, with no embarrassment. 'I had to sell the other one. You'd have liked the Labourdett. Now we've only got money to pay the bills and eat. Ranulfo was crushed; he didn't expect to find me penniless.'

She put her fan down and showed her bare hands, without a single ring. 'My son's death, gambling and drink left me this way. When Ranulfo came here, he understood everything.'

'Uncle Ran's got himself a job,' I said, without much conviction.

'What kind of fiddle's he into now? Is he helping your aunt sew buttons on?'

'He goes around on the boats.'

'It must be contraband,' said Alícia, winking at Naiá. 'Don't you want to work with him? You'd have fun, the two of you. Ranulfo's working with the natives . . . that's a good one!'

She gave the maid a cheque, asked her to get the money out of the bank and go and do the week's shopping. When Naiá left, she said: 'The poor thing does cleaning in the apartments on the Avenida Atlântica and contributes to our expenses. I've sold the jewellery I got from my father-in-law, all of it: rings, brooches, trinkets, bracelets . . . Jewellery made of Portuguese gold . . . Brazilian, that is – made by a Lisbon goldsmith. Palha tricked me: an accountant told me he sold my properties for less than they were worth. They brought a lot of money, but I had to ask for more to buy this apartment.'

I waited for about half an hour, and she finally touched on the subject: 'If it wasn't for my son, Naiá and I would be out in the street . . .'

She passed her hands over her face, sadly shaking her head. 'An art dealer in Ipanema got interested in Mundo's work. When I'm really short, I sell a picture or a drawing. Yesterday two watercolours went. Naiá went to get the money. I know it's not always that way, but I only managed to sell them after he died . . .'

'It's your son's legacy.'

She stopped shaking her head, and I had the impression my remark offended her less than it made her proud.

'I found out that in Europe Mundo sold a load of pictures and drawings for a song. You've no idea how he lived in London . . . the flat in Brixton . . . a mess, people from all over the place . . . white, black, mulatto . . . that neighbourhood looked like Brazil. Mundo was living with a film-maker friend. They had a goodbye party for him. The neighbours from Villa Road were there, and even some artists from Berlin. At the end of the party they slept on the floor, piled up on one another like animals. My son never stopped still, he was always going around, crazy to show his work. He sent drawings and objects to galleries and art critics, and dreamt of going to a London art school. He wanted to study at the Slade. "The Slade is my future, mother," he'd say. I said I hadn't got a penny left and that we were going to have to go back to Brazil. He was already ill, it wasn't Jano's illness . . . He always asked after you.'

She turned towards the kitchen, shouted Naiá's name twice and, when she noticed my surprise, she excused herself. 'I forget when she goes out. I live with my son's ghosts, Lavo, and that's the greatest suffering.'

She got up and went to get a bottle of whisky.

'I've stopped drinking, but because you're here . . .' she said, as she filled the glasses. 'Ranulfo led me to alcohol.' She took a sip, with no ice, closing her eyes and sighing. 'To alcohol and to bed too, for the first time. It wouldn't have worked with him, Lavo. It worked while I was with Jano and had Mundo near me. Without my son, I couldn't . . . Your uncle tried . . . he wanted . . . he tried to understand what only a mother feels deep inside. He still writes to me, you know? He loves writing sugary letters, full of obscenities, memories. He lives off the past; don't you think that's a bit cowardly? Don't you want any more? Just a little drop?'

She filled her glass again. 'Ranulfo didn't have the guts to tell me he's working. He thinks he was born with the vocation to be rich, and not to work. He'll die without a vocation. When the subject is work, your uncle knows how to lie. What sort of smuggling is it?'

'Little fish from the Rio Negro . . . cardinals . . .'

'Cardinals, of course,' she laughed out loud. 'And a good few river sirens too. The scoundrel! Over and over again he asked me for money to come to Rio, and I always refused. He came when he found out Mundo was in hospital. I asked him how he'd got the money for the flight. He laughed and said: "By banging on a lot of doors." But he liked my son a lot, loved him like a father. He went to the hospital every day.'

Glass in hand, she got up and made a gesture with her head, pointing to the rooms: 'Naiá sleeps in my room. Mundo slept in the other.'

We went into the room on the right of the narrow corridor: there was a double bed in the centre, a dressing-table, and hanging from hooks on a wall, a red hammock. The window gave on to the wall of another building, which blocked part of the light. Alícia took a key out of the dressing-table drawer and, at the end of the corridor, un-locked the door to her son's room. I smelt dried paint. From the window I could see the square: children running round the bandstand and the group of old men.

'He slept here for a few days. He was arrested and humiliated, only because he went walking round the streets naked. Then he was more than a week in the hospital, suffering . . .' She opened the wardrobe, and took water-colours out, thumbnail drawings, sketches and little paint-ings, cityscapes with distorted figures in the Kreuzberg and London neighbourhoods. Some of the works, in acrylic paint on aluminium plates, with an inverted version on paper, were portraits of friends: *Alexander Fleming and his Identities*, *A Jamaican Protests in Remnant Street*, *Mona and the Journey to Everyone's Body*, *Adrian and his Kinetic Pictures*.

From an oak trunk, she took out canvases rolled up in towels — seven, the last two heavier. She unwrapped them and put them, one by one, on the L-shaped bench, as if they were a sequence.

'Mundo asked me to show you these pictures. I had to swear a thousand times over I'd never sell any. It's the work he wanted to submit to that school . . . The Slade. He began it in Germany and finished in London.'

She went out of the room and came back with her glass full of whisky, and a sad but serene look in her eyes: 'I've never shown anyone. Well, your uncle's seen them. It's all very strange . . .'

In the first painting a male figure appears full length, with grey eyes in his severe face, still young, with a dark suit and a tie the colour of his eyes, holding a puppy in his hands, and, in the background, the big house at Vila Amazônia, with Indians, *caboclos* and Japanese working at the river's edge. Mundo, in the middle of the workers, is looking at them and drawing them. In the next four canvases the figures and the landscape gradually change, the man and the animal become more and more deformed, aging, acquiring strange features and grotesque forms, until the painting disappears. The last two, with a dark background, were more like objects: in one, nailed on to the wooden support, were the rags made of the clothes worn by the man in the first picture, which had been torn, cut and pierced; in the last one, the pair of shoes riddled with nails occupied the whole of the canvas, the shoes side by side but facing in opposite directions, and a phrase was written by hand on a piece of blank paper fixed to the bottom left-hand corner: *The Story of a Decomposition — Memories of a Beloved Son*.

While I was looking at each of the pictures and then at the whole, I discovered details, delicate nuances of colour, lines. There's something terrible and comic about this *Story*, I thought.

'It's the clothes Jano wore at our wedding. I looked for them when he died, but I couldn't find them. I thought he'd given them to the poor, but no . . . Mundo had taken everything to Europe: the suit, the trousers, the tie and the shoes. I only saw them again here. He showed me the canvases . . . he was proud, full of enthusiasm; I begged him to get that hatred out of his soul. He said he wasn't going to remove any remnant of the life inside him . . . "Memories", he said. Then he went out without telling me. He ran away . . .'

She went up to one of the paintings, the one in the middle, not daring to touch it: 'Look at this, Lavo. Doesn't that diabolical old man remind you of my husband? The dog's muzzle looks like a sad old man. The two of them looking at each other in the mirror. And those torn clothes, the shoes with all those nails . . . What do you think? Is that art?'

She stood there, stock-still, the empty glass in her hands, maybe without seeing that the seven pictures, with the story that her son had invented, didn't just allude to the life and death of the father – they translated Mundo's anguish and foretold his own death.

'Mundo spent a lot of time thinking about this,' I said. 'It was his way of expressing life. There's a lot of feeling . . .'

'Hatred . . .' she interrupted. 'Isn't that what you mean? Thank goodness he didn't paint my face in these horrible memoirs of his. I know Jano was hard on my son, still isn't it unjust to trample on the dead? The father . . . I was going to throw all these paintings away . . . your uncle wouldn't let me: he said it would be the same as killing Mundo. I felt remorse. But that's not the worst of it. One day I'll tell you . . .'

She covered the paintings, and I helped to arrange them in the box.

'Ranulfo said you wanted to see me. I'm going back tomorrow, Alícia.'

'Tomorrow?' she said, surprised.

She stroked her creased neck and her lips, and stopped two feet away from me. Uncle Ran didn't lie, I thought. She wants to tell me something and she's not prepared, or she's sorry she sent that message. Seeing her close to, I clearly remembered my friend: the same way of looking, as if the eyes hid a story.

Sweat was spreading over her face like a thin tissue-paper mask, wrinkling it. The scent of drink and perfume drowned the smell of wood and paint in the room; now she was looking at me as she'd never done before: serious, guarded, perhaps changing her mind over and over, studying the situation, calculating, until her voice murmured: 'Why don't you stay a few days? You can sleep here . . . in his room.'

I felt her wet hands on my arms, her warm breathing . . . Her voice asked again, this time without insistence, intuitively aware that I couldn't, didn't want to sleep in my dead friend's room, under the same roof as Alícia.

She went out: I was to wait for her in the sitting room, she'd not be long.

I noticed that none of Mundo's works were on the wall. Jano's books and records weren't in the apartment, nor his record player, the sofa, the card table or the chairs. The only familiar objects were the wicker chair and the crystal cabinet. I thought of the seven paintings: the perfect technique of the first, full-length portrait, with the landscape and the workmen in the background, and then, in sequence, Jano's face aging, in a time which he didn't live to see, as if the father had been alive until the moment the painting was done (and even some years afterwards), and only the clothes and the look in his eyes stayed immune to the passing of the years. The eyes disappeared into cavities or dark blotches, and features of a dog's muzzle appeared in the face, the canine teeth; both bodies were deformed and decomposed. There was the sharp awareness of an animal nature, with a more brutal, naked, sharp truth. But, unlike Alícia, I wasn't sure that the figures really represented Fogo and his master. They looked like unknown figures, which time distorted till they appeared grotesque. The Vila Amazônia house has features of the Manaus mansion, I remembered. But it evoked another place, which I searched for in my memory, ferreting in corners of the past . . .

Alícia had changed, and was now wearing a greenish silk dress; a string of imitation pearls accompanied her neckline. She was going to take me to one of the prettiest places in Rio. We went to Our Lady of Copacabana Avenue, and went along the Avenida Atlântica towards the end of the beach. Alícia wasn't carrying a bag, but she was somewhat apprehensive. She stopped to show me where two *carioca* friends of hers lived, ex-card partners, who'd lost money just as she had. Now they got together before Christmas to have tea and complain about life; one was married to a retired general, who had forbidden her to gamble; the other, the wife of a businessman, was still in the middle of a spending spree: she played in high-class clubs, paid for her friends' dinner and lent money on top of that. 'They're living the high life, just as I did in Manaus. They suffer because they're married but think of themselves as widows. They can't even imagine something that hurts more . . . They've not lost a son.'

She waved at the sentinels at the Copacabana Fort and greeted an officer of the Coastal Artillery Command. We sat on a bench shaded by a false-almond tree. Some soldiers were passing nearby; waves splashed on the rocks, and the spray formed a mist round the base of the fort. For a moment, the noise of the water and the beauty of the landscape distracted me. The blue water, the islands, the beach full of people, the hills, the mountains, the sea air, it was all new to me.

'When we came here on holiday, Mundo and I visited the fort. When we arrived back from London, we came here one more time. Rio was the city he chose to die in. In less than two weeks he lost an incredible amount of weight; the illness devoured my son's body, but not his soul.'

'Did he talk about coming back to Manaus? Arana kept on saying . . .'

'It wasn't because of Arana. My son never even mentioned that man's name. Mundo wanted to see Amazonas again. Here, on this bench, he said that when he looked at the sea, he remembered the Rio Negro, journeys by boat . . .'

'Did Mundo like Vila Amazônia?'

'He liked it and didn't want to like it, it was strange. When he was young, he was always in the houses in Okayama Ken: he wanted to play with the poor kids. Jano dragged the child back home. My husband detested play of any kind. Mundo stayed on his own on the veranda, looking at the river, and drawing. I think he did like Vila Amazônia, but he said that the poverty destroyed its natural beauty. He died with that rebellion inside him . . . And he talked a great deal about your uncle; thank goodness the two of them met again. In the hospital, he called you his. That's what he said: "Show my work to my cousin the lawyer."'

Her face turned towards the rocks and stones.

'Cousin?'

She gave a lifeless smile, pulled a white envelope with dark blotches on it from the top of her dress; she grasped my arm with her sweaty hand and looked at me. 'I only managed to tell the truth when he was in the hospital. It wasn't right, Lavo. My son would have died without knowing. So I told everything . . . It wasn't the moment to ask for pardon, but I couldn't hide it any longer . . . a secret that only I knew. He listened, said nothing, and wanted to be alone.'

She stroked the envelope with the tips of her fingers. 'Mundo left this letter for you.'

'Why didn't you send it me?'

'Fear,' she answered, point-blank. 'Fear and shame. I spent all that time wondering if it mightn't be better to tear it up . . . or forget it. But it was Mundo's last request . . . his last words . . . I haven't read the letter, Lavo, I swear . . . I haven't read a single line. And I'm not interested in what you do with it.'

She left the envelope on the bench and got up. She wasn't crying; more than two years after her son's death, her pain and suffering looked as if they were locked away inside. She kept her strength as she said goodbye. She wanted to go back to the apartment on her own.

'Well, I suppose we'll never see one another again,' she said, prophetically.

When I embraced her, I smelt an old-fashioned perfume and thought: that woman could have belonged to my family.

She stopped between the sentinels of the fort, quickly said goodbye, and the green, haughty figure disappeared along the pavement of the Avenida Atlântica. A reddish glow covered the islands and the ocean. I stayed there, listening to the crash of the waves on the rocks, looking at the buildings as their lights came on, and behind them, the hills blending with the night.

Hardly had I got on the bus to the centre than I opened Mundo's letter. The passage I read at random made me feel nervous. I read it again, slowly, and I couldn't get it out of my head. I got off the bus and wandered aimlessly around the hotel, between the Beco dos Barbeiros and the Rua do Rosário. How could Alícia have acted that way with her own son? I walked in a daze amongst people coming out of work, street salesmen, beggars, abandoned children, men and women selling flowers and manioc-flour biscuits, men playing draughts in the filthy doorways of shut-up shops, or standing, still, holding placards saying: 'I buy and sell gold.' In the bars, excited voices were discussing the end of the military regime. I put the country and the fast-declining power of the generals on one side, but I couldn't manage to go to the hotel: I went into the Beco das Cancelas and began to drink in the Devil's Gob. I was the last one to leave the bar, half drunk, thinking if it mightn't be worthwhile to put my journey off and see Alícia again . . .

I read the letter again several times in Manaus, even after Alícia's death, which Naiá phoned me to tell me about. She said that in the last year of her life her mistress had sold all her son's work, except the seven pictures. 'She did worse things, Lavo . . . but, all in all, she was a good person. I mean, she was fair to me; she put the apartment in my name. I was afraid of being driven out and having to go and live in a shack. She knew I adored Mundo. And who looked after Seu Jano? The food, the dinners, the cleaning of that house in Manaus. I knew she was on with your uncle. But Dona

Alícia was like a spider, she hid in the corner of the web and grew. She lied to Ranulfo . . . she wasn't going to call him when Mundo went into hospital. I threatened her: "If you don't tell him, I will." She was suspicious about something; she didn't want to say that the boy was ill. Her excuse? She said she didn't want you to see him that way, all skin and bones. "He'll get better; when he's well, I'll tell them," she said. "Then do what you've always done," I said. "Lie to them. Tell them he's had an accident and is in a bad way." She left a message for Ranulfo, asking him to come straight away to Rio, but didn't tell you. What I did was send you the paper with the photo . . . his arrest . . . I didn't tell Dona Alícia, she'd have been furious. She didn't let me open my mouth, wouldn't leave me alone . . . And I couldn't talk about those things when you came here. She lied to you, Lavo. She still had some necklaces and chokers, and only stopped gambling when the boy was near the end. She died alone, shrivelled up just like her son. In her last bout of drinking, it was dreadful to hear her crying. She went into Mundo's room and shut herself in . . . she shouted out his name and called for your uncle. Then I heard thumping, hammer blows. I got afraid, and called the neighbours and the police . . . they knocked the door down. She'd destroyed the pictures . . . she tore up the canvases, ripped everything up with so much strength, so much hatred, that all that was left was a pile of rubbish on the floor, twisted nails, bits of clothing . . . She was lying in the middle of all that, covered in cuts, and she'd been sick all over the place. We took the poor thing to a public hospital. And I was interrogated on top of it all . . . Now, when I'm alone, I pray for the three of them. They were my family.'

She stopped, and I realised she was crying. 'They were my family,' she repeated. 'I saw the boy being born.'

Alícia was buried in Rio, beside her son. The death of the woman Ramira hated so much put even more distance between her and Ranulfo. You hardly ever saw the two of them together, and I only saw them from time to time in Américo's house, on the Morro da Catita. They were the only relatives I had left, and their stories could provide material for another one, which I'd decided to write.

Ranulfo was no longer rude or coarse with Ramira. The punishment Uncle Ran applied to his sister was contempt. When she went after him on the Morro, my uncle would curl up in his hammock, letting silence mortify Ramira. She left Américo's house, went to pray in São Francisco church, and then walked under the few Brazil-nut trees to survive the devastation, shocked by the way the neighbourhood had grown; when she came back, she saw her brother snoring in his hammock, his hands on an open novel. She left a metal container with stuffed fish and, before she left, asked for a word or gesture of affection. With his eyes shut, my uncle wearily said: 'Now I want to be alone, sister.' Ranulfo's sincere voice was more cutting than his contempt. Then she went back to sewing her cheap clothes, to the solitude of an increasingly anachronistic occupation, without losing her courage, or the pride of a person who'd spent her life cutting and mending clothes. She said a lot of people danced, walked, studied and had a good time in clothes she'd made. 'Even the dead are buried in clothes that come out of here,' she'd declare, showing her hands.

Her pride won out over her strength, and she never again

accepted my help: the money with which she bought the complicity and the company of her brother. For good or ill, wasn't Ranulfo getting some money as the agent of fish smugglers? Didn't he live for free in Américo's house?

'What's more, your uncle was always an atheist and a useless vagabond . . . What he really wants is living flesh. The dead will never be born again in his heart. The spell's broken. My brother's been released from his enchantment!'

Ranulfo avoided me too, but with a different attitude and for other reasons. He knew I'd abandoned the established firm and was dedicated to trifles and to giving legal assistance to 'people heading for an unmarked grave', as he said. But he didn't celebrate the end of the military regime, only mocked Colonel Zanda, who, having destroyed part of Manaus and its history with his crazed mania for modernisation and urban reform, had retired and lived in Rio. Solitary, living off seasonal work, my uncle knew nothing of the history of the city and the country. His rebellion was personal, intimate, and raw. This could be seen in the mad political discussions he had with Chiquilito and Corel. His inflamed words didn't amount to an opinion; they were like absurd plants, with no roots in the earth or even in the air. They were like a child's rattle, completely useless.

When some time had passed, when the first civilian president was about to take office, I went to see Uncle Ran. One of the few trees remaining in the Castanhal cast a patchwork of shade which covered Américo's house. I saw the hammock stretched between the trunk and the post for the porch. It was heavy and full, and looked as if there was a body there, but when I opened it, I found only books. Ranulfo was dressed in shorts, sitting in front of a little table, tapping on a thick pile of paper with a pencil. I asked what he was writing.

'An account of Mundo's story,' he said, sadly but proudly. 'Stories . . . about me, Mundo and Alícia, the love of my life.'

Uncle Ran wouldn't say any more about his story, so I made a comment about the elections. He said that Arana had been invited to the ceremony in Brasília: he was going in an official delegation, taking animals and mahogany furniture to decorate the president's palace. He said this with no interest, looking greedily at the pages in front of him. He slapped the table, and his malicious voice came to the surface: 'Now go away, I need to be alone. I want to finish these stories quickly. Later, I'll give you the whole rigmarole . . . written in pencil.'

Ranulfo's greatest relief, happiness even, maybe, and the only triumph in a life full of disappointments of a hopeful lover, was to know that Mundo had deciphered Arana's character. What Ranulfo really wanted was to read my friend's letter. Alícia had mentioned it, and in hints and roundabout ways, he showed his desire to read it. I changed the subject, which made him more curious, and much more tortured by the doubt that, for me, no longer existed: he suspected his nephew was writing a book about Mundo. He wanted this to be true, because that was the only way he'd read Mundo's last letter, and at the same time he didn't want it to be true.

Before another trip to the Rio Negro, he handed me the manuscript, saying eagerly: 'Publish the story I've written straight away. Publish every word of it . . . in homage to the memory of Alícia and Mundo.'

I fulfilled my uncle's wishes, but not with the urgency he required – I waited a long time. As an epilogue, I added the letter Mundo wrote to me, before the end.

20

L AST NIGHT, not even my mother appeared . . . How difficult it is to find words . . . Even more when I'm lying down, destroyed inside and out . . . Mutterings in the corridor: nurses . . . The letter from Brixton . . . It took me more than a week to write it . . . I was already ill, but I didn't want to tell everything . . . I wasn't even going to write to you now, I didn't think I'd be able to . . . My mother promised she was going to give you the studies of the *Memories of a Beloved Son* series. When she saw the work, she got confused, and looked at the seven pictures hesitantly. The same hesitation she showed in the most decisive moments of my life. I'm sorry I showed her them now. Too late for everything . . . a story ending before it's ended. Life inside out, Lavo . . . Yesterday was a dark day, full of sleep and exhaustion, a day with my eyes shut. Today I woke up with not much pain; I saw the nurse's smile and remembered a nightmare . . . but I've no time to talk about dreams. It's a sunny day, my hand's less heavy, and I can write. At the end of one morning, Alícia, not Naiá, came to pick me up from school. She came on foot, without Macau. We went by taxi to Fifteenth of November Square; Ranulfo was on the pavement outside the Booth Line shop, he put me on his shoulders, played the fool, and gave me a box of sweets. One of mummy's friends, she said. We went along some streets in the area around the harbour, went down an alley that took us to the river, and got into a small motor boat. I thought we were going to Vila Amazônia, but that wasn't where we were going. We went to Chameleon Island, and my mother looked happy on the journey. Then Ranulfo would come alone to the school and take me to the Taquarinha bar; he had a beer and bought an ice-lolly for me. In the middle of the afternoon we went to the Manaus Harbour, and back home I asked my mother: 'Why isn't it my father that picks me up to go and visit the ships?' 'One day I'll tell you,' she'd say. Alícia brought me closer to Ranulfo, and told Jano I had private classes in the afternoons and asked me not to say anything. Ranulfo could have been anyone: a protector, a mentor, sometimes a strange and playful friend, anything but a father, I thought. Alícia wanted time for herself, gave money to Ranulfo and said: 'Buy the best books for my son; I want him to learn several languages.' Now I know it was your uncle who led me to art, more than Arana. I thought he was mortally jealous of Arana, but that wasn't it . . . Now the nurse is coming to give me an injection, my mother asks to come in, and I tell the nurse I want to sleep and I hate that soup, the smell of soup . . . My mother . . . Her mouth smells of whisky, she sucks a mint sweet, but the smell of the alcohol is stronger. I pretend to be asleep or sleepy, I pretend I'm dreaming and mumbling in my false dream. She passes her hand over my hot head and strokes my face with the tips of her fingers. Has she drunk a lot? She angrily denies it. In London I concentrated on the seven object-pictures, it was a way of freeing myself. The image of Jano wasn't alone in my head, it was the process that interested me, my life thought through, lived, and torn apart. Isn't painting a way of remembering with colours and forms? Of inventing life in extreme situations? I couldn't have gone to an art school. I spent weeks in the house on Villa Road, not going out, painting day and night, destroying things and painting again, trying to get an image in its moment of fullness. I don't know how much came from chance, how much from studies and sketches, the difficult balance between chance and intention. All I know is that I worked in a state of exasperation, almost delirious, sometimes laughing at my own misfortune. These were more or less figurative pictures, decomposing a family portrait, until I got to Jano's clothes and rejects. Ideas and emotions that move us. I freed myself from a weight when I finished the work, but I don't think of myself as an artist, Lavo. I only wanted to give my life some meaning. I'm afraid of dying with my sketches, and it would have been a emptied-out life . . . afraid because dizziness and weakness and pain were finishing me off . . . I remember my friends putting on a crazy show near Remnant Street: Mona fell over as if she was dead, and someone stopped the traffic and called the firemen while Adrian was filming; I just looked on, sitting under an archway. Suddenly I had a black out, and couldn't get up. I was an unknown person, ill and a foreigner . . . I phoned my mother, and in a way I gave in. She felt how distressed I was, my despair. She sold the Labourdett apartment, paid the debts and came to get me. Two sick people meeting. When she saw me, thin and with no strength in me, the world came apart. And, when we were back from London, she spent days in Rio promising to tell me a secret; she was going to tell it, and got stuck, and only managed to reveal that the pictures about Jano perturbed her. Now I know my work was a devil grinding in her conscience, gnawing her and burning her inside. Time, which was throwing itself against me, was giving her an ultimatum. My mother and I were hostages to each other, and both of us hostages to time. Not even in the last days we were together did she stop drinking. On top of that, she wanted me to destroy my own work . . . It was on the night I left the apartment, in the small hours . . . I sat on the bandstand in Bittencourt Square, thinking about my life. I waited for the dawn, the most beautiful moment, and the city was almost silent, the city of the abandoned, all the beauty of Rio for those who have nowhere to live, no shelter . . . people with nowhere to go. I thought: every human being at any moment of their life should have somewhere to go. I didn't want to wander around for ever . . . to die choking in a foreign land. Wandering wasn't my destiny, but going back to where I came from was impossible. In the early morning I walked along Tonelero Street . . . naked, with an Indian headdress, holding an oar. The people working in the bars and pharmacies laughed at me, but I wasn't going towards a tunnel in a carnival disguise. I was carrying the old Indian's oar, the one that died in Vila Amazônia . . . one of the Indians and *caboclos* I painted in the backgrounds of my paintings, in the hidden, shameful background of our history. When I got to the tunnel entrance I began to shout, as if I had the devil in me . . . Then came the beating in the police station, I couldn't put my feet on the ground . . . Now there were three, all dressed in white . . . The nurse came to take my blood pressure and inject some kind of medication into my vein . . . I didn't understand their talk, only my mother's words . . . 'He's strong, he'll live . . .' Naiá didn't come, apparently she was afraid, afraid of suffering as she saw me suffer. Then Ranulfo appeared. Grey-haired, his face hidden in a beard, and a look of shock and sadness in his eyes. He came in slowly, awkwardly, and knelt down beside me. He held my hands, with affection . . . he kissed me . . . And I wept silently, looking at him, remembering . . . My mother said again: 'My son is strong, didn't I say so?' I asked after you, and your uncle said: 'Look, Lavo's turned into one of those lawyers you see at the prison gate,' laughing, then crying . . . 'You'll see each other in Manaus . . .' 'Of course,' I said, as I felt the prick of the needle. He came to see me two or three more times, on alternate days I think. Night came, the doctor examined me, and I nodded off. The nurse brought the supper, and I heard my mother's voice, a conversation with the doctor. Alícia stayed with me, and wanted to sleep in the room. She asked what I was writing. 'A letter to my friend. When I finish it, give it to him. That's all I ask . . .' The best morning. I've got no more strength left, or energy, but I'm lucid, my mother's seen that. She kissed me over and over, wetted my eyes. She leant over the bed, her hair fell over my face . . . She said that she and Ranulfo fell in love when they were young. She was afraid of living with him, a poor young man, unwilling to work. The fights they had on that subject . . . In September 1951, in the Casa Colombo . . . 'My eyes were on stalks, admiring hats and posh shoes I could only buy in my imagination,' she said. 'A lad was choosing a cut of linen, and I interrupted him, gave him some tips, and he liked me. When he said who he was, I dreamt of another, much better life. Trajano Mattoso. Thin, timid, elegant. He liked me, and even forgot the cloth he was buying; he liked me so much he even invited me to visit the firm's offices on Marshal

Deodoro Street. Then he took me to dances in chic clubs. We were married quickly, almost overnight. That month I'd flirted with another lad; I wanted to make Ranulfo jealous. It was supposed only to be flirtation. Just one night . . . when I was coming out of a wedding party on my own. No one knew what happened that night. I was just a girl, only eighteen.' Her hands got warm, sweaty. My mother wasn't looking at me any more; she put her head on my shoulder, her left breast covered my face, and I could feel the beats of her heart, getting faster; the beats of an exhausted heart. Then she stuttered, confused, and uttered a name . . . It might have been your uncle's . . . Her body leaning over mine was trembling a lot, and she began to cry, and when she released my hands and got up, I saw silhouetted against the ceiling a face distorted by convulsive crying, sobs of the pain I heard for the first time. She wasn't weeping just for me, I thought at that moment; she's crying for herself, for a whole life of lying. I don't even know if Jano knew. Now she threw out this name in my face and confessed, too late, that that's the name of my real father. I try to remember every moment in the studio, each conversation and meeting, but all I can see is what's worst about that man: his cowardice, his opportunism and a feigned concern for the 'pupil' who was his son. I remember what he said to me one day: the pain of the tribes, of all the tribes. A great exporter of mahogany . . . Ranulfo told me those things, but neither he nor I, no one knew that my mother still kept in contact with Arana. She confessed to that too, she told all her shameful secrets, she even got money from Arana, money he wanted to send to me and which she used to buy the ticket to London and bring me back to Rio. The two of them pulled the wool over everyone's eyes. But she was lucky . . . I'm like her, not him. Jano's friends underlined the fact: 'Your son's just like his mother, the spitting image of her.' Now she's ashamed, she can hardly look at me, comes in bathed in tears, surrounded by doctors and nurses. Another reason to cry . . . And there's nothing more to say to each other. I thought of writing my life over again, back to front, or upside down, but I can't, I can barely scratch the paper, the words are blotches on the surface, and writing is almost a miracle . . . I can feel the sweat of death in my body. Friend . . . not cousin. This low ceiling, the empty walls, an absence of colour and sky . . . The sun and sky of Rio and the Amazon . . . never again . . . just these walls, and this unbearable smell . . . Now I'm listening to my own voice buzzing and feel sparks in my head, and my voice buzzing weakly inside me . . . I can't say another thing. What's left of all this? A friend, far away, at the other end of Brazil. I can't speak or write any more. My friend . . . I'm less than a voice . . .

GLOSSARY

Aero Willys: an American-designed car which was one of the first to be manufactured in Brazil, and popular in the 1950s and 1960s.

annatto **seeds**:   seeds from the fruit of a small tree, *Bixa orellana*, used to make red dye.

babaçu: (*Orbignya phalerata*) a palm tree whose fruit produces a valuable oil with many industrial uses.

beco: an alleyway.

bodó: (*Cascudo comum*) a mailed catfish of the Loricariidae family, common in the Amazon.

Boi-Bumbá: the Amazonian version of the festival commonly known as Bumba-Meu-Boi, a traditional dance and pageant surrounding the figure of an ox (*boi*), and which often contains irreverent and ironic meanings, directed at the rich and powerful.

Booth Line: the main steamship line plying between Liverpool, Portugal, Madeira, the Azores and the Amazon to Belém, Manaus and as far as Iquitos in Peru.

buriti: the name of various palm trees of the Mauritia genus, common in Brazil, and which grows in groups; the leaves are often used for roof-covering.

caboclo, cabocla: a person of mixed, indigenous and European descent.

cachaça: cheap and very strong liquor distilled from sugar cane juice.

caiçuma: a drink prepared from fermented manioc juice, originally made by the indigenous peoples of Brazil.

copaíba: (*Copaifera officinalis*) a plant common in the Amazon, which produces a clear oil used for medicinal purposes.

cupuaçu: (*Theobroma grandiflorum*) Amazonian tree whose fruit is a large velvety capsule like a cocoa bean, with a white pulp and large number of seeds. The seeds make a kind of chocolate; the pulp is used for drinks and sweets.

dendê: a thick cooking oil extracted from the African oil palm (*Elaeis guineensis*), much cultivated in Brazil.

DKW: (Dampf-Kraft Wagen: literally, 'steam-powered vehicle'); a German car popular in Brazil in the 1950s.

Domenico de Angelis: Italian painter (1852–1900) who spent many years in the Amazon area during the rubber boom and painted the ceiling of the Opera House (Teatro Amazonas) in Manaus.

farofa: a dish made with manioc flour, fried with pieces of egg, meat, etc. It is often used as a stuffing.

galego: an insulting word for immigrants of Portuguese origin, literally meaning 'Galician' (from north-west Spain) and implying they are ignorant peasants. Many immigrants came from bordering northern Portugal, and the two groups became assimilated in the collective Brazilian mind.

graviola: a fruit similar to the custard apple or cherimoya, with a green scaly skin and a sweet white pulp with black seeds.

guaraná: (*Paullinia cupana*) a climbing plant native to the Amazon, whose fruit is used to make a fizzy drink very popular throughout Brazil.

jaguatirica: (*Felis pardalis*) a spotted cat found in much of South America.

jambeiro: (*Eugenia jambos*) a tree of Asian origin with pink fruit, known in English as a rose apple.

jaraqui: (*Prochilodus taeniatus*) a fish common in the Amazon, which lives in shoals.

jatobá: (*Hymenaea courbaril*) a tree of the Leguminosae family found throughout much of Brazil and exploited for its wood.

jogo do bicho: a popular and illegal lottery game (literally, 'animal game'), in which bets are laid on which animal will be chosen. It is universal in Brazil, and associated with organised crime.

malva: (*Malva pusilla*) a plant of the Mallow family native to Europe and Asia, and cultivated in the Amazon area for fibres.

Manaus Harbour: originally the name of the (British) company which administered the Port of Manaus; the name came to signify the whole port area of the city, with its warehouses, docks, etc.

marajoara: a distinctive kind of pottery with bold geometrical patterns, from the Ilha de Marajó near the mouth of the Amazon where a complex society existed for more than a thousand years before the arrival of the Europeans.

maxixe: (*Cucumis anguria*) a common low-growing plant with small green spiny fruit, much used for cooking.

ocotea: (*Ocotea rubra*) known in Portuguese as 'red laurel', one of a family of tropical trees and bushes.

oitizeiro: (*Licania tomentosa*) a tropical tree of the Rosaceae family with pale yellow flowers, often used in Brazilian streets and parks.

paca: (*Agouti paca*) a spotted cavy, a small animal much hunted in Brazil.

pacu: a fish of the freshwater genus Characinidae, similar to the piranha, but herbivorous.

piassava: (*Leopoldinia piassaba*) a palm tree which produces a coarse fibre used for making brushes.

pirarucu: (*Arapaima gigas*) one of the world's largest freshwater fish which grows up to two and a half metres. Its meat is highly prized, and it has a rough tongue used as a grater.

pitomba, pitombeira: (*Talisia esculenta*) the small and red fruit (and the bush) of the Sapindaceae family.

samba-canção: a variant of the samba very popular in the 1930s and 1940s, in which the rhythm of the dance was adapted to sentimental lyrics.

seriema: (*Cariama cristata*) a long-legged, stork-like bird, found in the open country of central and south Brazil and the area of the River Plate.

seu: an untranslatable way of referring to someone – Seu Pedro, for example – with familiarity, but also with a certain respect. The word is a corruption of the more formal *senhor*.

tacacá: a porridge made with tapioca, flavoured with *tucupi* (fermented manioc juice and peppers), *jambu* (a herb), prawns and pepper. It is sold hot, in small gourds, in the streets of the towns and cities of the Amazon region.

tambaqui: (*Colossoma bidens*) a scaly fish prized for its meat, which also produces an oil used for cooking and lighting.

Ticuna: the largest indigenous tribe in Brazil, comprised of more than 30,000 people, which inhabits the area between Manaus and the Peruvian and Colombian borders.

tucum: (*Astrocaryum tucuma*) a palm tree which produces edible nuts and fibre used for making nets and hammocks.

tucumã **nuts**:   the fruit of the *tucum* trees.

tucunaré: (*Cichla temensis*) a brownish-green scaly fish much appreciated for its meat.

vila: a small group of houses, usually built around a short street or square.

A NOTE ON THE TRANSLATOR

John Gledson is Professor Emeritus of Brazilian Studies at the University of Liverpool. He is the author of books on Machado de Assis and the twentieth-century poet Carlos Drummond de Andrade. He has translated several works by Brazilian authors, including *The Brothers* by Milton Hatoum and a selection of the stories of Machado de Assis, *A Chapter of Hats*.

A NOTE ON THE TYPE

The text of this book is set in Bembo. This type was first used in 1495 by the Venetian printer Aldus Manutius for Cardinal Bembo's *De Aetna*, and was cut for Manutius by Francesco Griffo. It was one of the types used by Claude Garamond (1480–1561) as a model for his Romain de l'Université, and so it was the forerunner of what became standard European type for the following two centuries. Its modern form follows the original types and was designed for Monotype in 1929.